Only a Crush

Kasper Ridge, Book 2

Delancey Stewart

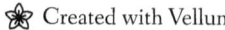

For Kelly, even if she does love pigs.

Chapter 1
The Woe of Short Legs

MATEO

I heard it again. The metallic snicker of the tape measure I kept in my tool bag schwicking back into its casing. I stirred, beginning to wake up even though I didn't want to.

"Twenty-eight inches, Poppy. Write that down."

"What are you doing?" I managed, dragging my exhausted brain out of the delicious shroud of sleep where I'd somehow found myself.

The tape measure slid out again, and I felt a small hand on my leg.

I pried one eyelid open and gazed down to the end of the couch where Lily was trying to attach the metal L on the tape to my big toe, which until one minute ago had been joyously asleep, along with the rest of my body.

"Your leg is short," she told me, looking into my face earnestly with the big brown eyes that made my heart squeeze every time I saw them. "Only twelve inches."

"That explains why it's so hard to walk," I said, waking up almost fully now.

Lily's expression shifted, her little lips pressing into a firm line and her forehead scrunching as she thought. "You walk okay."

I shook my head and sat up, stretching my arms over my head, and doing my best to shake off what had been a very long week. "No, it's been rough, actually. Especially at work." I slid off the couch onto the carpet and made a show of trying to walk around on my knees. "See, even you're taller than me," I told her, coming to kneel at her side.

"Lemme see," she said, sticking the end of the tape measure beneath my knee and pulling it up the front of my body and directly over my face.

"Hey," I said, lifting a hand to keep it from cutting my cheek.

"How long am I?" she asked, handing the tool to me.

I made a show of measuring my daughter as she stood as tall as she could, puffing her little chest out.

"Oh wow," I said, looking at the tape. "You're almost seven feet. I bet you're the tallest first grader in your class, right?"

She frowned at me. "Nope."

"Second tallest?"

She shook her head, and the little brown pigtails I'd put in that morning danced around her shoulders.

"I bet I am the strongest, though. I went on your scale while you were asleep and the number was big."

I loved that my daughter believed her weight equated to strength. I hoped she'd always feel that way.

"How big was the number?"

"Really big because I held Poppy too, and Poppy is super strong."

"What does Poppy think about you using her to make yourself seem stronger?" I asked, turning to look at the stuffed tiger that waited at Lily's feet. Poppy was her best friend and constant companion, and the thing went pretty much everywhere with her. It had stopped bothering me that she'd named the tiger for my wife, though it'd been hard at first. Now it was almost like having a tiny piece of my wife here, still part of our little family. Still with us.

"She thinks you're being a silly daddy." Lily threw herself against my chest and I pulled her into me, wrapping my arms around her small frame tightly and inhaling the sweet scent of little girl.

"I am," I told her, my voice quiet as I held my whole world in my arms.

"You gonna sleep some more?" she asked, sounding carefully hopeful.

I felt bad falling asleep on her, but construction was one of those jobs that took a lot out of you physically, and I came home exhausted most nights. For now, it was usually easy enough to turn in early, since Lily's bedtime was still eight o'clock. I couldn't imagine what things might be like when she stayed up later than I did. But those teenage years loomed ahead like a shadowed specter I knew would one day swoop in and scare the shit out of me. There was nothing I could do to stop it coming. But for now, my sweet innocent baby needed me to stay awake.

"Nope," I told her, standing with her still in my arms. She

wrapped her legs around my waist, her little arms twining my neck so she could lean back and grin into my face. "It's Friday night. Dinner and a movie, right?"

"Yay!"

"Just hope I can drive the truck with these short legs."

"Daddy," she groaned.

It was our Friday night ritual. Burgers and fries, and then back home for a movie. I would have enjoyed it only slightly more if the movie could have been something other than a choice of Lily's two favorite Disney movies, but for now, it was all part of the package. And I was doing my best to absorb and enjoy every second of the time I had with her. So *Frozen* or *Encanto* it would be. Again.

I got Lily (and Poppy) loaded into the truck and was just backing out of the driveway of the little house where we lived when the phone rang, interrupting Lily's favorite playlist (more *Frozen*. Sigh.)

It was Lucy, my boss, and I hit the accept button as I swung out onto the road. The sun was angling through the pine boughs overhead, sending a dusty orange light down to paint the asphalt, and my mind went for a moment to other fall evenings, other happy memories. Another lifetime ago.

"Hey Lucy. We're in the car." I wanted to make sure she knew Lily could hear her.

"Mateo, sorry to bother you on Friday night. I know it's date night." Lucy's voice came through the car speakers, confident and friendly as always.

"Hi Lucy!" Lily cried from the back.

"Hey you," Lucy said. "On your way to burgers?"

Lucy was a friend as much as she was my boss. I'd been working for Kasper Ridge Construction since I returned from the military after high school, and Lucy had taken the business over from her grandfather not long after that. We were close to the same age, but I had no beef with her being the boss. I had enough responsibility in my life as it was.

"Yep!" Lily confirmed happily. "And then *Encanto*."

"I didn't realize we'd decided," I said, feigning disappointment.

"I decided," she announced.

"Doesn't your dad get a say?" Lucy asked, a smile in her voice. "His favorite is *Moana*."

It was not. But it was the least played on our rotation, and the songs had less chance of winding up in my dreams or coming out of my mouth in an off-tune hum on the job.

"No." Lily was standing firm.

"My fate is sealed," I said. "What can I do for you, boss?"

"Just wanted to give you a heads up. There's some big event brewing at the Resort and Archie and Aubrey are in a tizzy about it."

"What does that mean?" I asked. We were still renovating most of the entertainment areas and many of the guest rooms at the Kasper Ridge Resort. A big event could mean anything from a party that only utilized the finished outdoor spaces we'd built this summer or a major inconvenience that would involve rushing through finishing some of the other things. And I was not a fan of rushing.

Lucy sighed. "Kind of a soft opening preview for some influencer types, I guess."

"Influencers?" I said, unable to keep the skepticism from my voice.

"Magazines, YouTubers, minor celebrities."

"Fun."

"Right," Lucy said, her voice carrying some of the wariness I felt when influencers were mentioned. I knew this kind of publicity was important to Archie and Aubrey Kasper—they needed the resort to do well. But I was leery of people who made a living judging other people. I'd never really understood the appeal, but Lily had begun watching YouTubers rate everything from brands of toothpaste to each other, and there was something about it that generated a worried little buzz in my gut.

"So anyway, that's happening in two weeks, and it's going to be a two-night thing, a preview of some of the attractions, a way for them to show off the food, the glamor, etcetera."

Glamor. I guessed the place was glamorous. It was also a construction zone. "Okay." I still wasn't sure if she was just giving me a heads up or whether there was more to it. Why was she calling me on Friday night to tell me this?

"Right, and the one guy with the biggest audience is the outdoor adventure guy. The one with that channel *Out and Out There?*"

"Douggie Masters!" Lily shouted from the back.

"You know this guy?" I asked, turning to look at my daughter.

She nodded enthusiastically as Lucy explained, "he has a huge audience, and the demographics—according to what Monroe told me—are super broad. Everyone from celebs to six-year-olds watch this guy do this adventure exploring thing."

"And he's going to adventure explore here? What does that mean?" I guided the truck into the parking lot of the Fox and raised a finger to Lily so she didn't start unbuckling.

"Well, here he wants to show off whatever backcountry fun the resort can offer."

"So the yurts?" I asked hopefully.

"I wouldn't be calling and bothering you if Douggie wanted to glamp." The yurts were Aubrey Kasper's idea, and so far we hadn't had luck getting them booked. At this point just Aubrey and Wiley lived out there behind the resort.

"So what then?" I asked, eager to finish my work week and spend some quality time with my favorite girl.

"Aubrey says there are four rustic cabins on the back of the property that she remembers from when she was a kid. I guess they're about seven miles from the main resort, down to the east, around the side of the mountain."

"So we need to drive back there and get them cleaned up?"

"If only we could."

Dread began to build in my gut. Lucy was about to give me a job I did not especially want. Right now, I liked things simple. Routine.

"No... these are hiking cabins, I guess. We might be able to get ATVs back there with some materials and tools. But for now, we just need to get eyes on them. We don't even know if they're standing."

"Send a drone?" I asked hopefully.

"Archie wants to send Monroe. And he thinks you should go with her."

Monroe was the events coordinator for the resort. She was also a former Navy fighter pilot and kind of a badass. Neither of those things was an issue. What was an issue was that I had an unnatural attraction to the woman, and I purposely avoided being around her. I was not looking for anything, and the uncomfortable prick of interest I felt when she was nearby made me feel like a dishonorable scum.

I had loved my wife with my whole heart—with everything in me. And I loved our daughter every bit as much. And that love still burned inside me, and would until the day I died. There was no room for anyone else, and the fact that my body seemed to believe differently when the smart, curvy blonde was around was unsettling.

"Pick someone else," I suggested. "Chris or Tony?"

"I have a vague sense you don't want to go for a hike," she

laughed. Little did she know my reasons. "It's gotta be you. I have to stay to focus on the restaurant, and no one else has the experience to evaluate those cabins like we need. Monroe needs to put eyes on them since she'd be the one developing the promo and sending the guy out there. Aubrey wants to go too."

Relief lifted some of the weight that had settled on me since Lucy started talking. "Okay. Sounds like I'm going for a hike."

"Perfect, thanks. That's why I called, so you could get your gear together. They're talking some time next week."

"Great. I'll dig out my boots." In reality, a seven-mile hike was not going to require any specific gear, but Lucy wasn't the hiking type so I didn't expect she would know that. I hung up with Lucy and took Lily inside. But the whole time we ate our burgers, I was thinking about hiking with Monroe. I didn't even know the woman's real name. I just knew that being around her too much was going to be a problem for me.

Chapter 2
Annalee's Antics

ANNALEE

"I just worry about you up there, darlin." Mama's voice sounded exactly as it had twenty years ago. Back when she was worried about me for completely different reasons. To her, worry equated to love. And since "I love you" was not something we said in my family, "I'm worried about you" was pretty much the same thing.

"There's nothing at all to worry about," I told her for the third time, leaning back into the couch in my suite and letting my eyes wander to the windows, to the deep blue Colorado sky outside, to the trees spotting the mountain. "This should be a whole lot less concerning than having me in a jet, Mama."

"I hated that too. Don't make me think about it, I'm likely to get a migraine. I swear, Annalee, you've taken years off my life with your antics."

My "antics" were essentially just me living a life that didn't follow the path Mama had expected me to follow. And if it had been up to her, I'd be following that path—which would certainly be strewn with pink glitter and silver tinsel—in four-inch heels with an apron tied around my waist and bright red lipstick perfectly applied at all times. Oh, and a collection of beauty pageant sashes displayed proudly around a pregnant belly and three kids hanging from my skirts.

"Okay," I sighed. "Well, I do need to get going. We're doing a soft opening for some writers and television people, and there's a lot to prepare."

"Once this place is open, honey... then you're coming home?"

Home. Not a concept that sparked even a lick of warmth in me. I hadn't been to the house I grew up in down in Honey Point, Georgia in at least a decade. And I had no plans for going back.

"We'll see, okay Mama?" I couldn't break her heart for good by telling her how I really felt.

She sighed, and for a second I imagined her sitting at the kitchen table, her slim shoulders becoming more frail than they were when I was a kid, her face beginning to show her true age, despite all her efforts to keep the ravages at time at bay. I knew I should plan a visit.

"We'd love to see you," she said, and the sadness in her voice plucked at the guilt deep inside me. "Your father misses you too."

"Tell Daddy I miss him." I swallowed hard, thinking of my

dad, trying to force my mind to see the strong smiling man he'd once been, not the smaller, frailer shadow he had since become.

"I'll tell him, honey. We'll talk soon."

I hung up the phone and set it on the table next to me with a sigh. My mother was an aging beauty queen, and I doubted she had ever considered a life where her darling daughters wouldn't want to be exactly the same thing. But the idea of settling in that tiny southern town with a pie in my hand and a flock of children at my feet didn't appeal to me. That pie and those kids might as well be an anchor, one that would keep me from ever seeing what else the world held.

After a few minutes where my mind roamed back through that tiny house, that teensy little town, I stood and pushed my arms up over my head with a deep breath. Here I could be big. Here I could grow. I could be whoever I wanted to be. And right now, I was about to be late for a meeting.

I made my way to the suite at the end of the hall where my old Navy pal, callsign Ghost, and his sister Aubrey had first settled when they'd inherited this old resort. Aubrey had since moved out back with Wiley Blanchard, a guy she and her brother had known since childhood, who'd built an incredible whiskey business and had come back to run the liquor program here at Kasper Ridge. Evidently their love story had been a whirlwind, and now they were rarely apart.

"There she is," Aubrey called as I strode through the door. Her freckled face broke into a grin and her long dark hair was in a messy knot atop her head. Everyone else was already settled around the big dining table that we used as a conference table.

"Sorry," I told them, giving them my biggest smile. "Calls with Mama are never brief."

"Family doing okay?" Ghost asked. His dark red hair was artfully messy, and his deep dark eyes held the same haunted look I'd come to know since the mishap that had ended his flying days. Though I was trying to get used to calling him Archie out here in the civilian world, he'd always be 'Ghost' to me.

"Sounds like everything's about the same," I said. "What did I miss?'

"Nothing," Aubrey said, "just getting started."

The table was packed with the team that had undertaken this somewhat insane project to relaunch the old Kasper Ridge Resort and try to turn it into a profitable ski and adventure destination on a timeline that most people would consider impossible. But thanks to one of my old squadron mates, Will Cruz, callsign Fake Tom, and the kickass construction foreman he was working with (and now dating), Lucy Dale, things were looking good.

"I've got a bunch of parts on order to get that lift running again," Brainiac said from beside me, his voice low and stoic as always. "But I'm not even sure new parts are the right move. We'll see how it goes."

"You think we might need to replace the whole thing?" Ghost's voice made it completely clear that this wasn't the outcome he was hoping for. The place was in the red right now —we all knew it—and every dollar mattered. Will had invested his own money to make the renovation happen faster, and at this point it felt like we all had some kind of skin in the game.

"Let's just take it a step at a time," Brainiac said, ever the voice of reason. "I'll see if I can fix it. If not, we'll move from there with the information we need to make a good decision."

"So logical," I quipped, poking him in the shoulder. Brainiac and I had been close friends in our squadron days. I'd been the only female pilot in our squadron, and he'd made it his personal duty to protect me—though I was never sure I needed any kind of protection. He was senior to most of us, being a couple years older and a rank above us, and he'd always been a good friend to me. And nothing more, despite ongoing speculation.

He gave me a frown that was pretty much the Brainiac equivalent of a grin—the guy was an engineering professor now, effusive wasn't really his style.

"What's the plan with the soft opening now?" I asked. There had been all kinds of ideas thrown out last week as Aubrey generated plans for things we could do with the list of folks I'd gotten interest from. "I've got about fifteen total confirmed for the dates we settled on."

"Douggie Masters still on the list?" Aubrey asked, her voice giving away her excitement.

"Yep. He said that if there was some kind of overnight adventure we could arrange, he'd bring his gear and do an episode here," I told her.

"Are we ready for that kind of exposure?" Ghost asked us.

Fake Tom and Lucy Dale exchanged a glance, and Lucy nodded. "The construction is essentially done. We can get the machinery cleared out by then for sure, and keep the work contained in the east wing guest rooms. The restaurant is partially completed, and we've got the temporary wall to erect in there. The bar is good, and the hot tubs are operational. There's no way we can get the arcade, bowling alley, or movie theater up to snuff in that time frame though."

"I don't think Douggie Masters wants to bowl," I said. "But I really do want to get eyes on those cabins at the back of the property." I was excited to see the old cabins because if they were in good shape, they expanded the world of events I could plan in the future tremendously. A mountain resort attracted different kinds of people, and we already had the luxury thing nailed. If the cabins were in good shape, I'd start marketing to the outdoor adventure set too.

"Yep," Aubrey confirmed. "Lucy, you gonna come out with us to see what needs doing there?"

Lucy shook her head, her dark braid swinging over one shoulder. "Talked to Mateo about it. He'll go with you to assess safety and see what kind of quick fixes we can make if the things are habitable."

I wondered how Mateo felt about that. The guy seemed to make a point of avoiding me whenever possible.

"And we're sure this Douggie guy wouldn't be happy in a yurt?" Ghost asked.

"The only person who said yes to yurts was the writer for the Glamorous Glamping blog," I told them. "Everyone else will be on the third floor, except Douggie, though he'll have a suite the first night and camp the next."

"And you're sure we need to bend over backwards for a guy who calls himself Douggie?" Fake Tom asked, looking skeptical.

"He could call himself Rooty Tooty for all I care," Aubrey said, her voice going shrill. "The guy has millions of fans. If he pimps the resort, we'll be turning bookings away, I promise."

I nodded. It was true. Attracting Douggie's attention had been no small feat, and now that he was interested in coming, we needed to make sure we had enough adventure to justify an episode of his show.

"Is he bringing Walter this time?" Lucy asked.

"I don't think so," I told her. "He didn't mention it." Douggie filmed about half his episodes with his husband Walter, but Walter wasn't the rugged adventurer Douggie was. "The lack of running water out there seemed to be the kicker for Walter."

"Gotcha," Aubrey said. "He could stay here, though?"

I shrugged. Whether Douggie brought his husband or not wasn't my main focus.

"When can Mateo go check those out?" Ghost asked Lucy.

"I talked to him about it Friday. Told him it would be this week," Lucy said.

"Monroe." He turned to me. "When do you want to head out?"

The idea of hiking out and back with the handsome contractor Mateo was appealing, I had to admit. But of course, Aubrey would be with us. Not that anything would have happened were she not. I did enjoy a handsome man, but I also knew this was work. I'd keep my flirting low key, even if I did entertain some thoughts of getting the guy to let down his defenses just a bit. He was so serious. So... hot. "I can go tomorrow. Or Wednesday, whenever Aubrey and Mateo can swing it."

"Tomorrow works for me," Aubrey said.

"I can let Mateo know. Maybe you can come down after the meeting and give him an idea what you have in mind for Douggie so he knows what to check on beyond the basics," Lucy suggested, looking at me.

"Sure," I said, shooting her a wide smile.

Lucy's eyes narrowed a fraction as she turned away, and I got the sense once again that I was not her favorite person. Not that it really mattered here—the rest of these guys knew who I was beneath the facade—but I supposed I should try to get a leash on the bombshell act. It had served me well for so long it was second nature now. But I liked Lucy Dale, and didn't really want her to dislike me. I'd always been better with men than women—Mama had taught me that—and close girlfriends were not something I'd ever had. But Lucy and Aubrey were candidates... and I wanted to work on it.

First though, I had an adventure hike to do.

Chapter 3
A Good Day for a Walk

MATEO

L ucy and I were standing in the area that would be the restaurant's dining room, discussing where the temporary wall would divide the finished portion from the larger space that we planned to work after the soft opening weekend. Because the restaurant seating area essentially curved around the kitchen, there was a natural narrowing where a wall wouldn't look too out of place, and we were discussing how to build it or whether it made more sense just to put up panels.

I felt the air stir to life when Monroe entered the space, and even if my body wasn't already certain it was the curvy fighter pilot so aptly named for Marilyn Monroe, I would have known by the way Lucy stiffened and her eyes narrowed slightly.

"Hey there," Monroe called in her subtle southern twang, and I turned to watch her approach, all graceful curves and wavy blond hair. She moved like a dancer, every step making me think of some routine choreographed to get my attention. I wondered how much of it was by design—no one spent every second of their existence playing the seductress. I decided at least half of it was just the way she was.

"Hey," Lucy responded, sounding about as thrilled as she would if she was about to have a few teeth removed.

Monroe's eyes lingered on Lucy for a second before sliding to me. She looked almost sad for a split second, the dark eyes shining, but then she smiled brightly. "Ready for a hike, Mateo?"

"I hear I'm taking one either way," I said, glancing at my boss.

"It's just a day," Lucy said. "Out and back. Take some photos, make some notes, and figure out if there's an easy way to get materials out there if we need to do some work. I can't imagine those things are standing there in pristine condition, considering Archie didn't even remember they were there."

"Probably not," Monroe agreed. "But let's hope they're useable."

"The guy wants an adventure, right?" I asked.

"He likes luxury at the end of his adventures," Monroe said.

"Then why's he coming to Kasper Ridge?" I muttered, half joking.

"Hey," Monroe said, pulling herself taller, which only made her sizable breasts push against the fabric of the soft-looking T-shirt she wore. "It's all in how you market a thing.

And Kasper Ridge Resort is the epitome of luxury in the mountains."

I looked around the restaurant space, which was in pretty desperate need of new carpet and a coat of paint at the very least. "Right."

"Okay," Lucy said, turning to me. "I'll focus on this, you guys figure out how much extra work on an insane deadline we have out there."

"Got it," I said, and Lucy moved to the other side of the restaurant with her tablet. I didn't mind the idea of getting outside for a day as long as I was home for Lily that evening. The only thing about this little excursion I wasn't excited about was standing in front of me smelling like orange blossoms and grinning at me in a way that had some part of my mind imagining what it would be like to put my hands on those hips, back her against a wall and... But I didn't want to think like that.

She wasn't Poppy.

And that was an understatement. We were also essentially coworkers, and I had a hell of a lot of other things weighing heavily in the keep-your-hands-to-yourself column, not the least of which was currently at her grandmother's, probably watching *Frozen* for the four millionth time.

"Just wanted to talk through what we need to head out there tomorrow," Monroe said. "Aubrey's got some walkie talkies since cell service only extends about two miles back."

Great. No service meant my connection to Lily was completely severed. It probably wouldn't be a problem, but in the past if she'd wanted to reach me and hadn't been able to, she'd gotten pretty upset. "That might be an issue," I said.

"I'm guessing you're not worried about being away from your Insta for a day," Monroe said.

"No. I'm worried about being away from my kid if she needs me. I'm all she's got." It wasn't exactly true, but the last thing

Lily needed was to worry if she couldn't get in touch with me. She'd lost one parent and she worried about losing the other. How did you explain to a seven-year-old that she didn't need to worry about that?

"Aha, right." Monroe lifted a hand to her mouth, holding her index finger against that plump bottom lip as she tilted her head to one side, clearly thinking. "Well, we'll be able to reach the resort," she said. "And you could make sure Ghost or Lucy knows how to reach your..."

"Daughter."

"Daughter," she said, a soft smile pulling her cheeks wider as her hand fell. "How old?" She asked.

"She's seven," I told her, feeling my own smile spread as I thought about my daughter.

"If you're worried, maybe Lucy can send one of the other guys on her crew? Or maybe Fake Tom could come."

"No," I said, maybe a little too quickly. I hadn't thought it through—the word had just leapt out of me. "I mean, it's fine. She can stay with my mother-in-law." Deep down, I wanted to go, I realized. I wanted to spend the day with Monroe.

I watched as her eyes swept my hands and then rose to my face again, a question there.

"I, uh..." Why was I about to explain to this woman why I didn't wear a ring on my hand? My heart was still with Poppy. But rings and construction weren't a great combination. I pressed at the ring hanging on the chain beneath my shirt in the same place I'd worn it since the day Poppy and I had gotten married. "My wife died," I said simply.

Monroe's lips pressed together and she laid a hand on my bicep, a little sympathetic noise escaping her throat. "I'm so sorry."

She was touching me, and I didn't want to like it. But I didn't move away, and I didn't ask her to stop. It had been a while since a woman I found this attractive had touched me. There'd been one brief relationship attempt earlier in the summer, but in the end, we were not a fit.

"So...gear," I said, prompting her to remove her hand. It left a warm tingle on my skin, and I had an impulse to find a way to make her put it back.

"Sturdy shoes, obviously. I'm guessing since you live up here, you're probably more prepared than I am."

I nodded. I was. "Water," I filled in.

"Right, and we'll bring lunch. I figure it'll be about three hours in and three back out. Sound right?"

"Depends on terrain," I said. "The elevation rises pretty fast depending which way we're headed."

Monroe looked thoughtful for a moment. "We'll leave extra early just in case. That gives us a couple hours of daylight to check things out and get the information we need."

"Pack a jacket and some rain gear," I suggested. "Weather can turn fast up here."

Her eyebrows pulled together as she glanced past me at the bright sunshine filling the windows of the dining room. "Okay," she said, nodding her head once.

"Some food, a first aid kit, matches." It had been a long time since I'd hiked any real distance, though Poppy and I used to backpack. My excursions in the past few years had been limited by the length of Lily's little legs—and by her endurance, which was limited unless bribes and snacks were involved.

"Right," Monroe said. "So what time? Six?"

Julia—Poppy's mom—was used to early babysitting calls. I was generally on site by seven in the morning. "Sounds good." I said.

"Perfect," Monroe said. "We'll meet you out back. The trail-head is just off the east patio."

"Okay," I said, turning to go. A thought struck me and I turned back around. "One more thing."

She waited, her pretty lips in a half smile.

"What's your actual name?"

A low laugh spilled from her. "It's Annalee. Annalee Alacaz Tyson. It's Spanish," she went on. "For cherry."

"Nice to meet you," I said, wishing I could pull the words back in. I hadn't just met her. My mind had just gone on a little excursion thinking about the cherry color of her lips, and other connotations of the ripe red fruit.

"We've met before," she said, laughing. "But it's nice to meet you too, Mateo."

With that awkward interaction behind us, I turned to get back to work, only glancing over my shoulder once to watch Annalee Tyson's sexy ass sway out of the dining room.

Tomorrow was going to be a long day. Thank god Aubrey was coming too. Her presence would definitely help cut the tension.

Chapter 4
Rufus and His Domain

ANNALEE

Those of us living at the resort had a bit of an unspoken ritual. We met downstairs for dinner at seven, and then often hung out in the bar or on the back patio until we each drifted off to our rooms. For a while, I'd been the designated chef at the resort, but we all agreed that it made more sense for me to focus on events and bookings, and so we'd ordered a meal service, each of us kicking in a bit for the cost.

"Spaghetti and meatballs!" Wiley had called out as he'd removed the top of the big family-style tin holding that night's dinner. It was his night to heat the meal, so he'd been in charge of setting things up in the kitchen. We took turns making grocery runs for produce and staples, and Aubrey had suggested we begin ordering double meals to freeze for winter.

"By the time snow falls, we'll have a full-time chef up here," Ghost had told her.

Still, having a few things in the big deep freeze wasn't a bad idea.

After dinner that night, I cleaned up my plate and headed into the bar. I wanted to get a good night's sleep for tomorrow's hike, but one drink with my friends wouldn't hurt.

"Good to see Rufus where he belongs," said Ernie Dale as I entered. The old man was a recent addition to the resort crew. He and Lucy had moved in just a couple weeks earlier. It was easier for Lucy to be close to the job, but mostly Fake Tom had insisted on it—since the two of them had decided they were in love, it seemed like they spent every second together. I didn't blame them for wanting to maximize their time. Life was short—you never knew what was going to happen. I got that.

"Good old Rudy Fusterberg," Ghost said, staring up at the stuffed bear that stood over the bookshelf on the side of the bar. "Our Hollywood mystery."

While renovating Kasper Ridge was our main focus, every person in the bar had fallen victim to Ghost's secondary obsession—the treasure hunt his Uncle Marvin had left him along with the old resort. So far we had half a map, a bunch of old movie posters, and a vague hint that some old screenwriter named Rudy whose fiancée left him back in the day had something to do with it. The treasure itself was still a mystery, and judging by the way the clues were lining up, I personally thought old Uncle Marvin might have been a couple sandwiches short on his mental picnic and that we'd probably end up finding a few hundred cans of Beanie Weenie or something.

Which was fine—who didn't like Beanie Weenie?

But I knew a lot was riding on the belief that the treasure was monetary, and that it might help Ghost and Aubrey get the resort back in the black.

I had slightly more actionable ideas about how to do that—beginning with this soft opening in a couple weeks.

"You ready to go in the morning?" I asked Aubrey, lifting the glass of pinot noir Wiley had just slid across the bar to me.

"What's happening in the morning?" Ernie asked, swiveling on his stool to peer at me through clear blue eyes.

"A couple of us are heading out to check the cabins at the back of the property. Hopefully they're still standing. We want to get one cleaned up enough to set up one of the influencers coming out for the soft opening with an adventure," I told him.

"That'll be an adventure, all right," Ernie said, a wry smile spreading over his face. "Damn, I almost forgot those old things were out there."

"Have you been back there, Papa?" Lucy asked her grandfather.

Brainiac and Fake Tom were at the other end of the bar, laughing about something together, but the rest of us were leaning in toward Ernie, who had known Marvin well when they were children.

"Oh yeah," he laughed. "It's quite a trek too, you sure it's a good idea?" He raised a fuzzy white eyebrow at me.

"Not too worried," I told him. "I'm in decent shape, and I've been up here long enough the altitude isn't really bothering me." You didn't pass the Navy fitness tests without staying in pretty decent shape, and I'd been on a hike or two in my time.

"Yeah," Ernie said, looking unconvinced. "This feller going with you?" He pointed his thumb at Ghost.

"No sir," Aubrey told him, her lips thinning a bit as she replied. "I hope you're not suggesting that we need a man along to look out for us delicate ladies." Aubrey could hold her own in just about any situation from what I'd been told. She was a black belt in some martial art I wasn't familiar with, and I'd personally seen her physically subdue her brother on several occasions when he'd insulted her in some way. She definitely did not need a man to protect her.

Ernie laughed heartily at that, glancing at his granddaughter, who waggled her eyebrows at him as if to tell him to tread lightly.

"You wouldn't flip an old man over the bar for insulting you, would you?" he asked Aubrey, clearly having been told some of the stories about Aubrey's 'arguments' with her brother.

"Of course not," she said, her shoulders relaxing slightly. "I guess I just get a little riled whenever someone suggests I can't take care of myself."

Ernie took a long sip of his beer and set it down on the bar top. "Course you can," he said. "But that's backcountry there. And there's a few things to keep in mind. Altitude and hydration for sure."

We nodded. We'd thought of that, but I was anxious to hear what other tips this old local could offer.

"The weather changes fast up here," he went on, but I'd checked the weather repeatedly and there was nothing to worry about besides a minuscule chance for a passing rainstorm. "Bears, bobcats, mountain lions, moose," he said, ticking these off his fingers. "Bigfoot, of course."

Wiley actually spit out a mouthful of his drink at this casual mention of Bigfoot, but no one questioned Ernie. Wiley wiped his mouth with a bar napkin as Ernie went on, ignoring him.

"Biggest thing you might want to think about is the ghosts."

"Ghosts?" I asked, trying to keep my smile under control.

He nodded, his expression severe. "That's why they quit using those old cabins back there."

"Because they're haunted?" Lucy asked.

"No, because of all the folks that died out there."

That little bomb landed softly as Ernie took another swig of his beer, and no one said anything. It was like we were all waiting for the explosion. My own mind had begun conjuring every horror movie I'd ever seen, and a glimmer of a second thought played through my brain.

"Ah, okay," Ghost said finally. "Care to elaborate?"

Ernie rocked back and forth on his stool, settling in for a story.

"Well," he began. "Tough to say for sure what really went on, since no one lived to tell the tale. But it started with a storm."

He went on to tell us about a group of guests who'd booked the backcountry cabins when the resort was a popular destination in the sixties and seventies.

"This was around 1970 or so, I'd think." He said. "Bunch of Hollywood types fancied themselves rugged and whatnot, and they geared up and headed out. It's about seven and a half miles to those cabins."

He described a group of socialites who disregarded weather warnings and didn't prepare properly for the terrain, suggesting that there might have already been an injury among them by the time they reached the cabins.

"There's no water or indoor plumbing back there, you know," he said, eyeing me. "And no electricity."

I nodded. I already knew all this. We were prepared, and Douggie Masters certainly would be.

"And that's all well and fine if you're just playing adventure for a night like this feller you're talking about is planning to do. But that's all these folks were doing too. Until the storm swept in and blanketed these mountains with more snow than we'd seen in a century."

"Shit," Wiley breathed, and like him, I could picture getting stranded back there with feet of snow piled along the trail leading back to the resort. You could survive it, I guessed, but not if you were unprepared.

"Wait, Papa," Lucy said. "This isn't going to be a Donner Party story, is it?"

It took me a second to pull up my memory of what the Donner Party was—a bunch of people stranded in the mountains who'd evidently turned to cannibalism when all else had failed. Ew.

"It ain't far off, I'd guess," Ernie said.

I shivered, thinking of the cold and the fear those people must've experienced.

"You'd expect they might build a fire, wait out the storm and head back," Ernie said, nodding at us. "And maybe if it'd been a day or two, they could have survived. But this storm sat over these mountains for seven full days, temperatures dropped below zero, and the wind probably took it a hell of a lot lower. They didn't have a chance."

"They froze to death?" I asked, unable to help myself. "Did they go back there in winter time?"

"It was June," he said, his voice serious. "Don't happen a lot, but it happens. And I suppose a few of them froze, yeah."

"What happened to the rest?" Ghost asked, hanging on every word out of Ernie's mouth as I was.

"No one really knows. Took a year or so to track down all the remains. A couple of them tried to head back, they thought. Found them about halfway back to the resort. One of them was out in the woods a mile or so from the cabins—no one knows what that fool was up to, but he met some animals up there, seems like."

Aubrey frowned at me as I met her eye. "We'll be prepared," I said, both to assure myself and to calm any fears she might have. "And we'll be extra sure about the weather. They didn't have weather apps back in the day."

"That's true," Aubrey said, her shoulders relaxing.

"And we'll take extra food and warm clothes. Maybe even plan to leave some out at the cabins for anyone else who goes back there."

"We'll definitely want them to be fully equipped for bad weather surprises," Ghost said. "The last thing we need is a lawsuit."

"Well, tell those ghosts hey for me," Ernie concluded with a nod.

"Sure," Aubrey said, looking a little uncertain again.

"Mateo's going with them," Lucy told her grandfather. "They'll be fine."

That seemed to satisfy the old man, and the thought of the burly contractor with the light green eyes put some of my worries to rest too. Mateo wasn't just nice to look at. Everything about him screamed capability and self-assurance. Of course that just made him hotter.

"Hey," Ghost said, turning to his sister. "You'll be sure to look around a bit right? For anything that might help us figure out the hunt?"

"That's half the reason I'm going," she told him.

"We'll all keep our eyes open," I assured him.

Chapter 5
The Insatiable Curiosity of Seven-Year Olds

MATEO

"If it's just a walk, why do they call it a hike?" Lily was brimming with more questions than I could rationally handle at six a.m.

"I don't know, honey." I was working on my second cup of coffee as I drove the curvy two-lane road between our house and Poppy's mother's. Julia had been a godsend since my wife died, stepping in to offer childcare whenever I needed it. She wasn't exactly warm to me, but she was amazing with Lily, and that was all that really mattered.

"Well, it's funny," Lily went on, still expounding on the confusing reality that was the English language. "And how come hike is a bad thing?"

"What do you mean?"

"Like, when someone is mad they say, 'go take a hike.' Is someone making you hike? Cuz they're pissed off at you?"

I lifted my eyes to catch hers in the mirror. "Did you just curse? At six o'clock in the morning?"

She had the presence of mind to look guilty, but then she asked, "What time can I curse?"

"No cursing." I took another swig of coffee. Between my over-chatty daughter and the day I was about to spend pretending not to be maddeningly attracted to Monroe, I was already exhausted.

"You curse," Lily said, pouting. "You say motherfu—"

"I'm gonna stop you right there," I said, lowering my voice in a warning.

"You do," she said defiantly.

I glanced at her again, my heart melting a little as I caught the exact replicas of my wife's eyes in the mirror, blazing with indignity. But Lily recovered quickly. "Do you think Grammy will let me make s'mores in the microwave again? If I do it right this time?"

"I'm guessing Grammy is probably going to ban you from any appliance use after that incident."

"It was an accident, not an incident."

"It was an accident that *you* didn't have to clean up."

"Grammy was kinda mad." Lily looked sad, and as we pulled into Julia's driveway, I scrambled to think of something to leave her with that would make her happy.

"Hey," I said, putting the truck into park. "I'm gonna do my best to catch some animals for you while I'm out there. To add to your collection."

"Get a bear!" she squealed, clapping.

I opened the door and helped my daughter out of the truck with her overnight bag and Poppy in my arms. "Maybe a bear," I said.

"Or a mountain lion!"

"I'm not a big fan of mountain lions, I'd rather not see one of those."

"But if you do, you'll get him for me, right?" She grinned up at me and I felt something chemical in my body shift. How was it possible to love someone so much?

I knelt in front of her, wanting one more moment with her before I had to share her with my mother-in-law. "I'll take the very best picture I can if I see one. Then I'll run for my life."

Her eyes widened and she shook her head, little dark pigtails flying. "No, Daddy. Don't run! You get big for a lion and yell at him a lot. That's when it's okay to curse." She was very serious, her voice low and stern.

"That's right. That's what I'll do. I'll scream as many curses as I can think of at that stinky lion."

"Yes," she agreed. "Call him a stinkerbutt and a pooper face. And a motherfu...you know. But take the picture first."

"Of course."

She nodded, one quick tilt of her little chin, and I lifted her onto my hip, carrying a little more than was comfortable between her overnight bag and her body, but needing to feel her close before I left her with her grandmother overnight. I'd arranged for her to stay over in case we got back later than planned.

"Good morning, you two," Julia said, stepping through her brightly lit front door wearing a long pink robe and holding a cup of coffee. "Lily, are you interested in some hot chocolate today?"

"Yes, yes, yes!" Lily called, wriggling to get free of my grip.

"Love you, bear," I told her, pressing my forehead to her warm little head. She stopped wiggling and threw her arms tight around my neck.

"Love you too, Daddy."

I let her down and she smiled up at me, reaching for Poppy. "See you tomorrow."

My daughter disappeared inside her grandmother's house, and Julia appraised me with her clear blue eyes.

"Thanks for this," I said, feeling the weight of her judgment despite the fact the woman was about a foot and a half shorter than I was and probably a hundred pounds lighter.

"Any opportunity to see my granddaughter," she said, her voice as cold as her gaze.

Julia held no real love for me, but I knew she lavished my daughter with warmth and affection. And that was enough for me. I deserved her scorn in some ways, and I'd accept it without complaint if it meant Lily had a woman in her life who loved her deeply. Julia wasn't Poppy, but she was as close as I was going to be able to give my daughter.

"I'll call and let you know when we get back."

"Sounds fine. You know Lily can stay as long as you need."

"Thank you," I said again.

I turned, feeling her eyes lingering on me as I walked back to the truck, the familiar cocktail of guilt and anger swirling inside me. She blamed me for Poppy's death—and maybe it had been my fault. But if I could go back in time and do it again... but then we wouldn't have Lily. The familiar pain lit through me, leaving a wretched path of regret and self-loathing in my gut as I backed out of the driveway and turned the truck toward Kasper Ridge Resort. What was done was done.

I might never be happy again, but I had to get on for Lily's sake.

I pulled into the resort's wide driveway from the highway, feeling the same sense of wonder I had the very first time Poppy had brought me here. We'd been young, and the resort had been abandoned, but the two tall stone markers had stood on either side of the wide entrance, the Kasper Ridge Resort plaque clearly visible. The entrance had been grand, even when the resort behind it had been sagging and lonely with disrepair, and Poppy and I had parked and wandered the grounds, imagining what it might have been like when this place was a destination for the rich and famous. Her parents remembered a bit of it, she said, but it had been abandoned for as long as she'd known anything about it.

Poppy grew up in Kasper Ridge, and she was the one who opened my eyes to the beauty and awe of this place when I'd come here as a teenager with my dad after my folks divorced. He'd found a job with Ernie Dale at Kasper Ridge Construction, and I'd found the love of my life at sixteen. She'd waited for me when I joined the Marine Corps, and we'd gotten married when I got back.

Today the resort stood proud and strong beneath the golden glow of the morning sun flooding the front drive. The turnabout out front had been reconstructed, and the revolving door to the lobby was ready to receive guests. The resort itself was a fitting mixture of wood and stone, exactly what you'd expect to see in a ski destination you'd paid a lot of cash to visit.

I pulled around to the side lot and parked, taking a few minutes to grab my gear and a few more to shake off thoughts of the past and force my mind to today's effort. Fourteen miles was not an extreme distance for one day by any means, but the weather app I relied on for accurate forecasts up here was calling for a summer storm, and it looked like we'd be getting some rain, but I wasn't too worried about getting wet. Still, I hadn't hiked more than five miles in a long time. I'd be sore tomorrow.

"Good morning," I said, walking around the back of the resort to the extensive patio facing the mountain. Annalee and Aubrey sat near the fire pit, each holding a mug between their palms.

"Morning," they said in unison.

"Quick cup of coffee?" Aubrey asked.

"Yes please. I never turn down coffee. Or a nap."

Aubrey set down her own mug on the edge of the fire pit and disappeared inside, and I tried not to notice the way the strengthening sunlight caught the flaxen gold in Monroe's hair. She'd pulled it back and wore a ball cap, but her ponytail waved through the hole behind the cap, and it looked so soft I had to remind myself not to reach for it to find out.

"Ready for a stroll?" she joked, turning the full force of her smile on me. Monroe—Annalee—had one of those smiles that got bigger than you expected it to, making you look twice. And her lips were generous and plump, staying that way even when stretched wide in a grin. I didn't think she'd put on lipstick for the hike, but her lips were a ruddy red anyway, a shade that made me think about what they might look like if I kissed her roughly, or if she took me into her mouth.

I cleared my throat, the only answer I managed to her question. The sound and action served to jar my errant mind from thoughts of Annalee's red lips wrapped around my dick. I sat, leaving three of the big Adirondack chairs between us as Annalee made a face of amusement.

"Not a morning person, huh Mateo?" she said, leaning back

into her own chair and tilting her chin toward the sun, letting her eyes drop shut.

Aubrey returned, handed over my coffee and sat between us. "We should head out soon," she said. She was small and spry, and I could feel energy jumping from her as she finished her coffee and looked between us.

"Looks like we might get wet at some point," I told them.

"Saw that little storm. It's flying by, though. We'll be okay," Aubrey said.

I was relieved to hear her say it. I knew she'd grown up here in the summers, and I'd been here for years now, but sometimes the mountains still surprised me, reminding me how small we were in comparison to their sheer magnitude. We were smart and prepared, but Mother Nature was so much more than that. I didn't believe in a hell of a lot, but I did have some respect for that.

"I have a raincoat in here," Annalee said, pointing to her pack on the ground. "And I packed in some warm stuff to leave back at the cabin too."

"Me too. And I've got a few things for you to put into your pack, Mateo," Aubrey said.

"Why are we taking stuff to leave out there?" I asked, not eager to carry more than I had to.

"So Douggie Masters doesn't end up like the last guests that went back there," Aubrey said, shaking her head.

That didn't make sense to me, but it was too early to ask questions. I accepted that something bad had happened at some point involving a lack of winter gear and rolled with it.

Once my bag was packed and we'd all finished our coffee and filled water bottles, we headed out, taking the trailhead that practically started at the edge of the east patio. Within ten minutes, we'd passed the yurts tucked into the clearing at the eastern base of the mountain and moved on into the dense forest, the elevation increasing rapidly with almost every step.

As the trail rose and narrowed, we were forced into a single file line, and somehow I ended up at the tail, directly behind a certain former fighter pilot's perfectly round ass, which was moving in ways that were extremely distracting as she hiked ahead in a pair of khaki shorts.

I needed to get a grip on myself. My only hope was that spending the day with this woman would relieve me of my attraction to her. I hoped she'd reveal some unattractive habits along the way or maybe I'd discover that she liked to kick squirrels or something. At this point, it was going to take a lot to turn off whatever roaring interest had been switched on by the fierce blonde's bright laughter and red, red lips.

This was going to be a very long hike.

Chapter 6
When the Rain Says, "Hold My Beer."

ANNALEE

I'd always thought I was in pretty good shape. I mean, you didn't get through Navy PFTs without training and maintenance, and everything I'd learned about physical fitness during those years was stuff I still practiced today. It was a little less motivating, of course, knowing that I wasn't at risk of losing my flight status or potentially going to be incapable of rescuing myself in the event of a problem in the plane. Now the stakes were more about fitting into my pants to avoid having to spend the cash to replace my entire wardrobe.

But this little backcountry adventure was kicking my ass.

"No one mentioned the extreme vertical rise," I huffed, slumping to sit on a rock at the side of the trail to guzzle some more water. It was getting cooler, but the sheer exertion had me wishing we'd come upon some kind of magical forest pond I could strip off my clothes and jump into. My legs were a little shaky and catching my breath felt like a lost dream.

"It is a little more extreme than I'd expected," Mateo agreed, making me feel slightly less incompetent.

Aubrey grinned at us, looking far less tuckered out than either Mateo or me.

"Damn, you'd think this wouldn't be a big deal after the Navy," I complained. "Guess I've let my training slide a little more than I should have."

"It doesn't look like you've let anything slide," Mateo said, and I felt a little surge of excitement at the comment, but then he quickly turned away, muttering, "I mean, also, you probably weren't training at this elevation. This would kick anyone's ass."

"Well, it's certainly kicking mine. Glad this cabin isn't any farther away." I said.

Aubrey didn't look to be huffing and puffing at all, but nodded her agreement and seemed happy to give us the time we needed to recover.

We sat for a few minutes, catching our breaths as the forest lived and breathed around us. I'd always thought of the woods as quiet, but once we stopped moving, I realized it was full of sound. Birds called, the wind rushed through the branches of the pine trees overhead, a distant stream trickled, and I had the constant sense of movement in my peripheral vision, a prickling awareness that we were not alone out here. The thought was equal parts comforting and disturbing.

Mateo was looking at his phone, his strong body perched on a rock on the other side of the trail. It was hard not to notice how the sunlight coming through the trees lit gold in his sandy hair, or how the bulging muscles on his arms flexed as he moved the phone around.

"We're officially out of the service area," he said. "At least for my provider."

Aubrey and I both checked our phones. "Same," I said.

"Good thing we have the walkie," Aubrey said, pulling it from her pack. "Aubrey to Archie. Come in."

We waited a minute, and the walkie talkie sparked to life in her hand.

"How's it going, guys?" Archie's voice sounded crackly and far away, but it was a relief to hear it. I didn't like the idea of being completely out of touch. You never knew what could happen.

"It's good," Aubrey told him. "Think we must be about halfway there."

There was a pause, then Archie's voice again. "Figured you'd be there by now."

I frowned, my eyes catching Mateo's. Was I holding us back? He shook his head a tiny bit and then reached for the walkie talkie. "Hey Archie, it's Mateo. Listen, the climb is a bit steeper than we'd been led to believe. We'll still get in and out today, but we're gonna be late."

"Okay," Archie answered. "Aubrey, you gonna make it back in time for dinner?"

We exchanged confused looks, Aubrey's face rearranging itself into an annoyed frown. She reached for the walkie and Mateo handed it back. "Doubt it. Why? You can't heat up your own raviolis, Arch?"

"Funny. No. Aunt Ida rolled in today by surprise, and I thought you'd want to spend as much time with her as possible."

Aubrey's face shifted from annoyance to a bright smile faster than I would have thought it could. "Auntie Ida?" She suddenly sounded like a little girl, and she literally sprang off the rock to bounce on her feet. "How long is she staying?"

"She said only tonight. That's why I'm asking."

Aubrey's face fell, and her eyes met mine. "Oh," she said. "I'll miss her then. Tell her I'll see her in the morning for sure."

"Who's Auntie Ida?" I asked.

Aubrey still held the device, but spoke to us now instead of into the face of the walkie. "Our very favorite aunt. Dad's sister. We spent a lot of time with her as kids. She's very...unique."

"You don't want to miss time with her," Mateo said.

Aubrey shrugged. "Too late."

I got to my feet. "Listen, no it's not. If you head back now, you'll be there for dinner for sure. Only, I suppose you shouldn't be out here alone..."

"Are you kidding?" Aubrey laughed. "I've been hiking out here alone since I was a kid. Plus, I know the trail now since we just walked it. And it's downhill. I could be back at the resort in an hour."

Mateo rubbed a big hand across his jaw. "I don't like you out here by yourself," he said.

"I'm a big girl," Aubrey said. "And I know these woods. Do you think you guys would be okay without me?"

Mateo frowned at me, and I got the sense he very much wished I was the one leaving this little adventure early.

I pushed my shoulders back and lifted my chin. "We'll be fine. We'll pick up some time on this last half, and be back in time to meet your aunt after dinner. You go spend as much time as you can with her."

Mateo continued to look at me, something in his eyes I couldn't quite read. It wasn't annoyance, but it didn't feel like happiness, either. I turned my attention to Aubrey. "Go see your aunt. If you'll be okay, we'll be okay."

Aubrey pulled her bottom lip between her teeth and shifted

her weight, then lifted the walkie talkie back up. "Hey Arch? I'm gonna head back to see Ida."

"She'll be thrilled," he said. "You guys sure you know where you're going?" That part was clearly for us.

"Trail's clear," Mateo confirmed. "It'd be hard to get lost. We'll be fine."

I thought I heard a low rumble of thunder just then, but a glance up at the sky revealed only a brilliant blue through the treetops. A little wave of uneasiness washed through me. Probably because I didn't love the idea of Aubrey out here all alone.

"Okay," Archie said. "Aubrey, if you're not back in three hours, we're coming to find you."

"Don't get your panties in a twist, Arch. I'll be there soon."

"I just worry."

"I know. That's your job." She smiled into the walkie talkie and I felt a little glow of warmth at how close the siblings were, the way they looked out for each other.

Aubrey unpacked her bag, stuffing things into each of ours, and handed the walkie talkie to Mateo. "Don't be long, guys," she said, turning back down the trail. "And keep in touch."

"We will," I assured her. "You hightail it straight on back and be careful."

"Don't worry about me," Aubrey said, grinning and then loping off down the trail back the way we'd come.

"Just you and me, Tex," I said, smiling at Mateo.

He frowned back at me. "Let's get moving."

Mateo took the lead, and he set a pace that had me wishing I'd done a bit more hiking and a little less drinking in the time I'd been up at Kasper Ridge. I'd liked to have made conversation to occupy my mind while we hiked, but we were moving fast enough that I had to focus on sucking in enough oxygen to survive.

The trail felt like it was climbing practically straight up, and

I hoped Douggie Masters was prepared for this because I certainly hadn't been.

"Hold please," I gasped, leaning heavily on the side of a huge boulder flanking the trail after we'd been hiking another twenty minutes or so. Mateo stopped ahead of me, turning to give me a disappointed look. His face changed, though, as he watched me gasp.

"You okay?" he asked.

I nodded and grabbed my water bottle as the wind blew around me, cooling the sweat on my face. "Yeah, doing the best I can. Just need to grab a few breaths." My words were punctuated by very unladylike heavy breathing and possibly a bit of drooling. I was exhausted, but knew a few minutes of rest would help.

"We should only be about a mile or two away now," Mateo said, checking his watch. "The way back shouldn't be too bad."

I nodded, hoping he was right. Looking down the trail behind me had me a little skeptical though. It was steep enough that I didn't plan to hurry down it. Going down could be more dangerous than going up, since gravity was helping.

I was about to suggest we get moving again, when the forest around us grew noticeably darker and before I could comment, a brisk wind picked up and a loud crash of thunder slammed through the trees around us.

"Holy fu—" Mateo's exclamation was drowned out by the wind that gusted again just after the crash.

And in the next second, the darkness was illuminated by a brilliant slash of lightning.

"Shit," Mateo said, glancing around and reaching for my hand. "Let's get moving."

"This is the summer storm, I guess," I said pointlessly as we began hustling again, my legs moving with renewed energy brought forth by a tiny bit of fear. Mateo released my hand, but my skin felt warm where he'd touched me. Worry mingled in my gut with the strange giddiness Mateo's touch had brought forth. This storm was no minor rain burst. It seemed like it wanted to hurt us.

As if I'd called it forth by thinking of its malevolence, rain began pelting us in the next second, fat drops coming down in mad torrents.

"Shit," Mateo said again, and we both picked up a little more speed.

I was gasping, trying to stay on Mateo's heels as we continued the rocky climb toward what I hoped would be a warm, dry cabin. The temperature was dropping steadily, and something in me was beginning to trill a warning. This did not feel like a light summer shower.

The bright summer day we'd hiked out into had turned into a glowering darkness lit intermittently with terrifying flashes of lightning that were near enough that I could smell the ozone and feel the hair on my arms lifting with static. I was soaked to the bone, and beginning to shiver. The dusty trail beneath our feet was beginning to turn to brown slime as water ran along the sides of it in brown rivulets, making the going slippery and uncertain.

"This is not good," Mateo said, still moving forward ahead of me. "You doing okay?" He had to shout over the noise of the storm.

"As good as you are, I guess," I screamed back. "Let's just get to shelter." As I said this, the storm seemed to lull a bit, the rain tapering to a drizzle. It was freezing cold, and the sun had clearly abandoned us. The thick clouds felt like they were dropping lower to surround us, and bringing the frigid temperatures right along with them. The water on my bare arms felt like ice.

"Maybe that was the worst of it," Mateo said, and I wasn't

sure if he meant the storm or the trail, which had leveled out a bit and widened so we could walk side by side.

"Only about a mile more, you think?" I asked, my teeth chattering.

"Maybe. The GPS on my watch isn't working as well as it should. Maybe the storm or the dense forest is interfering"—he frowned at me, pausing—"You got a jacket or something in there?"

I nodded, feeling suddenly exhausted and a little bit afraid as thunder rolled again directly overhead. I shrugged the pack off, letting it fall to the muddy ground and pulled out the winter coat Aubrey had shoved in there before she'd turned around. I hoped she had gotten down before the storm had hit, or that maybe it wasn't as bad down there.

Mateo held the jacket up for me to slide my arms into, and for a moment I felt very taken care of. He had practice, I remembered. He had a daughter.

"Thanks." I looked up at him, feeling a little guilty for my warm coat since his hair was plastered to his head and his T-shirt was drenched, clinging to his chest. I could see the faint outline of something beneath his shirt, but it wasn't the time to ask about it. And if he wore it beneath his clothing, maybe it was something he didn't want to discuss anyway.

He nodded, looking grim as he glanced at me and then up at the dark clouds overhead. Just as he reached for the walkie talkie, a snowflake fell, landing on the ground at our feet and lying there, intact.

"That's really not good," Mateo said.

I looked around, realizing that snow was beginning to fall all around us. The cold was driving into my bones, and even with the warm coat, the cold wet clothing was pulling the warmth from my body. Mateo didn't look much better, as he tugged a sweatshirt from his own pack.

Within minutes, the snow was falling so thickly we could have been in the midst of a shaken snow globe, or a Hallmark movie. We were renovating an inn, after all.

"Crap. This is not what we planned for," Mateo said.

"Maybe we should go back?"

"This storm is supposed to be quick," he said. "Even though they didn't call for snow, they did predict it would be a blip, passing through. And you look like you really need to warm up. Maybe we just get to the cabin and wait it out?"

"Yes. It would suck to have come all this way and not see the cabins. At least we can assess them and do what we came out here to do. Maybe dry off a bit before we head back?"

"Yeah," Mateo agreed. He lifted the walkie talkie. "Hey Archie. Mateo here." We began moving forward again through the heavy falling snow as he tried to signal the resort. "Mateo to Archie."

"Hey," Ghost's voice crackled to life and relief surged through me. "You guys okay? Lotta rain down here."

"We're getting snow. A lot of it." Mateo said, and I noticed that we'd already gotten enough that it was starting to stick to the trail, making a smooth depression in the middle of the rough patches beginning to drift around the forest floor.

"Shit. Come back before you get stuck," Ghost said.

"We're almost there. We'll just check the cabins, dry off, hopefully let this storm roll through and then we'll head back."

"Hurry," Ghost said. "Just make sure the things are standing, then head back. Or better yet, just forget it and come back now. They keep changing the predictions on this thing." That got my attention. What did that mean?

"What are they saying now?" I asked.

Ghost must have heard me, because he responded. "They're calling for snow overnight up in the high country, and it sounds like the storm isn't going to just blow over like they thought. Sure you don't want to turn around now?"

"Nah," Mateo said, checking my face before answering. "We'll be okay. Might as well get eyes on them, dry off, and then head back."

I nodded. We hadn't come this far for nothing.

"Be smart, guys." Ghost said.

"We're fine, Ghost," I said. I doubted enough snow could fall to pose much of a problem in so short a time, even if our trek back home was looking more cold and miserable than we'd anticipated. "We'll be back soon."

Mateo put away the walkie talkie and we trudged forward, keeping our heads bowed into the thick snow as it fell.

Chapter 7
Got a Light Jacket?

MATEO

Each time we turned a bend, I expected to see the cabins pressed up against the tree line, waiting for us, promising shelter, if not warmth. But with each quarter mile we slogged through the worsening conditions, they seemed farther and farther away. I was beginning to worry that in the years since anyone had been up here, they'd fallen to dust, been taken back by nature. But surely there'd be some remnants —we couldn't just miss them completely, could we?

"You don't think we passed them somehow, do you?"

Annalee asked me, her teeth chattering loudly enough to make her voice judder and leap.

I glanced over my shoulder at her, worry beginning to seep in around the edges of my initial annoyance at the fact this little excursion was not going as planned at all. She wasn't dressed right for a snowstorm—neither of us was. Her arms were crossed tightly around her, and her cheeks were bright pink. The jacket she wore was nowhere near warm enough for this weather, especially since I knew the clothes beneath it were soaked, and her bare legs were bright red with cold.

"I'm not sure," I said, glancing around, trying to figure out what to do as worry and frustration warred for prominence in my gut. "We're seven miles in by my GPS, so if the maps were even close to right, those cabins should be nearby."

"Maybe they're off the trail. Maybe we missed a sign or something?"

"I don't think so. Archie and Aubrey said this trail leads to the cabins. And the trail is clear enough."

Annalee nodded, her whole body shaking.

"Do you want to keep looking? Or would you rather turn around and start heading back? We'll drop altitude fast and we might move out of the snow and back to rain, but at least it will be getting warmer, not colder." I didn't like this idea, based on how cold I knew she already was, but I wanted her to decide, because we were getting very close to the point where this outing was becoming dangerous. Annalee needed to get warm. Soon. So did I, I realized as I flexed my fists, trying to get feeling back into my fingers, which were burning with cold.

She straightened, her face grim. "Let's find those fucking cabins." She marched ahead, the snow swirling thick around us as the wind continued to blow, and I followed, worry and a tinge of fear growing in my gut.

The trees were becoming sparser up here, thanks to the

elevation, and while it exposed us to the onslaught of the storm, it also made it less likely that we'd walk right by some tiny shack huddled in a stand of pine trees. We walked another fifteen minutes, the storm behaving like the evil villain in our story, actively trying to stop us with icy fingers of wind and snow that was coming down almost horizontally, forcing me to shield my face with already frozen hands.

I was about to demand that we turn around and get down as fast as we could when Annalee spoke up.

"Is that?" Her voice was small and frightened, and I had an urge to put my arms around her, pull her close to try to give her whatever warmth I had left. It's what I would have done for Lily. Or Poppy. But Annalee was not part of my family, and I had no right to touch her.

I looked up, using my hands to shield my eyes from the blasting snow, and relief washed through me. There, maybe one hundred feet ahead, were four small structures, dilapidated and sad, but fully intact. "Yes!" I said, my voice louder than I'd intended. Annalee and I both picked up speed, heading for the little cabins.

"Do we have keys?" she asked. "I didn't even consider that they could be locked."

"Yeah," I said, pulling out the old ring of keys Archie had given me before we'd left.

The cabins were built of timber, not log cabins like I'd expected. They had little roofs sloping down from a peak along the center and each had a brick chimney poking up from the top. One clearly had some damage, evidenced by an obvious hole in the roof, but the one we stood in front of looked intact, if neglected. The wood was worn and weathered, but it seemed to be sturdy, and the glass in the little window by the door was solid.

It took a few minutes of fumbling with the keys. My fingers

were so numb they were almost unusable, but eventually I managed to fit the correct key into the lock of the first little cabin after trying all four.

The door swung in with a groan, and Annalee and I practically tumbled in on top of one another, the dark quiet space a welcome respite from the relentless wind outside.

I pushed the door shut behind us and we both stood in the center of a small room, looking around, dripping and shivering.

"Not much warmer in here," she said, though the cabin did hold some remnants of what had been a warm summer day until a few hours earlier, and it was better than being outside. I moved to push the curtains from the small square windows, letting the glare of white snow illuminate the space around us.

The cabin was two rooms. We stood in the living room, which also doubled as a small kitchenette. There was a basin, a wood stove, some cupboards and a little table pushed up beneath one of the square windows. On the other side of the room was a fireplace, a couple upholstered chairs and a low table. In the corner was a stack of wood that looked to be crumbling to dust. In the second room was a double bed, a small table, and a dusty, broken mirror hung on the wall. The place was in pretty good shape, all things considered, and I was relieved. Douggie Masters would be fine in here for one night.

"Five-star accommodations for sure," Annalee stuttered, the joke losing its punch in the face of her shivering.

"Better than being out there," I said. "There's wood in here. Might be dry at least."

I looked around, taking in Annalee's shaking form and putting together a plan in my head.

"Let's take our packs into the bedroom and empty them out, see what dry clothes we've got. Then you get out of your wet stuff and put on whatever you can find. I'm gonna get a fire going." I glanced at the sad pile of wood. "Somehow." I wondered at what might have taken up residence in the chimney in the years since a fire had burned in this place.

"I'd make a joke about you trying to get me out of my clothes," she said, "but I'm too damned cold."

I stiffened a bit, mostly because my mind had gone to inappropriate places as I pictured Annalee pulling off her wet shorts, exposing all that silky skin. "Ha," I managed.

I dropped my pack on the bed and pulled out all the extra stuff Aubrey had shoved in there. I had a couple pairs of thick socks, some sweatpants, a thermal shirt and a few long sleeved T-shirts in various sizes. Monroe pulled similar things from her pack. There was enough here for both of us, and relief replaced some of my worry. We would be able to get warm. That was something.

She was moving slowly, her fingers fumbling as she tried to unzip the jacket she wore over her wet clothes. I turned and helped her, trying not to think about other situations in which I'd unzipped a woman's garments, trying to remind myself that Annalee was off limits.

"Just get it all off," I suggested. "I'll step out." I grabbed the dry thermal shirt and moved toward the door to give her some privacy, but she stopped me.

"Mateo?" Her voice was small, frozen. "Could you help me a little more? My fingers..."

My heartrate galloped at the need in her voice, and at the idea that she wanted me to strip her completely. But I knew she wasn't asking like that, and I tried to swallow the attraction I couldn't shake for her.

"Yeah." I pulled my own shirt off fast, eager to put on something dry. I shrugged on the dry thermal shirt and moved toward her. She stood shivering, looking smaller, her drenched hoodie clinging to her curves. "Uh," I let my fingers slide under the hem of her sweatshirt, grabbing the other layers beneath it too. Her eyes found mine, and held there for a flash, and something inside me stirred. I pulled my gaze away as my fingers brushed her bare, icy skin and lifted.

"I'm too cold to be modest," she said, meeting my eyes again for a brief second with an expression of pleading mixed with something else, something vulnerable and soft.

"Arms up," I told her, trying to tell myself this was just like helping Lily dress. That worked right up until Monroe stood before me, shivering in a pink lace bra that barely contained a set of glorious, plump breasts. I swallowed hard, getting a grip on myself before the shirt was off her head.

I dropped her wet clothing and turned to pull one of the long-sleeved T-shirts from the bed. "Here," I said, turning back to her only to find she'd shrugged out of the bra, leaving her exposed from the top up and sending my brain clunking to a standstill. "Uh..."

"Shirt," she said, meeting my eyes with something like a dare.

"Yeah," I managed, holding it up so she could slip into it. When she was covered again, my mind began to regain standard functioning capacity. "Uh, sorry."

"If you hadn't reacted at all, I guess I would have been disappointed," she said, pointing at a sweater on the bed. "Can I have that too? This is so much better already."

"Yeah." I grabbed the sweater and held it open for her, feeling ashamed at having taken such a bald look at her—but god, it was a vision I wouldn't forget anytime soon. "You okay with your, uh..." I couldn't speak as my mind began to imagine me helping her out of her shorts.

"I can do it," she said, and when I looked back into her face, she wore a knowing smile, as if she understood exactly what had shot through my head.

"Okay, yeah." I moved to the end of the bed and snagged a

pair of sweatpants that looked like they might be a little snug, but I needed to be dry more than I cared about fashion. "I'm gonna go get that fire going."

I went into the living room, shrugging my hiking boots and pants off and pulling on the sweats. They weren't just snug. They fit me like leggings made for a six-year-old girl. But they were warm and dry, and they'd have to do for now. At least they were grey and not bright pink or something.

Alone in the front room, I had a moment to think about the situation we were in. I had been worried about controlling my attraction to Annalee on a day hike, but now we were potentially going to be stranded here overnight, and I was going to have a very rough night as my mind insistently replayed the moments we'd just shared in the bedroom. Her, shivering with nothing on except her shorts, her glorious breasts practically begging me to touch them.

Shit, I needed to get it together.

The wood in the corner was crumbling with the ravages of time and insects, but I found a good amount of soft dry shards that would work as kindling, and several larger logs that might burn for a little while. Hopefully long enough for this storm to pass. There was a little box of matches atop the mantel, and I was happily surprised to find it almost full. Soon, a merry little flame blazed to life in the grate. A few minutes later, the entire space was filling with smoke.

"Uh, so you've got the fire going, I smell," Annalee called from the bedroom.

"Shit, shit," I said as I scrambled around looking for a way to open the flue. There was a lever at the side of the fireplace, and after a few tugs, it ground open and the flames in the grate swelled with the increased airflow.

I moved to the front door and pulled it open, gratified as

some of the smoke rushed out into the cold, replaced by a bracing blast of clear cold air.

After a moment, the cabin was mostly clear, and the fire was steadily burning, radiating a tiny bit of heat into the room. I closed the door and for the first time in hours, felt myself relax. Annalee moved into the room wearing sweatpants that fit her perfectly and an oversized sweater that could have fit two of her.

She made a beeline for the fire in a pair of thick socks, and held her hands out in front of her. After a moment she turned and shot me a dazzling smile. "I think I'll live. Thanks for the—" her smile wobbled as she began to laugh. "Mother of cornbread, what are you wearing?"

I shrugged. "This is all there was."

"Those pants are painted on," she giggled. "I guess we can give up this treasure hunt."

"What?"

"I've located the family jewels." She laughed hysterically, covering her mouth with one hand and squeezing her eyes shut. "Oh God, I need to take a picture." She moved back toward the bedroom, clearly going for her phone.

"Don't even think about it," I warned. "Desperate times call for desperate measures. No need for photos."

She laughed some more, tears squeezing out the corners of her eyes, and even though she was having fun at my expense, it was a relief to see her warm and happy.

"Go on, get it out of your system," I said, pulling my hiking pants from the wet pile on the floor. "This is what we've got until these dry." I spread my pants out in front of the fire, trying not to dissect her tone or her words to see what she might be thinking about my family jewels.

"Oh man," she said, sinking into one of the cushioned chairs, which made a cloud of dust puff up around her. "That makes the whole march of near death almost worth it."

"Glad you're enjoying it," I told her.

"Oh, I am," she said, her eyes dropping a couple more times to where my junk was very clearly outlined by the tight pants. I swallowed hard as her eyes widened slightly, pushing any thoughts of Annalee and my dick as far down as I possibly could. Nothing good would come from that train of thought.

Chapter 8
Ignoring the Ghosts

ANNALEE

Now that I was actually almost warm again, my mind was working slightly more functionally than it had been for the last hour or so when I really thought there was a tiny possibility of death in my near future.

The thing about freezing though, I was realizing, was that once you were past a certain level of cold, you just began not to care as much. Almost as if your mind was too cold to plow forward with its usual efforts at resisting things like freezing or worrying. I hadn't quite been there, but I was able to admit now that a nap had been beginning to seem like a good solution to the freezing issue. Of course that would have been the kind of nap people don't wake up from.

My mind strayed to the story Ernie had told us, the people who'd died right here, maybe close to where I was right now.

Maybe we weren't quite that near to being in real trouble up here. I didn't care now, though, since there was a fire glowing in the fireplace, I was covered in warm, soft clothes, and Mateo was parading around with his very impressive goods fully on display.

He was definitely nice to look at, even if he was a little grumpy and serious for my personal tastes. He had that soft looking sandy gold hair, which was beginning to make a nice little scruff along his tanned jaw. And those eyes. I'd never seen quite that shade of green before, like watered down sea glass. Mystical and strange.

The body didn't hurt the total package either, that was for sure. He was strong and built, and the parts that hadn't been carved through years of hard work in construction looked to be equally well-sized.

All that said, I'd spent plenty of time around guys I worked with, guys who looked good but were strictly off limits. And while this might be a little different than being in a squadron, it was mostly the same situation. Here was an attractive guy I could flirt with, but could not touch. And based on the way his pupils had dilated when he'd helped me out of my shirt and gotten a look at my chest, I suspected he might have similar thoughts about me.

Hell, I knew he did. Women could tell when a man was interested.

But this man wasn't some twenty-something sailor looking for a quick fling with no attachments. He came ready-made at a whole other level, one I had no interest in reaching. The family level. The one where you had to think beyond yourself and start worrying about things like whether your proclivity for the F-word would fuck up the next generation and if you were even close to the kind of role model you needed to be. I already knew the answers to those questions, and I'd built myself that way by design. I was not mom material. Not that Mateo was asking. Just thinking ahead far enough to see that no good would come of pulling those skin-tight sweats off his incredible body.

No good at all.

"You hear me?" he asked, and I realized Mateo had been speaking to me and that I might have been staring at his junk. It was hard not to.

"Sorry, yeah." I had no idea what he'd said. "I mean, no. What?"

"I said I was gonna radio the lodge and let them know we're okay. What should I say our plan is?"

"I guess that depends," I said, holding my hands out to the lovely fire. "What is our plan?"

Mateo sank into the other chair and reached his own hands toward the fire. "I don't know." We each stared into the flames for a moment, and then he said. "The snow isn't slowing. But maybe Archie can give us an idea what the forecast is at this point, and we can plan from there. I don't want to head back out as long as it's falling like this."

"He said it was supposed to snow all night," I said.

"Maybe it's changed." Mateo's voice didn't hold much hope.

I glanced out the window. The snow was dropping heavily, making it hard to see past the thick flakes still rushing around in the wind. "Yeah. I'm not anxious to go be cold again."

"Thing is," Mateo said. "If we stay much longer, we're not gonna have enough daylight to get back today anyway."

I felt my spine stiffen. I hadn't really thought about that.

"Not sure I want to spend the night up here." It wasn't that I was scared. It just felt like a much more real crisis if we were stuck here overnight, and part of the reason I'd come to Kasper Ridge was to avoid serious crises. I'd had enough of those to last me a lifetime between my childhood and flying in the Navy.

"Yeah." Mateo blew out a breath and rubbed a hand over his forehead and through his hair. "Lemme see what Archie has to say." He went to the bedroom to retrieve the walkie talkie and came back carrying that and the rest of our wet clothes, which he took care to spread on the little coiled rug to one side of the fire. I watched with amusement as he gently set my bra down to dry, spreading the cups out with something approaching reverence.

"Hey Archie, come in," he said, sitting back up in the chair and holding the device in front of him. "Archie, it's Mateo and Annalee. Come in."

There was a bit of static and some crackling, and then a buzzing noise. Finally, a voice broke through. "Hey guys. It's Aubrey."

Relief soothed a bit of the worry I'd been feeling. Aubrey had made it back. Good.

"Where are you guys? How's the weather up there?"

"Hey," Mateo said, meeting my eyes for a moment and then turning back to the fire. "We made it to the cabins. Four of them, all standing. We got inside one and made a fire. We're wet and cold, so thawing out and trying to wait out the storm."

"Good," Aubrey said. "You might need to wait a while. This thing took everyone by surprise. Now they're predicting a foot down here and more at higher elevations. Snow's supposed to last into tomorrow night."

"What?" I stood, shock at this news making me feel like I needed to spring into some kind of action. Only, there was nothing I could do.

"Shit," Mateo said. "Aubrey, could you call Julia for me? Let her know."

"Yeah, of course."

Static filled the line again, Aubrey's voice cutting in and out.

"Hey, missed that last part," Mateo said.

"I said, don't forget to look for clues while you're up there." Mateo looked at me, and we each rolled our eyes. We were potentially stranded in a snowstorm, and they were worried about their treasure hunt. Though really, I was curious whether we might find anything up here too.

"Sure," he said. "Keep in touch."

"We will. Stay safe, guys."

Mateo set the walkie talkie on the table between us and we both spent a long moment in silence.

"So," I said. "The plan then... sounds like we'd better find some more wood and figure out what we're having for dinner. Maybe check these other cabins."

"You okay with spending the night?" he asked. There was a note of concern in his voice that reminded me of my dad, of the way he'd looked out for me when I was little. I hadn't thought of that in a long time; I'd spent most of my adult life ensuring I could take care of myself.

"Sure," I said, filling my voice with bravado. It was the same tactic I'd used when I'd been preparing to launch off the carrier the first time. Back then I'd found that if I pretended to be brave, I became brave. Figured it would work now too.

"You warm enough to go out and get eyes on the other cabins? See what kind of shape they're in, grab whatever wood we can, and look for clues? Gonna be dark soon."

I didn't love the idea of going back outside, but we wouldn't be going far. "Sure."

We both pulled our boots back on and Mateo picked up the rusty key ring he'd tossed on the windowsill. A few minutes later, we were back out in the frigid cold, huddled against the second cabin as Mateo struggled to find the right key. When the door finally creaked open, we both peered in.

Shock rumbled through me, a low warning deep in my bones. "Holy shit."

Chapter 9
Luxury Accommodations

MATEO

The door to the second cabin swung open, and despite the cold behind us driving us inside, the smell alone pushed us right back out.

"What happened in here?" I asked aloud, though it was somewhat clear. The place was a disaster of shredded furniture, animal scat, and demolished blankets and cushions. Something had been nesting in here, and from the smell of it, it died here too.

"Next cabin," Annalee suggested, stepping backward, out into the driving snow again. I wasn't going to argue with her, and I didn't see much point in locking the door to this cabin. It was in far worse shape than the one we'd lucked into the first time, probably because of the hole in the roof. We moved to door number three, and after a few minutes, I got the key into the lock and the door open. We stepped inside, pushing the door shut behind us. We shivered and gasped—the temperature was still dropping, and though I wasn't soaked through anymore, I missed the relative warmth of the little fire we'd built. However, without more wood, we wouldn't have a fire for long.

"What are we looking for?" Annalee asked as we stood side by side, gazing around the darkening space. Her shoulder pressed into my arm, and the warmth generated there was comforting. I had that urge again, to put my arm around her, to pull her to me. But again, I resisted, stepping toward the fire-place at the side of the room.

"Wood, food, blankets. And clues, I guess." I wasn't convinced there was any real treasure, but like everyone else, I was a tiny bit captivated by the possibility. We were here. We might as well look.

"Right. The hunt. Very important." Annalee began looking around the kitchen area of the small room, opening the few cupboards along the wall, while I looked for a woodpile like the one in our cabin. "There's a good amount of wood here," I said, moving aside the few disintegrating logs on the top of the pile as relief lightened my mood.

"Bedroom's clean," she said. "You want me to grab these blankets? Couple here in a chest at the end of the bed."

"Yeah," I said. "We'll need them."

It was as if we both had the same thought at the same moment, because Monroe stepped into the bedroom doorway, one of the blankets pulled around her shoulders and her head tipped to one side. "Mateo," she said slowly. "Are we planning to sleep together tonight?"

Her eyes danced with mischief, but it was a legitimate question. I had kind of assumed, but now that it was clear there was at least one other workable cabin, it wouldn't be strictly necessary.

"I mean..." I tried to imagine each of us alone in one of these stark little cabins, burning wood for two fires. "It would make more sense to conserve supplies. And it would be warmer to stay together. Two bodies generating heat." It was hard work not to picture us together in that little bed, sharing body heat. But this wasn't about attraction, I reminded myself. It was about survival, really.

"We could each have our own little cabin," she mused, poking around the space. This cabin had a small bookshelf under the window, some ragged paper in a pile on one of the shelves. "It would be like having separate bungalows in Tahiti. We could just imagine the ocean beneath us, the sun beating down..." she trailed off and I wondered for a moment if she was suffering from some kind of hypothermic mania.

"A little colder here."

"A lot fucking colder here," she said, turning to face me, a wry grin on her pretty full lips. "Yeah. Makes sense, I guess. Conserve heat."

I didn't answer, since it seemed like it was decided. The two of us were spending the night up here. Together. In a tiny cabin with one small bed and a storm raging outside.

The warm glow that sprang to life inside me at the thought of holding Annalee in my arms in the darkness of the long night was nothing, I decided. Probably my fatherly instincts. She was vulnerable. I would do my best to protect her. Only... looking at her now, her mass of golden waves spilling down her shoulders and her curves encased in layers of fabric — she didn't look especially vulnerable. That was the thing about her, I decided.

Monroe—Annalee—was no delicate little woman to be

protected and shielded. If anything, she might be able to protect me, and she could certainly take care of herself. She'd held her own against who knew how many cocky men who thought they were better than her just by nature of what hung between their legs. If anyone could take care of themselves, she could.

Why was that so fucking attractive?

"There's a pile of stuff over here," she said, pulling my attention back from ruminations about my inappropriate interest in her.

"Yeah? What stuff?" I moved to her side, pulling my phone out and using the flashlight to illuminate the shelf she was leaning over.

"Like... a manuscript, maybe? Look, all typed out."

I reached out to flip through the tall stack of typewritten pages, coming to a blank one about one third of the way down. I pulled the top stack off and looked more closely. "Not a manuscript," I said. "A script. Like for a play. Or a movie."

Annalee lifted the next pile into her hands, moving closer to share the light I was aiming at the papers. "This one too. 'The Map,' it's called."

"That's a little ironic, no?" I met her eyes, a jolt of heat rolling through me at the amusement I saw there, the warmth and life.

"Maybe we can take these back and read a bit later. Like in front of the fire?" She shivered, a whole-body shudder that reminded me exactly how frigid it was growing as the sun slid down the sky outside.

"Good point. Any food?"

"Nothing." Annalee piled the scripts into her arms, I scooped together as much wood as I could carry, and we headed through the snowfall back to the first cabin.

As we stepped inside, it was comforting to find the little fire still burning and the room much warmer than the temperature outside.

"Should we check the last one?" She asked.

I didn't want to. It was cozy and warm in here, but there was a chance we'd find something really useful in the last cabin, and it would be silly not to look.

"I can go if you want to stay here," I told her. Annalee put the scripts on the little table, and tugged the blanket tighter around her shoulders.

"No way," she said. "We stick together."

"Okay," I agreed. "While we still have a bit of light then."

She followed me back out, shutting the door tightly behind her, and we trudged to the farthest cabin out. This one was set a little ways beyond the others, almost as if there had been one other between the third cabin and this one at some point, but there was no sign of a fifth cabin. We opened the door and pushed inside.

"Nothing died in here, so that's a plus," she said.

"Pretty sparse though," I added, looking around. This cabin was barely furnished, the coiled rug in the center of the room exposed by the lack of a couch or armchairs atop it. There was a small table in the kitchen area with two straight-back chairs, and a double bed in the bedroom, just as in our cabin. But no wood-pile, and nothing on the kitchen shelves. No mysterious scripts, either.

"Nothing useful, I guess," Annalee said. "Let's get back."

I agreed, locking the door to this cabin behind me and following her through the little rutted trail we'd left in the snow back to the first cabin. As we stepped inside, she said, "home, sweet home," and turned to me with a bright smile.

"For one night, I suppose it will have to be."

"At least it's warming up," she said, moving into the bedroom and beginning to pull the covers from the bed.

"What are you doing?" I asked.

"Checking for snakes and spiders."

"Probably too damned cold for them."

"Can't be too careful."

I nodded, letting her go about her business. I wandered into the kitchen, taking inventory of supplies. "I'm gonna get some snow to melt over the fire for water," I told her. We had whatever was left in our water bottles, but there was plenty of snow at this point—might as well use it.

Annalee gave me an uncertain look, pulling one half of her bottom lip between her teeth. "What do we do about... I mean, there's no bathroom."

I frowned. "If you have to go, we go together."

"Not my favorite plan."

I imagined her wandering out to the trees behind the cabin alone in the dark, stripping half naked to take care of business. I didn't like the idea of her being exposed like that, even if the thought of getting her clothes off was becoming more appealing by the minute. "I'd just stand guard, Annalee. I wouldn't look."

She stopped remaking the bed and moved to the doorway to look at me, a strange expression on her face. "You called me Annalee."

I shrugged. "Seems more fitting than Monroe. Feels a little weird to call you by a nickname forever."

"I like it," she said softly, and then she turned and went back to the bed, fluffing tatty old pillows and pulling on the extra blankets we'd scrounged from the other cabin. When she was done, she came back out to stand by the fire. "Okay, then," she said. "Let's take care of business."

Together, we went back out into the cold darkness, and we each did what needed doing, my ears alert the whole time for anything outside of the quietly falling snow, the occasional gusts of wind. The storm was calming, though the snow was not letting up. At least the freezing wind had lessened.

It occurred to me that we were not in any real danger of freezing now. But as I followed Annalee back into the tiny cabin that would be our shared home for the night, I wondered if I'd survive the growing temptation I felt to move closer to her.

"Aubrey planned well," she said, moving to the counter in the kitchen where we'd lined up the supplies Aubrey had insisted we bring. There was a pile of protein bars, several cans of tuna and chicken, and a few more of beans and vegetables.

"I guess these were the things we were supposed to leave up here in case someone got stuck," I mused.

"I think that ghost story really freaked her out," Annalee said, examining the cans lined up before her.

"Ghost story?" I said, shaking my head.

She turned and looked at me, evidently weighing something in her mind. "You don't look like the type to scare easily."

"I'm not."

She nodded once, seeming to decide something, then said, "dinner first. Then ghost stories."

We agreed, and when we were both settled in front of the warm fire with bowls of beans, chicken, and corn in our hands, I pressed again.

"So, this ghost story..."

"Right." She told me a story about some resort guests who'd ventured up the trail we'd just hiked, in the summertime. And had encountered a freak storm, just like we had. Only in her story, something went really wrong. The people got separated somehow, a couple of them wandering out in the storm and dying there. And the rest—well, it sounded like maybe they'd died here in one of these cabins.

I shook my head. "That's really terrible. But it's not surprising. Stuff like that happened a lot back then, I think."

"But how?" She asked looking around. "There's shelter. Firewood. Food."

"But that's the point, I guess. Back then, there was only the shelter. And you said it snowed for a week."

The horror of the situation those folks had been in must have set in, because Annalee set her bowl down and stared into the flames for a moment. "They might have sat right here. Talked about what they were going to do. Before they..."

That deep worrying dread threatened to wrap around me too, but I shook it off. "Yeah."

Chapter 10
Science Experiments

ANNALEE

I didn't like thinking about the people who'd been here all those years ago, about what had happened to them. I'd been cold today. I was still a little cold, but I couldn't imagine the way they must have felt—the fear layered on top of that frigid worry seeping through their very bones. The desperation of knowing there was no real way out.

The snow was still falling in thick drifts outside, piling up against the walls of our cabin. I hoped it didn't plan to fall for a week. But we'd know, wouldn't we? Weather forecasting had come a long way. Maybe this storm had packed a bigger punch than the weather people had predicted, but no way could it go on for seven days with no one calling that kind of longevity.

"You okay?" Mateo's soft voice broke through the worried thoughts in my mind, and I turned away from the dancing flames to look at him.

God, he was handsome. He had a square jaw, and a look about him that just told you he was a good person—but it was those eyes that really got me. It felt like he could see right through me, and I wondered how much he'd already figured out about who I really was. Under the "Monroe" shell I wore.

"Yeah," I said, not bothering to coax any of the usual brightness into my voice. "I'm okay. It's just hard thinking about those people dying up here. About how they must have felt—so helpless and alone."

He was watching me now, those eyes undoubtedly seeing far more than I'd meant to show him. But I was tired. And the pretending grew difficult the later it got at night.

His voice was soft, and I had to rip my gaze away from those eyes, or I'd lose my mind and push myself into his arms and beg him to help me forget everything, just for one night. That was what happened sometimes, when it was too hard to carry things myself. I'd find someone to distract me, to carry some of it for a little while. One night, maybe a week. But Mateo was not that guy. We worked together. We had the same friends. Besides, I'd already decided that coming to Kasper Ridge was about breaking patterns.

"Yeah," I said, standing and taking both our empty bowls to carry to the kitchen. I put them in the basin, and then moved back to the fire with a towel wrapped around my hand to take some of the hot water steaming in the pot Mateo had pushed into the coals. "I'll just get some water so these can rinse. They'll be a bitch to scrub in the morning."

He watched me, and I could practically hear the wheels

turning in his mind as he put the pieces together—the few he had, anyway.

I finished filling our bowls and looked around the sparse little cabin. The light of the fire filled it with a cheery glow, and the white frames made by the snow against the windowpanes almost made me feel like we were in a charming little painting.

"Be better if we'd thought to bring some whiskey up here," I said, looking around for a bottle of Half Cat that I already knew we didn't have.

"We would have if we'd had any idea we might get stranded," Mateo said, rising. "I did find this, though." He moved to the stack of firewood he'd piled when we'd come back from the other cabins and reached beside it, rising to show me a full bottle of brown liquid.

"What is it?"

He squinted at the label, which was yellowed with age, as I stepped closer. "Some kind of bourbon?"

"Sold," I said, going back to the kitchen area and returning with two tin cups.

"Does alcohol have a half life?" he asked, pulling the seal from around the cork and then pouring a splash into each of the cups. One side of his mouth was pulled up into a skeptical expression, but his eyes danced with amusement when they met mine.

"I have no idea, that'd be a question for Wiley, I guess."

"We'll find out," he said. He lifted his cup to mine. "For science."

"Science?"

"Yeah, it's our duty to learn whether a bottle of bourbon abandoned in desolate cabins for decades is still good." He waited for me to touch my cup to the rim of his, which I did, a tinny clank sounding merry against the crackling background of our fire.

"To science."

We each took a sip, our eyes holding one another's as we did. There was something intimate in the action, in the whole setting. Just the two of us, up here miles away from anyone or anything—away from reality.

Mateo must have felt it too, because he tore his eyes from mine and took a step back, moving back to his spot by the fire. I joined him, keeping my distance as I sank into my own spot.

"Hit me," I said, holding out my cup again.

He refilled us both and put the bottle down. We were silent as the seconds ticked by, the fire filling the awkward quiet around us. Finally, Mateo said, "Where are you from, Annalee?"

I felt a door creak open somewhere inside me, the things I kept hidden behind it creeping toward the sudden opportunity, their yellow eyes glowing with anticipation at being let out. "The south," I said, knowing that wouldn't end the conversation, and hating myself for wanting to tell him more. I didn't talk about the past. Not usually.

He shot me a smile, and said, "Okay. Let's see... I don't think you're a Texas girl, and I don't get a Florabama vibe from you."

"What do you know about Florabama?" I asked, laughing as I recalled the bar on the Florida-Alabama border where we'd hung out while we were in flight school down in Pensacola.

"Enough," he said simply, shaking his head. "I get more of an antebellum vibe from you. Big dresses, sweet tea on the porch swing, that sort of thing. Tennessee?" He seemed to be asking himself, his eyes raking my face as he thought. "No," he amended after a second. "Georgia. Am I right?"

I let out a little puff of air. "You ain't wrong, sugar."

Mateo's grin spread wide at the long-buried accent I whipped out for him.

The bourbon was creating a spreading warmth in my chest,

slowly working toward the ends of my cold fingers, my toes. It was hard to believe that just a few hours ago, I'd really thought I might freeze. "Your turn," I told him.

"I'm from here," he said. "Easy. Next question."

I raised an eyebrow at his invitation. "All right. Tell me about your daughter."

He stiffened just slightly before dropping his gaze to the liquid in his cup for a second, and I suspected he had a door sealed up somewhere inside too. He must have. "Lily," he said, his voice soft like a daddy's gentle hug. "She's seven, and she's my whole fucking world."

I nodded, part of me envying the little girl suddenly—less because it was Mateo who clearly thought she hung the moon, more because I knew she had the kind of love a little kid deserved. No expectations. Just acceptance.

"She's a live wire," he said. "Always curious, always testing me, testing the world."

I watched him, waiting for him to mention her mother, to tell me more. But he didn't, and I held my tongue, though I desperately wanted to ask.

"Why'd you join the Navy?" he asked.

"Oh, your turn again, is it?"

"Seems like."

"There was a recruiting office in town. Talked to them a bit in high school. I had good grades, and they pretty much promised me jets if I did ROTC in college, so I stepped on the path." It wasn't the whole answer, but I thought it might satisfy him.

"Why jets? Why the military at all?" He shuddered slightly as he asked this. "I can't imagine flying like that," he added.

"You don't like to fly?" I probed. I couldn't imagine life without the sensation of soaring over the tops of the gathered clouds, feeling free and lucky, like I was one person in the whole world who got to experience that rush.

"Did it a few times. Hated it. Almost died. Never getting in a plane again."

"Died?"

"Maybe that's an exaggeration. But my first flight was a rough flight. And it scarred me for life. They made an emergency landing. That was enough for me. I had to fly a few times in the Corps and gritted my teeth the whole time."

I thought about that. This hot strong man was afraid to fly. Interesting.

"So," he prompted. "Why flying for the military?"

I swallowed more of the bourbon, enjoying the burn, the heat of it. "I needed to get far away from Honey Point, Georgia," I told him. "As far as I could get."

He watched me for a moment after I said this, his eyes narrowing slightly. I could feel the next question about to spring forth, so I asked one instead.

"Lily's mom." Okay, maybe it wasn't a question. But he knew what I wanted to know.

"Died," he said, and the word hung in the air, turning and twisting like a living thing, begging to be considered, understood.

It wasn't polite—hell, if my southern roots taught me anything it was that, but I asked anyway. "How?"

He looked at me, those pretty eyes hardening before they became soft again. He let out a breath and then turned to look into the fire. "The doctors told her she shouldn't get pregnant. She had a condition called aplastic anemia." He closed his mouth, and I watched the Adam's apple on his throat bob once, twice. "We wanted a family."

"She died in childbirth?" I guessed, thinking how hard it must have been for Mateo to go on, to raise his daughter alone.

"No. Two years later. But she was never the same. She had a bone marrow transplant, but it didn't help. She died after that." This part was delivered in a monotone, as if the only way he could say these words was to keep emotion from them entirely.

"I'm so sorry," I said. And I was. Sorry I'd brought it up, sorry I'd pried. I knew better than anyone that there were some things people didn't need to talk about, things that only made life harder if you took them back out to examine.

He nodded. He didn't tell me it was okay—clearly it wasn't. He didn't ask me another question.

I wondered what came next as we both sat stiffly, the specter of his dead wife in the room with us like one of those ghosts who roamed these cold lonely hills.

"More?" he asked, holding up the bottle.

"Just a splash," I told him.

He refilled us both and then got up to stare out the window. "Still coming down heavy," he said. "I'm gonna check in once more." He went to the table where the walkie talkie lay, and picked it up.

"Shit," he said, almost immediately.

"What?" I put down my cup, went to his side.

"Battery's dead."

Something like fear raced through me, cooling my warming veins and pricking my skin with worry, with what ifs. "We have more," I suggested, hoping if it wasn't a question, it would be true.

He moved to the table where we'd unloaded our supplies. "Let's see."

He picked up a few batteries Aubrey had packed, and I smiled with relief. "See? Always prepared!"

The batteries, however, didn't work.

"Does the cold affect them?" I asked.

"Maybe. I don't know." Mateo put the walkie talkie down

on the table and picked up his cup again. "It's late anyway. Nothing they tell us will change anything. We're stuck here tonight."

I tried not to let the words hurt. I wasn't forcing myself on Mateo—I hadn't conjured this storm. But I didn't like the idea of him feeling stuck with me, either.

I was tempted to offer to sleep in one of the other cabins again, but I didn't. It would have been a hollow offer. I couldn't imagine myself going outside now, trudging through the cold wet snow and trying to sleep in a frigid old cabin alone. It didn't make sense, and I knew Mateo wouldn't let me anyway.

"I think I'm going to turn in," I said, the atmosphere between us still awkward, his wife still wafting through the ether.

"Yeah," he said. "Be there in a bit. Gonna shore up the fire."

I went to the little bedroom, leaving the door open for warmth, and pulled open one side of the bed. I removed the bulky sweater, but left the rest of my clothes on. It was too cold to strip down properly, and I doubted Mateo would be thrilled find me in here in my birthday suit. Things were uncomfortable enough already.

As I snuggled into the icy sheets, I could see him out there, sitting in that chair and staring into the flames. What must it be like for him, I wondered. To love his daughter so much, but to understand that his own wanting of her had led to the death of his wife. Had he loved his wife, I wondered. The answer to that seemed pretty obvious. But also, his daughter was seven. So she'd been gone five years. And clearly, Mateo was still paying penance for whatever guilt he suffered over her death.

Sleep came pretty fast—the result of facing a seven-mile hike and a near-death experience all in one day, I supposed, and I awoke only when another body joined me in the tiny bed. The mattress depressed on the opposite side, and I couldn't help rolling in that direction. This was no high-tech tempurpedic mattress, after all.

"Sorry," I mumbled as I pressed into Mateo's sturdy back. I woke up enough to try to slide back to my side, but before I could manage it, Mateo's big hand reached around and landed on my low back, holding me in place.

"Stay," he said. "Warmer this way."

It did feel nice, pressed up against all that warm muscle, and I was too groggy to fight it or think clearly about putting up a protest. "Mmmmh," I mumbled, letting one hand slip over his waist and pressing the rest of my body against the hard planes of his.

If I'd been more awake, I might have thought about the way my breasts were pressed up against his back, or about the pleasure I took from the manly scent of him as my nose practically buried itself in his shirt. But instead, I fell into a deep, relaxed sleep, feeling safe for once. Even if it was just an illusion.

Chapter 11
That's Not a Pillow!

MATEO

I was in trouble.

I'd tried to slip into bed quietly, purposely waiting until Annalee was asleep.

The conversation we'd had wouldn't leave me alone, wouldn't let my mind go back to the place I tried to keep it. The place where I stayed busy and tired, where I didn't let myself think too much about the life I'd once had, and where I made sure I let myself feel even less.

But talking about Poppy, about what had happened—and learning even the little bit I'd discovered about my cabin mate—

had unlocked something, shaken something loose. And now I felt a little unhinged, like a boat whose anchor had slipped after it had been safely moored in one spot for years. I was adrift.

And the thing that worried me most was that it wasn't a wholly terrible feeling. But all of it was uncomfortable, and there were many reasons why the mounting interest I had in beautiful Annalee was something I needed to be wary of. Something I needed to stop if I could.

But the second I'd walked into the bedroom to see her golden hair spread over the pillow and heard her soft regular breathing, a little piece of my heart split open. It had been so long since I'd shared anything with anyone, let alone a bed.

It didn't help that my dick stood to immediate attention at the realization that I was going to climb in beside her. My whole body sizzled with awareness of her, dousing any drowsiness I'd managed to settle into by the fire.

It was impossible to get in without waking her, unfortunately, thanks to the size and age of the bed. And maybe I should have pushed her away, but I was out of strength and short on resolve. I reached for her without meaning to, every part of me wanting her close. Closer.

When she let out a soft muffled moan and her arm slid around me, it was like reaching a destination I'd been searching for after years on the trail. It was like coming home, only Annalee's soft warm body and sweet orange scent weren't quite right. She wasn't Poppy, and guilt threatened to swell inside me, pulling me under once again.

But God, I was tired of the guilt. I'd lived with it so long it was like riding a bus each day, always ending up sitting next to the smelly guy. Because you didn't want to be rude, and the guy had taken your lack of rudeness as acceptance. And so he stayed. Guilt was my smelly seatmate, and I was fucking sick of him.

So I closed my eyes and turned off everything except my awareness of the soft warm woman behind me in that little bed. I took my time, letting my mind drift over every single place where our bodies touched beneath that mound of covers, every spot where her softness pushed up against me.

Annalee's breathing was deep and even. I knew this because I could feel her chest pressed snugly up against my back, and her breath was hot between my shoulder blades. I laid there for what could have been hours, just letting myself feel. Her hand was splayed across my stomach, and as I settled, the T-shirt I wore had pulled up, so her fingers pressed into my flesh, skin on skin.

Part of me wanted to lay there forever, unmoving, just feeling her near, hearing her soft breath, inhaling her sweet scent—how did someone manage to smell like orange blossoms after hiking all day? I was pretty sure I wasn't smelling too good at this point, but Annalee's soft body against my back seemed to indicate she didn't mind.

I drifted for a while, tiptoeing the line between sleeping and waking. And then Annalee's hand dropped lower. I'd peeled off the ridiculous sweat pants I'd been wearing, leaving me in only my boxer briefs. Since she had been asleep when I'd come in, I figured it would be okay. She wouldn't know that I was mostly naked. But I hadn't counted on her pressing herself up against me. Or on me refusing to let her go back to her own side of the bed.

Now her fingers had slid just beneath the waistband of my briefs, and my entire body coiled in response. I didn't think she was even awake, but it didn't matter because I was. And now that her fingers lingered just inches from an erection that had only just begun to relax, I was becoming painfully hard again. If I'd been on my own, I would have reached down, pressed a hand hard against it, maybe given it a couple quick strokes.

Anything to relieve the need for pressure, something to take the edge off. But with her hand right there, it was a kind of torture I hadn't experienced in a very long time.

I must have moved, pressed back into her maybe. It was impossible to be still when everything in me wanted some kind of release and I knew it wasn't coming. I needed to get up, probably, to go in the other room and do something. Drink more, maybe. I definitely couldn't jack off with Annalee asleep just feet away, could I?

God, it was torture. She was right there, and my body wasn't willing to accept that I couldn't have her.

And then she moaned. It was a breathy soft little sound, accompanied by her shifting against me, rolling into me even more, and dropping that hand even lower.

My dick was at full attention now, pressing up and out of the elastic of my briefs, and her fingers dropped, grazing the side of it and sending a jolt of hot need sizzling through my body.

I laid there in agony for a long second, wishing she'd move, wishing she'd stay right there forever, my body like a fucking bomb about to go off. And just when I wasn't sure I could survive whatever this was, her fingers slid lower, tracking the length of me, and then they softly glided back up.

I didn't say anything, didn't let out the strangled moan trapped in my throat. I wasn't sure if Annalee was asleep or awake. I couldn't let this happen if she was asleep, couldn't take advantage of her like that. But it wasn't right if she was awake either. Was it?

Then her voice came soft through the darkness. "Is this okay?" As she uttered the question, her fingers wrapped me, and I nearly lost it.

"Yeah," I said, and it was half-prayer, half-grunt. "Yeah, but you don't have to."

"Mateo," she whispered, that silky hand wrapping my shaft

as her voice sifted into me, calm and smooth. "I've wanted to touch you since I met you."

Fuck. That was all I needed to hear. I pressed back against her body as her hand gripped me, harder now, beginning to work me up and down.

I reached around behind me, my hand finding the curve of her ass and pulling her closer, wanting to be enveloped by her softness, buried in her. She wrapped a leg over mine, and I let my mind drift to the way she was open for me there, pressing the center of herself up against me, using my body for heat, for pleasure.

Her hand worked in a steady rhythm as her hips rocked behind me and she let out raspy little moans here and there. I was so far gone, I had little ability to control the situation, so I just turned myself over to it. I knew that if I moved to face her, I'd be inside her within seconds, and that seemed like a big step too far. So I let her work me, and work herself against me, losing myself in the sheer ecstasy of being touched, being wanted.

I heard my own breath coming in pants, and felt Annalee's arousal rise too, as she practically straddled my side, thrusting against my hip as her hand drove me onward, closer and closer to the edge. There was one second where she paused, her hand moving erratically and then going still, and the woman riding my hip let out a shuddering moan that sent me practically over the edge. She released a few gasps after it, and I stilled, listening to Annalee come, wondering what she looked like when she did it, feeling both close to her and miles away.

But her hand gripped me tight again in the next second, and I didn't have the capacity to think anymore.

"I'm gonna..." I managed, wanting to warn her.

"Go ahead, baby," she purred, and those words were like the permission I wasn't able to give myself. Permission to come, yeah, but also like permission to feel again. Permission to live.

And I let go. Every part of my awareness was focused on Annalee, on her body, on her hand, on her mouth against my back, her hips pressed hot against my body. And when I came, it felt like something was physically ripped from my soul, dissected from my body through a jagged wound that had never healed.

She held me when it was over, her hand clasping me, though I knew she must be sticky and wet, wanting to clean up. But she stayed where she was, her body wrapping mine, her breathing calming me, and everything in that moment feeling softer and more right than anything had in years.

After a little while, she moved, removing her hand and taking her warmth away from my body. I could hear her moving through the dense fog of sleep that was coming over me. And just before it took me under, I felt her return, that soft body back against mine, her comforting breath hot on my back.

For the first time in years, I slept dreamlessly. But through every dark moment of that frigid night, some part of me remained aware of Annalee there, holding me.

Chapter 12
Don't Eat the Yellow Snow

ANNALEE

There was something so hot about a man as stoic and tortured as Mateo. I'd seen it the first second I'd met him, all that angst tied up inside him—guilt and sorrow twisted up together in a beautiful package of handsome man.

And maybe I should have kept my hands to myself, but I could sense his need there in the darkness, could feel it like a suffering animal in the room with us. And I needed something too.

Plus, I knew he'd never touch me. Mateo was a special

brand of chivalry and stoic guilt, and I sensed that he'd been trapped in his misplaced sense of ownership over his wife's death since the day she'd passed.

It was glorious touching him, feeling like I alone could give him some kind of release from the confines where he kept himself. It didn't make much sense, but in some crazy way, I told myself I was saving this man in my arms.

Saving him with a magical hand job. Ha.

But when the dim morning light turned our frigid little bedroom from murky black to gray, I wasn't sure what would happen next. A guy like Mateo—one so dedicated to his family and to the guilt of losing them—might not handle a morning after especially well.

Our bodies were still pressed together when I woke up, more out of necessity than anything else. The tiny cabin had cooled during the night, and I didn't hear the comforting fire sizzling and popping low in the grate anymore. It had certainly gone out, and the thought of moving away from the warmth and comfort of Mateo's strong back was a difficult obstacle to overcome. But I needed to pee. And I wasn't sure how he'd handle waking up together after what had passed between us the night before.

I wasn't sure I trusted myself to keep my hands where they belonged this morning either. I slid from the bed into the piercing cold of the room beyond the blankets and pulled on the heavy sweater as quickly as I could. I wanted to pull one of the blankets to throw around myself, but I knew it would wake Mateo if I did, so I decided I'd get the fire going before I went out to take care of business.

In the little living room, I peeked out the window, and my heart dropped. The snow hadn't stopped overnight. If anything, the storm had picked up some fury and intent, and the landscape out the window was practically unrecognizable. Everything was blanketed in white, a pristine wonderland that I would have guessed was a couple feet deep. Could we even find the trail to get back in this?

The sky wasn't promising. Though the snow wasn't falling, the sun wasn't shining, and it felt much more like winter than late summer. A dense grayness sat low over the mountains, and I couldn't see much beyond the trees outside, the next cabin over.

"Well, shit," I muttered, moving to the fireplace. There was still a good amount of wood, and I got to work coaxing the coals from the previous night back to life with a little kindling and some puffs of air. Once they were red and glowing, I added smaller sticks and then bigger ones until I had a few flames I didn't think were going to go out when I carefully settled on a larger log. When it had caught, I stood again, steeling my resolve. I needed to go outside, even though there was absolutely no part of me that wanted to do it. Nature called.

I shoved my feet back into my boots and pulled on the hat and gloves that Aubrey had been wise enough to shove into my pack before we'd left. And then I braced myself and opened the door.

A pile of freezing snow toppled inside as soon as I pulled the door toward me, scattering itself over my feet and onto the wood floor. I did my best to step high over the snow that remained piled just outside the door, and pulled it shut again. It was still freezing out here, possibly below freezing, and the wind was light, but had an ominous strength beneath it, as if it had been waiting for us to wake before it started its onslaught once again.

I hurried around to the treeline behind the cabins, but the going was tough through the thick dense snow. I couldn't imagine hiking the seven miles back to the resort in this. Every step was three times as hard as it should have been, since I had to high step, and the dense snow clung to my ankles and feet.

Delancey Stewart

Once I'd relieved myself, I followed my tracks back to the door, and practically fell back inside in my hurry to find some modicum of warmth. I wasn't especially quiet about it, and I glanced through the bedroom door as I pushed the outside door shut again, gasping with cold.

"It's okay," Mateo's voice came from the fireplace, and I swung around to find him standing there in those too-tight sweatpants again in front of the fire. "I'm up."

His hair was a mess, and his face was creased with sleep, but my god, he was handsome. So big and sturdy and sure. And when I glanced up, expecting to see traces of regret or blame in his light green eyes, I was relieved to find only a warm smile.

"I'm glad you're back, I was just about to come out looking for you."

"I'm glad you didn't," I said, pulling the hat from my head. "You would have interrupted my little tree squat."

"Still snowing?" he asked, moving to one side to let me have a spot next to the fire.

"No, but it feels like it wants to. And the snow out there is pretty deep. Not sure we could follow the trail at this point."

He didn't respond, but dropped his chin in a nod, as his eyes found the little coiled rug at our feet.

For a moment we both stood in front of the crackling flames, and then I braved a look up at him. "Should we see if there's any coffee?"

"Good plan," he said, one big hand rubbing over his head and standing that sandy hair on end in spots. "And then I'd better dig through our stuff and see if we've got more batteries. They'll be worrying about us pretty soon. I'm just gonna head out for a second too. I'll be right back."

Mateo headed out to use the bathroom, and I stood there warming up, trying not to think about the idea of being trapped up here another day or longer. The thing was, it wasn't conve-

88

nient, but it wasn't scary, either. We had enough food. We had water. We had a warm bed and shelter, and a fire. The only thing we might run out of was firewood, depending on how long we were stuck here, and with a forest around us, it was hard to worry much about wood.

I moved to the little counter and cabinets in the kitchen, and was rewarded with an ancient-looking tin of coffee grounds. I smelled it, and though it might have been slightly musty, it still smelled like coffee. Now I just needed to figure out how to brew it. I filled the little pan with snow and set it into the coals at the bottom of the fire. There was no Mr. Coffee, no French press. We'd have to improvise, I figured. I spooned a few heaps of coffee into the pan heating on the fire just as Mateo came back in, huffing from the cold.

"That's a lot of snow," he said, beating his hands against his thighs and stomping his feet just inside the door.

I looked at the pile below him on the floor. "It is."

"Out there," he said, chuckling.

"No fancy coffee maker here, but I found some coffee. Might be a little stale."

He shrugged. "I'll take what we've got." He stood in front of the fire for a moment, warming his hands, then moved to the chair where his pack sat. He began carefully removing things from the pack, placing them on the little table.

Aubrey had been prepared as she'd thought about what supplies to plant up here in case of emergency. She just hadn't known that the emergency would happen so immediately.

When Mateo had unpacked both packs, we had a first aid kit, a few more thick sweatshirts and several pairs of warm socks, a couple more hats, a utility knife, a water bladder that was half full, a bunch of purification tablets, at least twenty more nutrition bars, a map and compass, a plastic tube of matches, a couple rain ponchos, and a length of cord.

"She doesn't mess around," Mateo said.

"She did say she spent her childhood hiking up here."

"Well, we won't starve. And we might even be able to cut some wood with this if we need to," he held up the knife.

"How long do you think we'll be stuck here?" I asked, knowing he didn't know anything more than I did.

He shook his head and picked up the walkie talkie. "No idea. But I need to let my daughter know I'm okay if I can."

My heart dropped. I'd forgotten that this wasn't just inconvenient to him. He was a daddy. Of course Lily would be worried about him.

"She's okay with your mom, though?"

"My mother-in-law," he said, a hint of bitterness in the way he formed the words. "She's not my biggest fan, but she loves my daughter."

I nodded. "Batteries?" I asked hopefully.

He shook his head. "I think we're screwed there. Aubrey thought of everything, but she must not have tested the extra batteries." He deftly removed the batteries from the back of the walkie talkie. "We can probably get one last little pop from them though." Mateo moved back to the fire, the batteries between his palms. He rolled them back and forth in his hands in front of the fire, and cleaned the ends with his shirt. "Sometimes warming them up helps."

I'd never heard of that, but I wasn't going to be a doubter. I watched as he put them back into the walkie talkie and tried to raise the resort.

The walkie crackled to life in his hand and Ghost's voice filled the little cabin. "Thank god you guys are okay."

Chapter 13
Don't Die. But Don't Forget to Hunt for Clues.

MATEO

"Yeah, we're fine," I said, talking quickly. "Need someone to get word to my mother-in-law that we're stuck though."

"Done," Archie said quickly, certainly realizing that this was my top priority.

"We're outta batteries here too, so may not be able to get in touch again."

"Shit."

"It's deep up here, and still blowing good. Forecast?" My

words were rushed; I knew the walkie talkie was probably about to die again.

"More snow and freezing temperatures today. Warming up tomorrow."

"Plan to see us then."

"Be safe guys," Archie said. "When you—" the walkie talkie died before his last words came through, and I turned to look at Annalee.

"Think he was going to remind us to look for clues?" I asked.

Her face broke into a wide grin, and the laugh she let out untwisted some of the knots inside me. "Probably. He's pretty focused on the hunt."

"I guess if I thought there were millions waiting me for me, I might be too." I set the walkie talkie down and moved back to the fire.

"So you think we'll be here another night?" Annalee said, and I couldn't tell if her voice was hopeful or wary. Neither of us had addressed what had happened between us, and while I'd risen expecting things to be uncomfortable, they really were not.

"Seems likely," I said. We both raised our eyes to the little square window, just in time to see snow beginning to drift down again.

"Okay," she said, turning in a slow circle and looking around her. "Let's make one more run for wood in the cabins next door, and see if there are any more pots or pans for melting snow."

I nodded.

"But first," she said, moving to the fire at my side. "Breakfast."

We drank tin mugs of murky liquid that she assured me was coffee and ate protein bars. I wasn't hungry or thirsty at least, so all things considered, we were in good shape for people who were stranded.

Eventually we made the trek out for the rest of the useable

firewood, and Annalee collected some other items in her back-pack from the other cabins. We each made another visit to the woods behind the cabins, and soon were back inside as the storm outdoors began to pick up steam again.

"I hope we don't get a ton more snow," she said, her voice worried.

"As soon as the sun pops back out, it'll start melting," I assured her. "That's the thing about Colorado. The weather's a little wild, but snow doesn't stick around long unless it's the dead of winter. We'll be okay." I mostly believed my own words, but I wanted to reassure Annalee.

We'd each claimed a chair, and were taking turns feeding and poking the fire. Annalee had brought the rest of the pile of scripts back in her backpack, and we each had one on our laps, though neither of us was reading. It was only mid-morning, but the day seemed to have stretched on forever already. I glanced up at the side of her face as she stared into the fire. Her lips were full, pouty almost, and the waves of her hair fell around her face, escaping the knot she'd twisted the rest of it into. Her round cheeks were rosy, and it hit me again how pretty she was. There was a compelling combination of innocence and cunning to her looks and her personality. That sweet face coupled with curves that had me aching to run my hands over them, those innocent eyes combined with the vocabulary of a sailor. Hell, she was a sailor.

I tried to picture Annalee flying a jet, streaking through the skies at crazy speeds—dropping bombs or firing missiles in an actual war. It was hard but not impossible. Everything about her screamed of capability.

"You're staring," she said, her voice laced with amusement.

"Sorry," I said, pulling my eyes away. "I was just thinking about you flying jets. That must have been insane."

"It was fun," she said. "Scary too, but I never let myself think about that until it was over."

I nodded. Not that I could really relate. Terrifying was my first thought any time flying was the topic.

"I bet your family is proud of you."

She turned and looked at me then, a tight smile on her face and her eyes assessing me, maybe deciding what to tell me. How much to share.

"Not really. I didn't go the way they thought I should. I mostly went into the military because they thought I couldn't."

"Good reason, I guess."

"Not really. I did most things for that reason."

I shook my head. "What do you mean?"

Annalee put the script on her lap aside and rose, going back to the little kitchen area. "Would you say it's too early for whiskey?"

"Not when you're snowed in with nowhere to go and nothing to do," I told her. I wanted her to talk, wanted to understand her better. And if whiskey would help her do it, I could join in.

When she was settled again, each of us having traded shitty coffee for questionable booze, she spoke.

"My mother was a pageant queen," she said. "And when she had a daughter, there was no real question about it. I'd be a pageant kid too. Follow in her footsteps and all that. My aunts were in pageants, all my cousins did them, and so I did them. And I won them, because that was what my mother expected."

"You're gorgeous, that's no surprise."

She inclined her head slightly. "Thanks," she said. "But it's not even about that. Where I come from, in my family, it's a fucking lifestyle. We ate, breathed, and dreamed those fucking pageants. It was all I was allowed to think about, talk about."

"You didn't like it."

She lifted a shoulder, and sipped her whiskey. "I didn't like that they never considered anything else. I was smart. I did well in school. But I was trapped in this expectation. I'd win pageants, score an eligible businessman, and settle down to have thirty babies. No one ever asked me what I wanted. They just told me that's what I would do."

"What did you want?"

She grinned at me. "Thank you for asking." She raised her cup to mine and we touched them together briefly.

"I had no fucking idea what I wanted. No one had ever walked me through the possibilities. But I was good at math and science, and my high school counselor was the one person who saw something in me besides the pageant stuff. He suggested I apply to a few engineering schools, think about going into science."

"Bet your family didn't expect that."

"No one did. And when I got a full ride to MIT on an ROTC scholarship, they shit themselves."

"No way they saw that coming."

"Right?" She chuckled. "I mean, I didn't either, but the recruiter knew that a woman had a good shot at it, especially at a school like that, where they got about twice as many applications from men as women. So I agreed to join the Navy when I graduated. Figured I'd do eight years or whatever, and move on with my life. All I cared about was that it got me out of Georgia, and out from under all the stifling expectations my family had for me."

"They never gave you enough credit." I shook my head, making a mental note not to do the same thing to my kid.

"Well, I was a girl, you know." She pointed at her chest and wiggled a bit, reminding me all too vividly of her gender. A flash of heat rushed through me at the memory of her soft breasts pressed up against my back the night before.

"And once I was there, it was a whole new world. The Navy told me I could get jets, and so I went for it. And I never looked back."

"What'd your family think?"

She shrugged again. "Eventually they accepted it. Kind of. I sort of quit going home a while ago."

I nodded. My own folks had died when Lily was a baby, one after the other. I missed them, and couldn't imagine just never going home. But I'd had a different family than Annalee's, clearly.

We were quiet for a little while, each of us staring into the fire and sipping our whiskey. I was surprised how relaxed I felt, knowing my daughter was probably worrying about me. But I wasn't making a choice not to try to get to her, the choice had been made for me by circumstance, and the lack of options made it easier to sink into whatever odd comfort this was.

"Your childhood doesn't sound like a dream," I told Annalee after a while. "But earlier..." I paused. Maybe it wasn't right to dig. She'd told me a lot already. "You made it sound much worse."

She turned and gave me an assessing gaze, those big round dark eyes taking me in. Her head gave one little nod, and she turned back to the fire. "Don't miss much, do you, Mateo?"

"What happened?" I asked, realizing I might be pushing too hard. She wasn't volunteering whatever this was, clearly. "I mean, you don't have to tell me."

She sighed and put her cup down on the little table, leaning into the fire. "Pageant girls like me and my little sister," she said. "They don't bother to teach us much of use. You don't have to fish or hunt to win your crown. And you don't have to swim."

She went quiet then, and a cold understanding filled me. I waited, knowing she was about to tell me the whole story, the real truth about how Annalee had become Monroe.

Chapter 14
Staying Out of Jail

ANNALEE

"My sister and I might have been my mama's little dress-up dolls, but we were still kids, and we grew up country. We wandered around and got into some trouble here and there, exploring, climbing rocks and trees, poking around the neighbor's land. That kind of stuff." I took a sip of whiskey and glanced up at Mateo. His eyes were on my face, his expression open. I continued. "When I was about ten, there was a boy I thought I liked. A kid who lived down the road from us. My sister and I rode our bikes down there, and we all went back on his land to the lake where his daddy kept a fishing boat."

The familiar darkness welled up inside me as I recalled that bright summer day, the carefree way we'd yelled and run and jumped into that boat. I took a deep breath and went on, steeling myself against the guilt.

"We were all messing around in the boat. It was tied up at the end of a dock, so we figured we were pretty safe. We didn't plan to go in the water. Plus, Joel—that was his name—he could swim."

"What happened?" Mateo whispered, and I could tell he already sensed the answer.

"I don't know really." I squeezed my eyes shut, wishing I could stop seeing it before me, wishing I could banish the feeling of worthlessness, helplessness. "Joel was balanced on the side of the boat, and he fell. Maybe my sister jumped at the wrong time, maybe I did. Cause and effect aren't huge factors when you're little. You don't think about it."

Mateo nodded, and I went on, trying not to relive that awful moment, peering over the side of the boat, searching for my friend.

"But we didn't worry much when he first went in, because he'd been making a big deal about how he swam across the lake every summer. Swimming seemed like magic to us, since we never got in past our knees. Mama was terrified of water and the thought of us swimming was something she couldn't handle. So we never learned."

I swallowed hard. "We sat in the boat and waited, watching for him. And when he didn't come popping right back up, we didn't know what to do."

No matter how I tried to push it away, the memory took me again, making me feel so powerless as life was draining out of my friend, just feet away from where I sat, useless.

"We waited, watching for him, and eventually we started racing around the boat and looking over the edges."

I leaned forward and picked up my cup again, draining it. "They fished him out later. He'd hit his head on the dock as he fell in. I guess the only good thing was that he didn't know he was drowning. He was unconscious before he hit the water."

"Oh god." Mateo let out a breath.

"If I'd known how to swim..." I said.

"You can't think like that. You don't know that you could have helped."

"I could have fucking tried," I said, bitterness coloring my words, darkening my mind. I was angry at myself, but angry at my mother too. It was her decision that we didn't need any useful skills. It was her fault I couldn't save him.

Mateo nodded, and the look in his eyes told me he understood a bit about feeling helpless. "I'm so sorry. That's awful."

I looked at him then willing determination to replace the guilt and misery that memory brought back. "That's why I quit. I wasn't going to be a pretty girl sitting in a boat while people died around me."

Mateo held my gaze. "You're so much more than that."

There was a strange look in his eyes. I just hoped it wasn't sympathy. I couldn't stand people feeling sorry for me. Especially now. There wasn't a point to it. I was strong, I was well past the events of my childhood. If anything, I tried to honor them for making me who I was today.

"I brought a few things I found in the other cabin," I told Mateo, standing to refill both our cups and working hard to change the subject.

His eyes tracked me across the room and back, and I felt warmth bloom in my chest... and lower. I wanted to touch him again—the guy was a mountain of solid muscle and warmth, and with a freezing storm raging outside, who wouldn't want that?

It might have been a bit deeper than just seeking warmth on a cold day, of course. But I wasn't thinking about that now.

"Monopoly," I said, pulling the ancient set out of my backpack.

"You're kidding."

"Why do you not sound excited?" I crossed my arms and stood before him, looking down at him with mock disappointment.

"Maybe it's because every time I've ever played Monopoly, the game has gone on for hours and the people playing end up pissed off at each other."

I pulled the board from the box and set it on the little table between the chairs. "We have plenty of hours, so that's not a concern." I handed him the little metal thimble. "And you could never be pissed at me." I batted my eyes at him, slipping for a moment into my familiar façade.

"I already feel grumpy," he complained. "I don't want the thimble."

"Fine, what do you want?"

"Let me see. I don't remember what the options are. I remember the boot and the dog. I'll be the dog."

"You'll be the dog," I repeated, handing him the little metal scotty dog. "I'll be the cannon."

We set up the board and got the money distributed. We were missing a few playing pieces, but the dice were there and most of the set was in relatively good shape. Then I made sure our cups were full. "You can go first," I told him. "Since you still look pouty about having to play."

"I'm not pouty," he said, a smile tipping up one side of his full lips.

"Just roll," I suggested.

In the first six turns, Mateo collected three properties,

including Boardwalk, while I paid taxes and went to jail. "I think you're cheating."

"Hey, this was your idea."

"Want to make it more interesting?"

His head snapped up and those light eyes scanned my face. Neither of us had addressed what had happened in the dark the night before, but the heat in his gaze told me he hadn't forgotten it, either. "Just being here with you is the most interesting thing I've done in years, Annalee," he said softly.

I felt my eyebrows rise. I liked his directness. But I wasn't quite ready to push the board aside and attack him, and I wasn't sure he was hinting at wanting that anyway. There was something sweet about Mateo, and there was a chance he was just giving me a compliment.

"Thanks for that," I said. "But let's add a few things here." I slapped a five-hundred dollar bill into the center of the board. "Free Parking," I told him. "And every time you land on a railroad or utility, or you have to draw a card, you drink."

"I'm drinking anyway." It was a mild protest, and it was accompanied by the sly smile that sent a bolt of want through my core.

"Then it should be no issue." I rolled, finally leaving jail behind and heading directly for the railroad in the center of the row. I took a sip, and then bought the property.

Mateo landed on Chance, and took a swig before pulling his card. "Jail," he said.

"Ha!"

"No, not going. Getting out free next time I go. Be nice and maybe I'll bail you out sometime."

"I'm not going back to jail."

He raised an eyebrow at me.

We rounded the board another few times each, and by the time I had all the railroads laid out in front of me, along with no money at all, thanks to Mateo buying up the whole side of the board with Boardwalk, we were both giggling.

But a light dread filled me as I rolled and counted spaces for my next turn.

"Boardwalk," Mateo announced, grinning like a kid.

I dropped the little cannon on the space and sighed. I hated losing. "I don't have it. You win."

"Not like that," he said, sounding sad. "You can mortgage stuff, take a loan..."

"I don't like accumulating debt. It's not responsible." I was also ready to move on to other things.

He nodded gently, then looked up at me, those green eyes dancing. "I can think of another way you might work off what you owe."

There was no questioning the suggestion, and heat flashed through me. "You can, huh?"

"I can think of a few ways, actually." His eyes dropped to my lips, and I felt it as surely as if he'd run a finger over them.

I put my mug down in the center of the board and stood, stepping between him and the fireplace. "Show me," I said, reaching a hand down to him.

He took my hand and stood, inches from my face. I could smell the whiskey on our breaths, and the heat emanating between our bodies, which were just inches apart. I stared up at him, tilting my chin to meet his eyes as he looked down at me, that sexy half smile on his lips.

Anticipation built within me, sending blood pulsing to my center, my limbs tingling with want. I reached up and ran a fingertip over his full lower lip, pleased when his eyes dropped shut.

He leaned closer and I let my other arm lift to place my hand on the back of his neck, feeling the soft hair there, threading my fingers into it. His hands found my waist, and as I stepped into him, one of them slid lower, down to cup my ass in a possessive move that sent fire licking through me. His head dropped, and our lips met.

For a second, neither of us moved, or breathed, and it felt like the world stopped spinning, the fire stopped crackling, and time stood still.

Mateo let out a sound, low and heavy with want—or need— and it did something to me, pulled at me, twisted me up inside. And time unfroze as I pressed into him, my mouth moving on his. His tongue found mine and we were devouring one another, the push and pull of our mouths and bodies mimicking the flirtation we'd enjoyed before.

His hands slid along my body, lifting my shirt and pressing against the skin of my back, moving down the curve of my ass beneath my jeans. I explored him too, my hands greedily finding handfuls of hot muscle on his broad strong back as I lifted a leg, wrapping it around him, desperate to be closer.

He took my thigh in his hand, holding it around his hips, and lifted me with his other hand, so that I was basically clinging to him, my legs around his waist. It gave me leverage, hoisted me slightly higher than him, and I took his face in both hands, kissing him with every ounce of sheer desire boomeranging around inside me.

I'd wanted Mateo since the first second I'd seen him, but had done my very best to stay away out of respect for his situation. Single dads were off limits for me usually. For one, because I respected that they had a load of responsibilities that I'd never understand, and for another—kids were something I planned to stay far, far away from. I had no idea how to raise them, I only had examples of how to do it wrong.

Mateo lowered himself back into the chair, and I faced him, my legs on either side of his hips. We made out in a way I hadn't done in years, our bodies sliding together, as our mouths explored one another completely. Those sexy full lips I'd dreamed about traced kisses down my jaw, my throat, crossing my clavicle, as Mateo's hands pulled me ever nearer, touching my ass, my breasts.

We were both breathing hard, little moans and grunts escaping each of us as we became sensation and nothing else, hands and tongues and bodies, seeking, finding, needing more.

I pulled back, only to remove my shirt to give him better access, and he watched with eyes full of desire.

"You are so fucking beautiful," he said, his hands staying put on the arms of the chair once I'd removed my shirt and bra. "Completely fucking perfect. I knew you would be." As his hands skated up my waist, finally palming my breasts as I tipped my head back, I let that sink in.

"You imagined what I'd look like?" I asked him, my voice a breathy whisper.

"Of course I did. Every man who sees you imagines it."

I tipped my head back to look at him, taking his face between my palms. "Yeah?"

"You know that's true."

I did. I'd had enough years to prove it to myself. But that was the problem. I'd always wanted to be more. To be more than the pretty girl.

"But that's not what's so hot," he went on, pulling my attention back to those incredible lips, even as his fingers explored my breasts. "It's everything else, coupled with the way you look. You're so fucking smart it's scary."

I leaned in, kissing him again.

"It's fucking intimidating," he said, moving back to look at me again.

"Nothing to be scared of," I assured him, sliding back and reaching a hand to him as I stood.

"You're wrong there," he said, and I wasn't sure exactly

what he meant. But in that moment, as I led him to the bedroom, I didn't care.

"Were there condoms in that emergency pack?" he asked.

"You don't carry them?"

He dropped my hand and looked at me as fear that this was ending before it had even gotten going threatened to swamp me. "I haven't been with anyone in a while. It was a short thing this summer..." he trailed off, his eyes leaving mine. "I don't have a condom."

"I'm on the pill," I told him. "And I'm guessing you're clean."

He nodded, taking a tentative step forward. "I am. I've always used protection. I mean, the few times since..."

"I am too," I assured him, though if he'd been worried, he was right to be. My reputation preceded me, I knew. But it had been a few years since I'd worked a room the way I used to. That kind of affirmation ceased to be fulfilling after a while. This, however, felt different. Mateo wasn't some guy collecting notches for his belt. I wasn't a conquest or a score. There was more to it, I just didn't know exactly what it was.

Mateo stepped close, taking his time as he peered down into my face, one hand tracing the line of my cheek. "You're so beautiful," he said in a voice so soft I could barely hear him.

Chapter 15
Paying Debts. One Way or Another

MATEO

Annalee led me to the bedroom, taking my hand and leading the way. There was something so fucking hot about her sheer capability. She wants something —she takes it. She thinks something—she says it. And though she clearly thought about the past, hell, it sounded like the past had made her exactly who she was today, she wasn't going to let it determine her future. And that was where we differed.

I pulled my shirt off over my head as I followed her to the bedroom, dropping it in the doorway as we stepped into the room, which was noticeably colder than the cozy spot we'd had by the fire.

"Shit, it's cold," she gasped, giving my hand a tug as she dove into the bed and huddled under the mountain of covers.

I was beyond feeling the cold. Every single part of me was burning for the woman I'd found myself trapped here with, the woman I'd imagined finding in my bed a few too many times to pretend I wasn't interested.

I peeled off my jeans and climbed in beside her, letting my body cover hers as my mouth found her soft lips again.

Her hands traced my chest and stopped, her lips going still at the same time. I looked down to see her holding my ring, which had dangled between us on its chain.

"This is..."

"Yeah." It was strange, seeing the ring my wife had put on my finger all those years ago in Annalee's hand. Especially at this moment. But the stranger thing was that I didn't feel the hard punch of guilt I expected, didn't need to gather my things and get away. It was part of me, and right now, the rest of me only wanted one thing. Her.

I leaned in close again, taking her mouth in mine, and her hand released the ring, sliding around to my back, pulling me close.

She moaned into my mouth even as her body melted into mine. The contrast between the cold sheets of the bed and the fiery heat of our bodies sent my mind spinning. Or maybe that was the ancient whiskey we'd been drinking. Or maybe it was just Annalee.

Mouths still attached, tongues exploring one another, our hands roamed beneath the covers. I braced my weight over her, letting just enough of my body press into her to warm her up but not enough to crush her. And her hands slid down my sides, pushing down the waistband of my boxer briefs. I pushed them off, suppressing a groan when the length of my erection pressed against the firm softness of Annalee's belly. But in the next moment, there was no stifling the sound that escaped me when her hands grasped me firmly and began to stroke me with a soft, determined motion. One of her soft hands slipped to cup my balls, and then she began playing with them, and my capabilities for rational thought slid even further away.

I rolled onto my side, determined to do more than hover over her while she drove me to the edge, but Annalee surprised me by rolling on top of me, pushing me to my back.

Her warm, soft weight pressed down into me as her mouth moved from mine to the line of my jaw. Her hair tickled my face, and every breath I took smelled like whiskey, sweat, and sex, combined with something floral and light that was all Annalee. I didn't think I'd ever been more turned on in my life.

She moved like she was going to sink lower, take me in her mouth, maybe, and my hands stopped her before I could get words out.

"You don't want me to?" She sounded confused, almost hurt.

"Fuck, yes, I want you to," I managed. "But it's been years. Literal years. And I won't last if you do that."

She climbed back up my body, smiling down into my face as her hair framed her beautiful pink cheeks. "Well, I don't want you bailing out early," she murmured. "I've been imagining what this would be like, so you have a bit to live up to. My imagination was pretty damn good."

My ego inflated a bit at that, and I wrapped her in my arms. "This time might be fast and hard," I told her. "But the next time... I'll do my best to live up to your imagination."

Her eyes glittered, and she gave me that wicked smile before kissing me again. And then her hand was between us, positioning me at her entrance, which was so soft and wet I could have come just like that. Still, even though I didn't expect to last long, I wanted to give her more than that, and I gritted my teeth, fighting for control as she eased herself onto me. She moved so slowly it felt like a delicious torture she'd devised to drive me insane, but I was too lost in the sensation to do anything about it.

She let out a soft little moan as she drove me closer to the edge, and as she got close to having me all inside, I couldn't take it anymore. I gripped her hips and pushed upward, taking the last couple inches for myself.

Annalee let out a throaty noise as I felt myself seated completely inside her, and it almost pulled my orgasm from me in that second.

"You feel good, baby," she whispered, bracing her hands on my shoulders and pressing herself upward. The change in angle sent off a whole new round of sensation, and I couldn't answer her, I was too lost in the feelings shooting through me and the emotion welling behind a gate I'd lost the key to long ago.

When Annalee began to move, I felt things inside me unraveling. Her fierce softness and the way she took what she wanted was nothing like Poppy, but they had the same steely core, the same unquestionable determination pushing them forward. I didn't want Annalee to be like my late wife, not at all. But feeling that vague similarity was reassuring in some way.

I didn't have the capacity to think when Annalee was moving above me, taking me in all the way and then sliding backward slowly, her channel like a vice as she pulled me out and then took me in again. I kept my hands on her hips, feeling like I needed that small amount of control in order to hold on, to give Annalee half the pleasure she was giving me.

Her breath was coming faster, and her head was tipped back, her delicate chin in the air as those perfect breasts jutted forward and bounced with every thrust. "Ohhhh," she moaned, and the sound had me coiling up inside, every atom, ever fiber, ready for release. But I wanted to wait, I wanted to be sure she had what she needed. I just didn't know if I could.

"I'm not gonna last," I bit out, sounding desperate, because fuck, I was.

"I'm right there with you," she said, and one of her hands moved between us, finding what she needed to tip over the edge. She let out another cry that was so heady and erotic, I lost myself in it as she came. And when I was sure she was coming, when I felt the spasms of her tight pussy around me, I let go.

I might've roared with my release—hell, I might have lost consciousness or recited the Pledge of Allegiance. My mind departed my body completely and I was pure sensation. And the sensation was like nothing I'd ever experienced. Annalee was holding herself over me, and I thrust up into her, fixing her hips with my hands as I took what I needed greedily.

When I was done, I pulled her to me, coaxing her body down to lay over mine, our hearts aligned as our breaths slowed. I was still inside her, and there was something so comforting about the feeling. It was erotic, of course, but it was also a reassurance. I'd been alone for so long.

"What do you think?" Annalee's soft breath was on my neck as she spoke.

"Uh." Was she looking for a clinical assessment of the sex?

"Did I work off what I owe?" she asked, saving me from having to form ridiculous words that might ruin everything.

I looked down at her as she tilted her face to meet my eyes. "I'm afraid not," I said, relieved that the most intense orgasm of my life hadn't rendered me permanently speechless.

"No?" she sounded skeptical, but not disappointed.

"Tell you what," I said, rolling to my side and keeping her in my arms. "I'll give you another chance. In fact, I'm willing to give you as many chances as you need."

She batted those long lashes at me and my chest tightened for some reason. "I might need a lot," she purred.

We didn't leave the bed for hours, napping and fucking as the storm outside beat at the walls of the tiny cabin. It felt like we were in another world, an isolated mountaintop perch away from the responsibilities and requirements of our regular lives. And while my daughter crossed my mind several times, I knew she was safe, and I hoped that if her grandmother reassured her that I was fine, she wouldn't worry. Lily could be anxious, but there was nothing I could do from here. I had to trust that Julia was doing everything she could for my daughter while I was away.

When the dim gray light began to fade from the little window and I'd made Annalee come at least four more times, she stirred in my arms and stretched.

"I suppose we should get up," she said, though she didn't sound especially motivated.

"We should," I agreed, holding her tighter against me.

"Can we heat a little water?" she asked. "I need some kind of sponge bath or something."

I pressed my lips together, feeling a little guilty for messing her up when we were so far from a shower or any way to comfortably clean up.

She frowned at me. "Not because of the sex," she said. "Well, partially because of the sex, but also just because it's been a couple days. I probably smell like a compost pile."

"If you do, I don't notice because I'm sure I smell worse." I lifted my head and sniffed her dramatically.

"Don't!" She swatted my chest.

"Honey, you don't smell like compost. You smell like sex and flowers. And a little like oranges."

She frowned at me, but those dark eyes sparkled. "I'll smell better if I get to clean up a bit. But first," she glanced out the window. "I need to go outside. And I'm dreading it."

"I do too," I said, feeling the same way. The last thing I wanted was to tromp through the snow, freezing my balls off right now, when I was relaxed and warm and satisfied. But I needed to pee.

We rolled from the cozy warmth of the bed, each of us pulling on layers of clothing. I stoked the fire and added a log, and Annalee filled a pot with snow and then set it close to the coals before we headed out.

The wind had stopped, and it wasn't snowing. But the snow was deeper than I'd expected it to be. Shit, would we be stuck here another day? As I watched Annalee disappear behind a stand of trees nearby, I found my own screen of trees and thought about that as I went to the bathroom. Something had lightened up inside me, as if the heavy burden I carried through each day had been cast aside somewhere up here in the snow.

There was a faint trace of guilt trying to sink claws into me, a flicker of a feeling I didn't want to acknowledge. But mostly, I felt freer than I had in years. Poppy wouldn't want me to slog through my days, never feeling anything but remorse and sadness over her loss. She'd want Lily to know joy, to find happiness and light despite losing her mom. And she'd want the same for me. I knew it was true, had known it for years, but it was hard to put into practice.

"You about done?" Annalee's voice came through the trees. "Don't make me come in there hunting for you."

"I'm coming," I called back, her voice reigniting the happiness I'd been feeling.

"Good, cuz after I get cleaned up and we eat something, I'm going to have my way with you again," she said, and I would have thought I was too exhausted to respond, but desire zipped through me.

"One thing at a time," I said, stepping through the thick snow to meet her behind the little cabin.

She took my hand, and we went back inside, like a happy couple living in an isolated little house away from the rest of the world. I guessed in some ways, that's what we were. For one more night, at least.

Chapter 16
Too Smart to Fall

ANNALEE

W hen we got back inside, had stripped off snowy boots and gloves, and found ourselves alone and facing each other once more, a strange atmosphere settled between us. I stood in the center of the little main room, watching Mateo put another log into the fire. And I felt something I rarely felt: awkward as hell.

He turned and gave me a look that was at once amused and heated, his eyes tracking from the top of my head down to my thermal-clad legs. "What?" he asked, laughing a little as he stood and crossed his arms, facing me.

"I don't know," I said. "Is it weird that I suddenly feel weird?"

"This whole situation is completely weird," he said. Then his smile faltered a bit. "Weird how, though? Like regretful weird?"

I didn't want him to think that. "No, not even a little bit."

The smile was back. "Good."

I didn't know how to explain the feelings growing inside of me because I wasn't sure they were feelings I could identify. That happens when you have feelings you've never experienced before, I guessed.

"I'm gonna grab that water if it's warm, and maybe step into the bedroom to clean up a little," I said, moving toward the pot of water.

"I can go in there," Mateo said. "You stay out here where it's warm. Just holler when you're done."

I smiled my thanks at him, and waited until he'd moved into the bedroom and closed the door. It was much warmer in this room, and the thought of stripping down in there without plans to be immediately warmed up by Mateo was not especially tempting.

There were a few little rags folded in a cabinet in the kitchen, and I pulled a couple out and shook them out. I had no idea how clean they actually were—they smelled musty—but they had to be cleaner than I was at that moment. I used the little hard bar of soap from the kitchen too, and slowly did the best I could to freshen up. When I was finished, and dressed again, I felt better, and the odd feelings swirling inside me were a little better too, if not gone altogether.

I knew they related to Mateo.

I knew they were dangerous.

"All done in here," I called when I was dressed again. I

sipped a big mug full of water and settled back into the chair in front of the fire to clean up the forgotten Monopoly game.

Mateo emerged from the bedroom, and immediately moved to the fire to warm his hands, which he extended before him. "Feel better?" he asked.

"I do, yeah." I smiled at him, meeting those disarming eyes and feeling my emotions rise again. Looking at Mateo now made my chest tighten, my stomach drop. He was gorgeous, but as he leaned down to help me put things away, I realized it was much more than that.

"I might go out once more while we've got some light," he said when the game was packed away. "The whole point of me coming up here was to evaluate these cabins to see if we need to do any refurbishing."

"Can you even tell when they're covered in snow?"

He shrugged one shoulder and his smile became slightly skeptical as he looked around. "I mean, I can tell a lot just by being inside here. These things were actually built pretty well."

"Need help?" I asked, hoping I didn't have to go outside again. The snow had stopped, but I could still hear the wind blowing. I'd just gotten clean and warm. But I'd go if he needed me.

"Nah." He pulled his coat back on and shoved his feet into his boots. "I'll get some photos with my phone and check on a few things. I'm guessing we'll have Douggie Masters stay in this cabin, though. It seems the best set up."

"Okay," I said. "Maybe I'll do a little reading." I pulled one of the yellowed piles of scripts onto my lap. The one called "The Map."

"Be back in a bit." Mateo's eyes lingered on mine for a beat longer than they might have a few days ago, and my stomach twisted under his gaze.

He disappeared out the door, letting a burst of cold air in

when he went. I watched him pass by the little window outside, and then it was silent, and for a moment I just sat there, thinking about the handsome man I'd been lucky enough to be stranded with. He'd spent the last twenty-four hours making sure I was safe, warm, and comfortable. And giving me more orgasms than I'd had in a row in... ever.

The man was handsome, there was no doubting that. But there was something else about him that was getting to me. Most men focused on what I looked like, or got some kind of kick out of believing they were bagging the hotshot female fighter pilot, like I was one kind of Pokemon they hadn't caught for their collection yet. But Mateo was different. I didn't think he saw me as Monroe—I was pretty sure he saw the real me.

He was polite and considerate, careful and sweet. In twenty-four hours he'd learned more about my past than I'd shared with anyone in years. Maybe ever.

And that, I decided, was what was making my stomach feel so flighty and my chest so achey around him. I felt close to him because of the conversations we'd had. I didn't want to acknowledge that it could be more, even though I knew it was true. I wasn't the girl who fell hard and fast for the handsome guy who paid attention to her. I'd never been that girl.

But no one had ever really paid this kind of attention, either.

I pulled my eyes from the dancing flames and my mind from the curious examination of my feelings, and forced myself to read. This script, like the others, gave no indication of who had written it, or whether it was ever produced. I doubted it had been, since the script had been abandoned here in this place for years.

But it wasn't bad. The story was, ironically, about a treasure hunt, and about two brothers working to beat one another to the eventual prize, though neither knew what it was.

Pretty on the nose, considering Ghost had us all chasing

some treasure he believed his uncle had left him, and none of us had a clue what it was.

The story was absorbing enough that I didn't realize how much time had passed, but when I glanced at my watch, I found that forty-five minutes had gone by, and Mateo was still outside.

A quick rush of worry tumbled through me, and I moved to the window, peering out to see if could spot him out there. He might be in one of the other structures, I realized, and for a moment I debated whether he might need help. Was he in trouble? What would I do if he was?

My mind flashed to that dock long ago, to my sister and me sitting in a boat, waiting for Joel to come back. We didn't know he was in trouble, didn't know he needed help until it was too late. I shook my head. I wouldn't let that happen again.

I shoved my feet into my boots, pulled my rain jacket back on and put on my gloves. I moved to the door and pulled it open almost violently in my rush to get out of the house and out of the shadows of my past. And there was Mateo, standing just outside.

"Hey," he said, surprise lighting his eyes and the smile on his full lips widening. "I was just coming back in. How was that script?"

I swallowed hard, let out a sigh that surprised even me. What was happening here? Suddenly, I felt like a forlorn housewife, waiting at home for her husband to come back. My mind flipped to thoughts of my mom, primping and sliding on her signature burgundy lipstick as she waiting my father's return from work each day. When I was really small, I'd been charmed by her late afternoon beauty routine, but as I grew older, it seemed more like a cage my mother lived inside of. My father's expectations, her expectations for herself—and those that were projected on my sister and me—they were all so pointless.

That was not my life. I'd done everything in my power to

make sure that was not my life. Joel drowning had been the event that finally opened my eyes to how pointless—how literally dangerous—it was to raise daughters incapable of doing anything more than wearing a pageant banner or making a perfect coconut creme pie.

I would never be that kind of woman.

Chapter 17
Lions, Tigers, and Mateo

MATEO

I hadn't been expecting the door to fly open just as I reached for it, or for Annalee's face to hold an expression of angry determination. For a moment I wondered if I'd done something wrong, but I'd been outside for the past hour. Last I heard, she was reading the scripts we found, so I asked her about that, and the hard glare slid gradually from her eyes.

"I was getting worried," she said, stepping back to let me inside. "Was coming out to see if you needed help."

That was a surprise—I was pretty used to doing most things alone, after all. And no one really worried much about me, except for Lily, and I did my best to make sure she didn't ever have anything to worry about. "Thanks," I said. "Everything's good, though. The sun's pretty determined to get through those clouds. Should start getting some melt here soon. Temperature's already rising."

Annalee moved inside and stripped off the gloves, jacket and boots she wore. "It does feel warmer."

"Maybe the weather's actually remembering that it's supposed to be summer." Even as I said the words, I felt a little twinge of regret. But we couldn't stay up here forever, of course. This was just a blip on the radar of our real lives. We needed to get back. Soon.

"You find what you needed?" she asked, standing with her arms at her sides and one foot on top of the other in the middle of the room. Something in the posture was so vulnerable, I had an urge to sweep her into my arms. I pushed off my coat and decided to go with it. Who knew what would happen when we headed back to the resort tomorrow?

I stepped closer, stopping when our chests were nearly touching and looked down at her, giving her a second to tell me this wasn't happening again. But Annalee's hand rose to my chest, tracing a line between my pecs, over the shape of the ring hanging there, and then sliding around my waist. I pulled her into me, loving the solid warmth of her, the soft reassurance of her body responding to mine.

"I could make a comment about how some of what I need is right here," I told her quietly. "If I was a different kind of guy."

She tilted her head up to smile at me. "Oh yeah? Well, what kind of guy are you, then?"

I hesitated, but decided to just be honest. "The kind who really wants to take you into the bedroom again, but who also worries about what happens when we get back to the resort tomorrow."

She dropped my gaze and pressed the side of her face into my chest, tightening her arms around me. "We don't need to think about that."

So much for reassurance. "This is just a stranded in a mountain cabin kind of thing, then?" I wished I hadn't asked. The second the words were out, she was stepping out of my arms.

"I don't know what it is," she answered. "I'm not really the kind of girl who does forever."

"I'm not asking for forever," I said, forcing a laugh into my voice as if it hadn't crossed my mind. Even briefly.

"Well," she said, clear relief in her tone, "you're welcome to what's left of today and all of tonight." Her voice was a sexy purr, and while the words were welcome, I had the distinct impression they were constructed to distract me from my original line of questioning. And as I took her hand and led her back to the bedroom, I shoved it aside in my own mind. What had I expected? Just because Annalee was the first woman I'd been close to since Poppy didn't mean anything. This was a crush I had, one I'd gotten to explore pretty extensively. I'd be happy for that and not worry about tomorrow.

Annalee backed toward the bed, still holding my hand. She stopped as her knees hit the edge of the old mattress and took my shoulders, spinning us so the bed was behind me. Then she slid her hands to my waist, pulling my T-shirt from my waistband and lifting the sweatshirt I wore up my chest, her hands palming the exposed skin. I lifted the shirts over my head and bent my neck to take her mouth.

As I devoured her, Annalee's soft tongue sliding over mine and sending sharp chills skittering through my body, I pulled her shirt up, breaking the kiss to pull it over her head. I watched as her soft light hair fell back down around her bare shoulders.

"You're beautiful," I whispered. And she was. With no makeup, none of the trademark lipstick she usually wore,

Annalee was much more beautiful than I would ever have predicted. I wondered if the makeup and the attitude were an armor of sorts. What was she protecting herself from?

Annalee gave me a hard shove then, sending me backwards onto the bed, where I fell happily, waiting as she pushed off her thermal leggings and then reached to remove my jeans. When we were both undressed, she climbed over me, hovering for a moment on her hands and knees, looking down at me through that wavy hair.

"You're beautiful too," she murmured, and then she kissed me again, still holding herself over me. My body longed for contact, to feel her softness pressed against my length once again, to revel in the warmth and friction created between us. But she was teasing me, holding herself away, and my body was coiling with tension.

I reached for her, my hands finding her generous hips, marveling at the perfect swell below her taut waist. Her skin was smooth and so incredibly soft, and a thought floated through my mind then, a realization that I'd never get enough of her. That I would always, always want more of this.

As I gave myself over to sensation, experience, I kept concrete thoughts as far from me as I could. But as Annalee moved over me, finally sliding one small hand down to grasp my length and forcing a rough gasp from my chest as she stroked me between us, I couldn't help wondering what might happen in the days to come. Could I see her again? Might she want anything like a relationship? Did I?

Annalee teased my tip, sliding me through the wet welcome of her entrance over and over until I thought I would explode with the need to be inside her. And then finally, as my hands became more insistent on her flesh, my fingers digging into her as I tried to pull her closer, she opened for me, letting me inside.

And sliding into that heavenly heat was like coming in out of a raging storm.

Every muscle and nerve inside me was focused on that incredible feeling, the tight, hot beauty that was everything Annalee.

She moved over me, sliding me in and out, grasping me with every centimeter within her as her hips made slow, maddening circles.

"God, you feel good," she breathed, dropping her mouth to my ear before sliding my earlobe between her teeth and then biting me gently. The spike of near-pain combined with the pleasure wracking through me had me groaning as I pulled her tighter to me, tried to get more and more of her.

"You're killing me," I told her.

"I can stop," she teased.

"Don't you fucking dare."

I almost lost it when Annalee's breath started coming faster, when she cried out and froze over me, her body pulsing around my cock and her hair spread over my chest, tickling my chin. And when she began to move again, I let go, my own release ripping out of me with the force of all the emotions I wasn't going to share with her, all the questions I knew she didn't want to answer.

This, I realized, as I pulled her close and held her to me while our heartbeats aligned, would have to be enough for now.

Chapter 18
Indecent Proposals Only

ANNALEE

We spent most of the rest of the evening in bed together, like lovers who knew their inevitable goodbye was on the horizon. Because that was exactly what we were. The sun had come out in the late afternoon, and the sound of the howling storm was replaced by the steady dripping of snow melting off the roof and the trees around us. What had been a foreboding and wintry landscape that morning was already shifting into scenery that looked much more like what I'd grown used to this summer at Kasper Ridge.

And so holding Mateo, getting as much of him as I possibly could in the time we had left, felt like an extended daydream.

As day melted into darkness, I nestled against his chest, my fingers tracing lines over the perfect smooth skin there, avoiding the gold band hanging around his neck.

"I just need to know," he said, a vulnerability in his rich deep voice I hadn't heard before. "What happens when we get back? Do we pretend none of this happened?"

My heart twisted a little inside me. It would be so easy to ride along, see what happened. I certainly wouldn't say no to more nights like the past two. But that wasn't something he could offer.

"Mateo, you're a family man," I reminded him, sliding my hand around his torso to hug him tightly. "And that's just something...that's not something I can do."

He stiffened beneath me. "Hey." His voice held a steely edge. "I'm not asking you to take her place, you know."

I sat back, looking at him though the fading light. "That's not what I meant."

"Look. I don't need anything serious. God knows I've had enough serious to last me a while," he said. "I just think we have a good thing here. We're compatible."

"Sexually, you mean," I laughed. I knew it was more than that, but something in me wouldn't allow me to admit it out loud. Because then what?

"For starters, yeah."

"So what are you proposing?"

"Let's not use that specific word," he said, "since you seem particularly commitment averse. I will promise you right now that there will be no proposals between us."

"Only the indecent kind," I purred, hopefully covering up the strange sadness that floated through me at his proclamation.

"Only the indecent kind," he agreed. "Would that be okay?"

"Nothing serious. Just having fun." I laid back down, my body missing his in the few brief moments I'd pulled myself away. "You sure you can do that? I mean... you're a dad."

"Trust me, I haven't forgotten Lily. But I think, for the first time in a long time, maybe I deserve to have some kind of life outside of her." He sounded uncertain, like maybe it had cost him a bit to admit that.

He did, and I was glad I could help him see that. I breathed out against the heat of his chest, let my fingers trace the lines of his pectoral muscles again. "What do you say?" he asked, his voice a rumble that vibrated through me.

I slid myself over him, letting every nerve in my body appreciate him—his solidity, his warmth, his constancy—while my mind turned over the potential downfalls of letting myself enjoy him for longer than these two nights. I knew exactly what I was afraid of—that I would become attached. And attachments were one thing I'd tried most of my life to avoid.

"We can try," I agreed, letting my mouth open against him as I uttered the words, slipping my tongue out to taste his skin and moving myself against the thickening length I felt at my hip.

"Good," he breathed, his hands finding the globes of my ass, pulling me into him tightly. "That's good. Because I don't know if I could stand seeing you every day and not being able to have you."

And while I hid my reaction to that statement by dropping my head and taking one of his nipples between my teeth, worry shot through me. He already had me. In a way that made worry and fear compete with the lust I felt suffusing my body. I knew I'd need to cut this off before either of us got too deep, but now was not the time. I could enjoy him for a little bit longer. I had years of experience holding back just enough to make sure I didn't fall too deep. Only, with Mateo, I knew it was going to be harder.

. . .

The morning sun seared a line down my back as I woke, sprawled with half my body twisted around Mateo. His arm circled my waist, and his leg was wrapped over my own as his breath came in soft reassuring puffs.

I took a moment to study him as he slept—dark, thick lashes arced against the tan smooth skin of his cheeks, those full lips pulled into a tiny frown, as if sleeping was something he didn't really approve of.

He was a good man, I knew, and my heart thudded a little harder inside me as I considered him. He was a good man, and he deserved to be treated well. I could do that, I told myself. At least for a little while. Whatever was between us could run a natural course, I decided. Who knew how long I'd be staying in Kasper Ridge? And with him having family responsibilities, whatever this was would certainly fizzle out at some point without me even having to engineer it. And until then?

"Are you watching me sleep?" he asked, his voice deep and scratchy.

"Maybe," I laughed, tracing a finger down the angle of his jaw, over the scruff that had grown in over the days we'd been stuck here.

"It should be creepy, but it's not," he said, a slow smile pulling those perfect lips wider.

"Sun's out today," I said, pulling back a bit so he could see the glaring window. "Like it means it."

He nodded. "We'll give it a little while to melt and then head back, I guess."

His hand slid down my back, pulling me closer to him until I felt his morning erection press against my belly.

"Good morning," I said, dropping a hand to rub along his length.

"Morning," he growled, taking my mouth in his.

As the sun crept up over the trees, we clung to each other and to the fantasy we'd enjoyed for the past few days, taking what we could from each other's bodies, realizing that even if we agreed to see each other in the real world, things were about to change.

Chapter 19
Wearing Another Man's Shirt

MATEO

Eventually, we pulled ourselves out of bed. Annalee stripped the bed, stuffing the bedding into a pillowcase and pushing it down into her pack. With the warm clothes being left here and the food we'd eaten gone, there was room, and we figured Douggie Masters would probably appreciate clean sheets.

"Ready?" I asked her, lifting my pack to my shoulders and glancing around the little cabin that had been our home for the past couple days. We'd tidied up, tucking away the Monopoly game, and putting the scripts into Annalee's pack, even though I worried it would be too heavy for her.

One thing she proved over and over—she was ridiculously fucking capable—and questioning that only seemed to make her more determined.

"Yep," she said, meeting my eyes.

There was something dancing in her gaze, something that pulled me across the little space to stand close before her and push the lock of hair back from her forehead. I loved the look of her, the stark contrast between this soft beautiful package and the fierce spirit that lived behind those eyes. I leaned down and kissed her one more time. Just in case.

"Let's go," I whispered, pulling back. Her eyes were closed, and one of her hands had risen to clasp my neck.

"Let's go," she agreed with a sigh.

Soon, the little cabins were behind us, and the trail in front of us, visible mostly as a smoother spot in the melting snow, a depression between the trees and rocks that lined the path. In some places, the smooth dirt was visible, in others, the trail was slick with ice. But everywhere around us, the snow was melting fast, and little rivers of water rushed downward along the sides of the trail as we descended.

"This is almost as hard as going up," Annalee said, sliding a little on an icy spot.

"Be careful," I said, even though it was pointless. I was pretty sure telling people to be careful had never actually averted an accident, but my dad brain was kicking in again, the closer we got to the resort. I missed Lily. As much as I wanted to live in the separate world of the isolated cabin with Annalee and never-ending sex forever, that was a fantasy. And my daughter needed me.

We stopped for a breath at one point in our descent, resting on a sunny rock for a moment side by side. As we stood to begin moving again, Annalee captured my hand in hers, pressing my knuckles to her lips and looking at me with a deep searching gaze.

"What?" I whispered, fighting an urge to pull her close, strip her down and plunge myself into her again.

She smiled faintly and shook her head. "Just needed to touch you," she said.

And something in my chest loosened. Before I could respond, she'd moved on ahead, and soon the roofline of the resort came into view. It was odd seeing it now—in some ways I felt like everything in my life had changed, and yet I knew nothing really had.

I followed Annalee across the wide back patio of the resort, and in through the sliding glass doors to the lobby, which was in the final stages of refurbishment. Lucy stood in the center of the big space as a few guys pushed the front desk back into place.

"Hey!" she called when she saw us. "You're back! You okay?" Lucy smiled, but I could see the concern etched into the lines around her mouth. She was a good friend.

"We're fine," I said. "Just a little behind schedule."

"That storm was ridiculous," Lucy said. "Does Archie know you're back?"

"Not yet," Annalee said, gazing around the opulent lobby. "It looks fantastic in here." There were small sitting areas arranged, the floor shone beneath the overhead chandeliers and canned lighting, and the walls had been hung with old photographs of the resort in wide frames.

"You guys want to get cleaned up a little and I'll get Archie?" Lucy asked. "We can get the quick debrief and then you can go to your daughter. I bet she misses you."

"I bet Grandma has kept her distracted with Disney movies and cookies," I joked. But I knew Lily had probably had enough of Grandma by now. We both loved her, but Poppy's mother wasn't Poppy, and for Lily, I was the only one she really wanted.

"I wouldn't mind a real shower," Annalee said, glancing between Lucy and me. "Meet you back down here in twenty?"

It felt strange to let her go, but I smiled and nodded, conscious of Lucy's eyes on us.

"Mateo, you can clean up in our rooms if you want," Lucy offered. "I'm sure Will has an extra shirt you could grab."

I'd been suspicious of Lucy's fiancé at first, but it was clear he was a good guy. "Yeah, that'd be great."

"Come on," Lucy said, and I followed her up the sweeping staircase behind the front desk as Annalee disappeared into the elevator.

It felt strange being apart, knowing I wouldn't be climbing into bed next to Annalee's sweet body tonight. Or maybe ever again. We'd never really figured out what "normal" was going to look like on the back of our time together. I missed her already.

"So are you starving?" Lucy asked me.

"No, we actually ate okay," I told her. "The cabin was stocked with some things, and we went through the supplies we'd been planning to leave up there."

"How do the cabins look?" she asked as we moved down the second floor hallway to the main stairs.

"All in all, they're in good shape. We cleaned as best we could, at least in the one we used, and—"

"You and Monroe shared a cabin?" Lucy stopped on the stairway, blocking my ascent. She turned to face me, and the look on her face was a mixture of surprise and what seemed like anger.

"We had limited firewood and warm clothing. It made more sense to heat a single cabin than to split our resources." I explained this, hoping Lucy didn't ask about the sleeping arrangements. If Annalee and I were not going to continue doing whatever it was we'd been doing, no one ever needed to know what had happened between us.

"How was that?" Lucy asked, smirking. She'd never been the biggest fan of the buxom fighter pilot, and I suspected that at one point she'd worried that maybe Annalee and Will had something going on.

"It was fine. We survived." My voice was tight in an effort to keep any emotion at all from coloring my words.

"Well, I'm sure that was interesting. I'm just glad you're back." Lucy turned and led the way to the suite of rooms she shared with Will. Relief replaced my anxiety that she would press for more information about sleeping arrangements at the cabin.

Will was inside, seated at the desk near the window and frowning at a computer screen when we stepped in. Just as Lucy didn't seem to warm to Annalee, I knew Will had never been my biggest fan. I might have threatened him once or twice when I wasn't sure what his intentions were toward Lucy. But that was water under the bridge. I hoped.

"Hey, you're back," he said, rising. Will was big, but not enormous. He was a well-muscled, fit guy who was really too good looking to be fair. He had this golden boy thing going on, and it made me happier than it should have to know that his callsign had been "Fake Tom" in the Navy because he'd evidently shown up sure he would be called "Maverick" like his idol from *Top Gun*. Since his last name was Cruz, he figured it was a slam dunk. I liked imagining him receiving the news that he'd be Fake Tom instead.

"Yeah," I agreed, not sure what else to say. I was fine with the guy now, but we weren't exactly old friends.

"Babe, I'm gonna grab a shirt and some other things for Mateo, okay? He's gonna clean up here, give us a quick debrief, and then head out to get Lily." Lucy informed Will rather than asking him, and I grinned at him, shrugging as I dropped my pack next to a chair and then followed Lucy down the hall.

"You can use this bathroom," she said, indicating the guest bath off the hall. "And I'll grab some clothes and put them on the bed in here." She pointed to the second bedroom in the suite.

"Thanks, Luce," I said, happy to have a few minutes to myself.

"Sure. Can't wait to hear everything."

I closed the bathroom door between us. No one was going to be hearing everything, I thought. And depending on Annalee, even I might be doing my best to pretend none of it ever happened.

Chapter 20
Maps and Movies

ANNALEE

S oon, we were all around a table in the restaurant, glasses of soda and tea in front of us as we gathered. Ghost and Aubrey sat at my side, practically buzzing with anticipation. I was pretty sure they were going to be disappointed at what we'd found—or hadn't found, really—in terms of treasure or clues. Wiley sat across from me, Lucy and Fake Tom were next to him, and Brainiac was next to Mateo, stoic as ever. Ernie, Lucy's grandfather, had come down to hear our recap too, and he pulled a chair up next to Lucy.

Though the restaurant was otherwise empty, noise from the

never-ending renovation of the rooms overhead filtered down through the air.

Mateo sat at my side, and even with everyone here, even back in the "regular world" of the resort, it felt like he had a magnet attached to his side. I longed to touch him, at least to scoot closer and get a better whiff of the clean manly scent that surrounded him... but I wasn't sure how we were going to handle things. Or what I really wanted. Besides him.

"Okay," Ghost said, his eyes shining. "How are the cabins?"

I looked at Mateo, trying to figure out if I was going to tell this story, or if he was, and the second our eyes met, a sizzling heat drilled through my core. Luckily, he started talking. I wasn't sure I trusted my voice right then.

"The cabins are in good condition," he said. He went on to talk about the structures, the foundation and the roofs, and the state of the window seals and weatherstripping on the doors, which I wouldn't have even thought to check. That explained why he'd been out so long the day he was looking at the structures.

"We'll probably want to stock in some more firewood, and we'll definitely need food, water, first aid kits, flashlights, and batteries."

"We brought down the bedding to wash," I added.

"For all the cabins?" Aubrey asked.

I swallowed hard. "No, just for one."

She frowned, and I imagined she was trying to figure out whether that meant what she thought it did.

"We stayed in one cabin to conserve supplies," Mateo explained. "It would have burned through the wood twice as fast to split up." Aubrey was still looking hard at him, her eyes narrowing slightly. "I slept on one of the chairs by the fire," he added quickly. "To make sure it didn't go out."

There. We'd explained the sleeping arrangements now.

There should be no more questions about that. But Aubrey still looked like she was thinking about this information, and now she glanced at me with a little smile forming on her lips.

"We found something," I said, hoping to distract from whatever might be going on in her mind. "Could be a clue, I guess."

I pulled the scripts out from beneath my chair and stacked them on the table.

"Did you write a report for us, Monroe?" Brainiac asked, leaning in.

"Funny. No. These are movie screenplays. We found a stack of them up there." I pointed at the one on top. "I read this one. It's called 'The Map.' Felt kind of on the nose."

Aubrey and Ghost were both staring at the screenplay. "And?" Aubrey asked.

"It's okay," I told her. "I felt like there were a couple actions on the part of the characters that lacked sufficient motivation and were only there to make the plot work." I'd taken a film critique class as an elective once. I couldn't help the joke, plus I liked drawing out the anticipation.

"Thanks, but I don't think we were looking for a plot analysis," Brainiac said drily.

"What was the Rotten Tomatoes score?" Wiley joked.

Aubrey smacked his arm. "Did the script say anything about the hunt?"

I lifted a shoulder. "It was kind of all about a treasure hunt," I told them. "And there was actually a scene where they piece together the map, but there was no actual drawing of a map or anything in the script."

Ghost and his sister exchanged a look. "There's all those old movie reels in the theater," he said. "Any of them called *The Map*?"

"I think we should go find out," she said.

"Can we get to the part about preparations for *Out and Out*

There going up to use these cabins?" I asked, the exhaustion of the last couple days beginning to set in.

"So the first cabin in the row, the one that is basically at the end of the trail, is probably the one to direct him to. We should make sure they have keys to all four, just in case there are any issues," Mateo said. "But we can get back up there and install a few conveniences, supply it with fresh firewood, give the place a better cleaning than Annalee and I could do with limited supplies."

"Can we take up a generator or something?" Archie asked. "I'd rather not have anyone die on my watch."

"We could get it at least partway up on a four-wheeler when the snow's gone," Mateo said. "But part of the trail is really steep. We'd probably just have to carry it. Not a bad idea though."

"When do people start arriving?" Ernie asked, leaning in with glowing eyes. I had a feeling living here at the resort was probably a little more excitement than he'd had in the last few years.

"We have ten days," I told him and the rest of the group. "Are we ready to go here?"

Wiley nodded. "Bar's stocked for regular service and the whiskey and wine tasting we discussed."

I felt like I'd been on vacation, and it was taking a bit for my mind to kick back in, but the schedule of events for the soft opening was my responsibility. I pulled my phone out and checked the list I'd made. "We need to place an order for groceries. Did we find a sous chef to help while everyone is here?" I'd taken on the role of chef for the event, which was fine, but a lot of pressure.

"You've got me," Aubrey said, smiling.

I shook my head. "You're going to be busy with rock climbing and hikes." I looked around the table. Wiley would be in the bar, Ghost would be schmoozing, Lucy and Will were handling all things operations. I glanced at Brainiac, but he shrugged apologetically.

"I can barely make toast," he said.

My gaze fell on Mateo. He technically worked for Lucy. He definitely couldn't be my sous chef.

"We'll need to hire someone short term," I told everyone, looking back at them.

"I can cook," Mateo said quietly.

Now everyone was looking at him, and a tiny surge of excitement rushed up my throat.

"If Lucy can spare me," he added.

"We're halting renovation on the rooms while guests are in the hotel," she said. She was looking between us with that same narrowed gaze, and I guessed that if anyone was going to suspect what happened at the cabin, it was going to be Lucy. "So you're clear to help in the kitchen."

"Okay with you?" Mateo asked, his voice the same low rumble I'd heard in the darkness the last couple nights, the resonant timbre that sent nerve endings deep inside me buzzing with want.

I swallowed hard. "Sure. Yeah." I said, afraid everyone at the table could see how completely okay with me it really was.

"Great," Ghost said. "Get us a list for groceries, we'll finish getting the rooms sorted. Aubrey, keep up the inventory and cleaning of outdoor gear, and once the front desk is in, we can start installing the computer system. Hopefully that'll go smoothly and be operational when everyone gets here."

The little meeting broke up, and I watched as Aubrey and Ghost gathered the scripts and headed back to the wing where the movie theater was. Despite the fact the soft opening was the biggest thing to happen at the Kasper Ridge Resort in decades, they were single-mindedly focused on the treasure hunt. I guessed I didn't blame them. I hoped they found something interesting in that pile of old movies.

"Hey," Mateo said softly at my side. He leaned his head in, his breath warm on my neck. "I'm gonna go get Lily. I'll see you later?"

I looked up at him, conscious of Lucy just across the room. "Okay," I said, and sadness threatened to swamp me. I'd wanted to be strong, to pretend nothing had happened, but my heart was protesting. Or maybe it was my body. Either way, it pressed me to hold out my phone to my former cabin mate. "I don't have your number," I said.

A hint of a smile pulled one side of his mouth up as those light green eyes regarded my outstretched hand. "Here," he said, tapping the screen and creating a contact. "Sent myself a message. Now we're connected."

And as he walked away, I realized he was right.

Chapter 21
The Song You'll Never Forget

MATEO

I had called my mother-in-law as soon as we were back in cell service range to let her know the details about what had happened, to say hello to Lily quickly, and to assure them both that I'd be there soon. And as I drove away from the resort to go get my daughter, emotions whirled within me, warring for attention.

When I thought about Lily, my heart surged and my foot dropped heavier on the gas pedal. I didn't like being away from my little girl and I was eager to sweep her into my arms, to hear her carefree laughter and smell her little girl skin again. Still, as

I put distance between myself and the resort—between myself and Annalee—I felt a strange longing I hadn't experienced in years, if ever. I wanted to pull her into my arms too, and my whole body reacted to the idea.

I didn't know what lay between us. I'd thought it was lust, that the day and nights we'd spent in bed together would dampen the feeling, or at least make it manageable. Instead, the time I'd spent wrapped around Annalee's soft body, our heads together and our voices sharing soft whispered words, only made me want more. More of that intimacy, more of that connection.

I pulled into my mother-in-law's driveway, parked, and leapt from the truck, bounding up the front steps with excitement building inside me. The front door flew open just as I was about to knock, and a wild streak of little girl flew at me, slamming into my knees and nearly knocking me over.

"Daddy!"

"Hey baby girl," I said, bending down to scoop her up for a hug and bury my face in her hair. "I missed you."

"I missed you too," she said. "A lot."

Poppy's mother stepped through the door then, holding Lily's little backpack.

"Hi," I said, shifting Lily to a hip. "You survived. How many times did you have to watch *Frozen*?"

"I'll be singing 'Let it Go' for the next twenty-four hours, whether I like it or not," she said, smiling.

Lily lifted her head from my shoulder at the mention of her favorite song. "The snow glows ..." she began, her little voice serious as she sang.

"No, no," Julia cried in mock desperation. "No more, Lily!"

"Thanks again," I told her. "I'm really sorry about the last-minute change of plans. We knew there was a storm, but we'd expected a quick passing thunderstorm, not three feet of snow."

"I heard it was quite a lot at elevation," she said, her voice carrying a note of worry that touched me. "You had shelter, though?"

"The little cabins we'd gone up to check were in good condition. We were fine."

She nodded. "So you and two women? Stuck up there?"

"I, uh." For some reason my arm tightened around Lily as my mind reeled back to the days I'd spent with Annalee. "Just one other person, actually. Aubrey got called back to the resort."

A look of understanding crossed Julia's face. "Oh." She was assuming a lot, I could see. And I couldn't exactly correct her. Still, I hated the feeling of betrayal that washed through me at her appraisal.

"Anyway, I guess we'd better get home," I said. "But I really appreciate you taking Lily and keeping her so long. I honestly don't know what I'd do without you."

"You know it's never a problem," she said.

"Thanks." I turned, ready to go back to the car, then spun towards her again. "Did I already ask you about the weekend of the soft opening?"

"You told me about it, but I didn't know you'd need me. It's the twentieth, right?"

"Right." Something in her voice made me worry. "I'll need to be there pretty much all weekend since they need me to cook."

"You're cooking, Daddy?" Lily laughed.

"Hey, I'm a good cook," I told her, feeling my heart lighten immediately when I glanced at her face, full of amusement. I knew she was picturing me in our kitchen at home. I'd taken to wearing Poppy's apron when I cooked, and it wasn't the most masculine of garments with the soft yellow birds across the front and the bright pink ruffle.

"Mateo, I'm so sorry," Julia said, her mouth pressing into a frown. "That's the weekend I'm taking that cruise. I'm certain I told you about it. I'll be gone all week."

She had. And I remembered now that she'd mentioned it. "Oh that's right. Yes, you told me."

"What will you do?" A worried wrinkle appeared between her eyebrows, and for a second, I saw my wife in her mother's face. Poppy used to make that same look when she was worried. A flit of deep anguish pierced me, but before it could become crippling, it was gone.

"It'll be fine. I'll figure it out." I had no idea what I'd do with my daughter if I was supposed to be in the kitchen at the resort all weekend. But I would have to do something. "No worries. You deserve to have a fantastic time."

"Well, I am looking forward to it," she said apologetically.

Lily had buried her face in my shoulder again, and her breathing was becoming deeper, steadier.

"She missed you," Julia confided softly. "Didn't sleep well."

I nodded, my heart twisting inside me. I hated the idea of Lily having to worry about me, of her ever having to wonder if I was coming back. Losing her mother made her especially sensitive to any changes in plans that kept me away longer than I should have been, and guilt wracked me for enjoying the unexpected delay. How selfish I'd been, wrapped up in Annalee while my daughter laid awake concerned that she might lose another parent.

"I'm here now," I whispered to my little girl, and her arms tightened around my neck. I took the backpack from Julia's outstretched hand, and thanked her once more.

"See you soon, darling," she called to Lily.

"Bye Grammy," Lily's sleepy voice mumbled back.

. . .

The weekend home with Lily was quiet and peaceful. We went fishing and spent time at our favorite lake with a picnic, but mostly stuck around the house.

In the evenings, when the house was quiet and Lily was tucked into bed, I took a glass of whiskey out to the back patio and pulled out my phone.

When I'd first gotten home after picking up my daughter, my phone had chimed with a text.

Annalee: Is it weird that I kind of wish we were still snowed in?

My heart had jolted when I read her words, and I'd responded before I overthought my answer.

Me: We're both weird if it is.

That exchange had begun a flurry of messages between us, and the longer I went without seeing Annalee, the more honest our dialogue became—and the more I wanted to hold her again, to feel her softness against me, to be the victim of one of her sarcastic comments.

As Sunday evening lit the woods with a golden glow from the setting sun, and the birds chorused their goodnights from the treetops, I typed a note to her, my heart thumping harder than it should have.

Me: I don't know what we decided, really. About us. But I miss you.

Annalee: Yeah?

Me: Yes.

Annalee: Which parts of me do you miss?

My heart tried to press into my throat. Was she taking this where I thought she was? I didn't want to jump to conclusions.

Me: Your mind. Your voice. Your eyes.

Annalee: Nice answers. Very careful. But I like them. I miss you too.

Me: I'll see you tomorrow.

Annalee: I wish I could see you now. What are you doing? Right this second?

Me: Sitting on my back porch. Wishing I was stranded in a little cabin in the snow with a beautiful woman.

Annalee: might need to be more specific...

Me: A woman who goes by a nickname that doesn't begin to describe her.

Silence. I went on.

Me: A woman with a brilliant mind and sparkling eyes who keeps half of herself hidden from everyone she meets.

She didn't reply, but I could almost feel her there, across the space between us, reading my words.

Me: A woman so utterly attractive she can make a man forget every reason why he isn't supposed to touch her. And so addictive that he's still thinking of her even though they've agreed it's only going to be casual between them.

It was quiet for a little while after that, and I sipped my whiskey and tried not to be disappointed. Annalee was a mystery. It was part of what made her so interesting. But it was also what made it so dangerous to be this attracted to her. She had power to hurt me, whether I'd meant to give it to her or not.

Annalee: Maybe there is something more.

Annalee: Between them.

We both knew there was. Something. Hope sprang up inside me and I tried to quash it down. Why was I thinking about things with her, real thing?

Annalee: I'm lying in bed. Wishing you were here.

Fuuuck. Every fiber of my body sprang to attention.

Me: If I was there, you'd already be coming.

Annalee: What would you do to me?

Shit. I put my glass down on the deck beside me, sank lower in my chair and imagined Annalee in bed, alone in that big hotel, her hands roaming her beautiful body.

Me: I'd tease you at first. I'd skim my fingers over every inch of your skin, kiss you until you were gasping for breath and begging for more.

Annalee: More. I'm begging.

Me: I'd use my tongue and my mouth to explore your neck. I'd let my fingers go lower. Getting you ready.

Annalee: I'm ready now.

Dammit. My dick was throbbing painfully, clearly not having gotten the memo about sexting being virtual.

Me: Patience.

Annalee: Fuck patience. Fuck me.

Me: Oh, I will.

Me: First I'm going to open you with my fingers so I can feel how wet and ready you are. Then I'm going to taste you, working with my fingers while I fuck you with my tongue.

Annalee: Oh my god.

Me: And then, when you're moaning my name, I'll take my time...

Annalee: You know how I feel about waiting.

Me: It will be worth it.

Annalee: God, I'm so ready. I want to feel you inside me.

Me: Imagine I am. Imagine me

"Daddy?" Lily's voice cut through the growing darkness on the back porch, bringing me bolt upright out of the chair and to my feet.

"Honey?" I spun to find her standing in the doorway, the light from within making her curls stand out around her head like a halo.

My tiny angel.

"I woke up and called for you, but you didn't come. I thought you were..." she trailed off, her voice becoming tiny as she hiccuped a sob.

"I'm right here, baby." I went to her, knelt in front of her and wrapped my arms around her, pulling her onto one knee as her arms went around my neck. "Let's go inside."

It was more than an hour later before I found myself in bed, my phone in my hand once again.

Annalee: Don't stop!

Annalee: I was right there...

Annalee: Where did you go?

Annalee: Hey, is everything okay? Now I'm worried.

Me: Sorry. Got interrupted. Everything is fine. I'll see you tomorrow.

It was late, and there was no answer from Annalee. Just the steady need I felt inside me, matched only by the painful thought that I wasn't ready for this. That Lily and I were not ready for anything like this.

Chapter 22
Sugar and Spice

ANNALEE

With the soft opening just days away, the resort had begun to look like an entirely different place. The lobby was finished, the massive front desk wired with state-of-the-art computers for check-in and consoles that controlled pretty much everything else in the hotel. Beyond the phone system, the keypads there controlled the electric doors and locks in all the downstairs amenity areas, the music throughout the resort, the temperatures of the hot tubs, all the lights in the hotel, and much more.

Brainiac had hooked us up for it with a guy who taught at

Sterling Hill University with him, some Uber-rich entrepreneur who taught students about the business of startups. The guy had already made a fortune designing smart homes, and somehow he owed Brainiac a favor.

Ghost and Aubrey had been racing around like people possessed, but I knew everything was on the line for them. They spent all their free time searching through the movie reels in the old theater, which were evidently not all labeled and in some cases had to be rewound or even repaired before they could be viewed in the old reel-to-reel projector.

But one morning Aubrey strode into the kitchen where I'd been working on perfecting my creme brûlée, to demand my attendance at a movie showing that evening.

"Did you figure something out?" I asked.

Aubrey just grinned at me. "Theater, five o'clock, okay?"

I nodded, almost as pleased to see her happy as I was to find that the sugar I'd burned on the top of my dessert was perfectly crisp, forming a hard light-brown shell with little bubbles on it. "Yes," I breathed.

"Talking to yourself, Annalee?" Mateo's rich voice rolled through the air, making my insides ache with want. I'd never met anyone who could turn me into a puddle of need with just his voice. But it had been more than a week since we'd been together, and every part of my body missed him. We'd taken to texting most nights and had almost moved on to sexting once, but had been interrupted. All of it left me wanting him more.

Seeing him at work, beginning to show him what we'd be doing in the kitchen when guests arrived, had been a special kind of torture. We were rarely alone, and the kitchen was always busy, since there was no official lunch schedule, and everyone was in and out at all times for coffee or snacks.

"Hey," I said, grabbing a spoon and thrusting the creme brûlée at him. "Try this."

He raised an eyebrow, but took the spoon from my hand, digging a bite of creme out from beneath the crystallized top. I watched, my mouth opening slightly as he passed the spoon between his perfect lips.

"That is amazing," he said. "Did you try that?"

"I was more concerned with getting the sugar right on top."

"You got it," he said, scooping out another spoonful. "But taste it. It's incredible." He held the spoon up for me, and when I leaned forward slightly, opening my lips farther, he gently slid it into my mouth.

The sweetness of the dessert and the sexy simplicity of the action had me ready to drop everything and beg him to take me on the countertop. If I'd thought it would be easy to explore my crush on Mateo and then walk away, I'd been dead wrong. I wanted more. I just didn't know what that was.

"Good," I moaned, opening my eyes to find him watching me hungrily.

"Are you busy right now?" he asked, his voice a low rumble and his liquid eyes never leaving my face.

Was he inviting me somewhere? I shook my head in hopes my instincts weren't wrong. He looked as desperate as I felt. "No. Not busy."

"Would you..." he paused, looking around the empty kitchen. Mateo set down the dessert and stepped closer to me, trailing one finger down the side of my jaw and sending my body into overdrive. I heard myself gasp when he touched me. "You have a room around here somewhere, don't you? A bed? A door that locks?"

"I have all of those things," I agreed, letting my eyes drop shut as his finger tracked along the side of my neck.

"Would you want to show those things to me? Before this movie?"

"God, yes," I breathed. Those of us who'd come to help

Ghost renovate the resort all had rooms in what we were now calling the staff wing, but would one day be more guest rooms. "Fourth floor. End of the hall. Meet me there in five."

I was half out of my mind, but I knew heading up there together would be a bad idea. So when Mateo nodded and turned, leaving the kitchen, I made myself wait. I checked all the burners and the oven, and tucked my notes onto the shelf above the prep counter. Then I practically sprinted up the stairs to the fourth floor.

He waited at the end of the hallway, the square window at the end of the hall illuminating his broad form as he watched me approach, leaning against the sill, arms crossed. The glare from the window made it impossible to see the expression on his face, but I could imagine it. Those sculpted lips in a little smile, the light eyes gleaming.

"Hey," I said, feeling shy for some reason.

"Hey," he said, pushing himself to stand as I slid the key into my door.

Mateo followed me inside, and for a moment we both stood, taking in the room with its soaring window opposite the door, the simple but comfortable living room before us. All the rooms at Kasper Ridge were suites, so the bedroom lay just beyond, off to one side of the space.

"Come on," I said, taking his hand and walking him to the door to the bedroom.

When we reached the doorway, Mateo tugged my hand, spinning me so my back was to the doorjamb. He caged me in, one hand holding the doorframe at my side, the other finding my face as he leaned close, those perfect lips just inches from mine. For a long beat, he just looked into my eyes, sending things jolting and jumping inside me.

"I missed being able to touch you," he said, barely audible over the pounding of my blood in my ears.

My hands found his chest, flattening themselves against the hard muscle there. I could feel his heart beating through the soft T-shirt he wore. I slid them lower, pressing the hem up and letting my fingers glide over the hot smooth flesh below.

Mateo hissed in a breath as I touched him.

And then he was on me, his mouth on mine, his hands gripping me, owning me.

We moved together on instinct, the push and pull between us as basic as the undulation of the tide or the movement of the trees in the wind. His hands stroked, teased, enflamed, and soothed, and soon enough I was on my back on my own bed, Mateo kneeling above me.

"I dreamt about this," he murmured, those glowing green eyes staring down at me. "Imagined touching every inch of your perfect body, hearing those noises you make. I thought I'd just remembered you wrong though, that you couldn't actually be this beautiful. But you are. So beautiful."

I could have said the same of him, if only his hands weren't stroking me in ways that made words impossible. I had become sensation alone, feeling him near me, on me, around me, and finally—inside me.

"God, yes," I said as he stretched and filled me, bringing a kind of satisfaction I didn't know I'd been missing but now felt maybe I couldn't actually live without. "How is this so perfect? How are you so perfect?"

Mateo leaned over me, his hands braced on either side of my head, and though his eyes had been shut as he first slid home, now they met mine, and there was a question there, deep within his gaze. "I'm not perfect," he breathed.

"But you're perfect for me," I said, the words out before I realized they were probably more than I should say, more than what we had agreed to.

Mateo stilled for a moment, hovering above me, his body hot

and tight beneath my hands and his cock pulsing gently inside me, making me want something I didn't even have a name for.

"More," I breathed. I wanted more of everything. Of him, of this, of the time we had, but mostly of this feeling. The feeling that he saw me, he knew me. I wasn't Monroe to him. I wasn't the girl with the armor and the chip on her shoulder. I was just a girl who he thought was beautiful. And it was so much more than I'd ever had before.

He moved again, thrusting into me with a gentle but steady rhythm that was building the need within me to a boiling point, pushing me higher and higher until the inevitable free fall that loomed ahead was both terrifying and impossible to deny.

My legs were hooked around his thighs, my hands grasping at whatever I could reach—his soft sandy hair, the globes of his perfect ass, his strong muscled back.

And when the motion of his movements became quicker, less controlled, I felt myself losing control simultaneously.

"Annalee," he whispered, dropping his head next to mine. "Oh god, Annalee." It was like a curse and a prayer, my name on his lips a whispered plea my heart echoed and my body answered.

"Yes," I murmured, unspooling beneath him as he thrust harder, crying out. "Yes," I heard myself gasp, my world flying away from me, swirling into the cosmos and then regrouping, slowing with my breath.

Mateo stilled and then pulled me toward him as he rolled so we lay face to face, still connected.

For a long moment, he stared into my eyes, and I could see the thoughts chasing one another through his mind, each one reflected in those light green depths.

"What?" I whispered, knowing there were words coming, and feeling less and less willing to wait to hear them.

"Nothing," he said. "And so much."

I let out a laugh, but it was more nervous than amused. "That's a lot."

"It is," he agreed, one hand tracing a line down my shoulder, my arm. "It's more than I expected. Close to everything."

He didn't have to spell it out. I felt it too. "Too much?"

He sighed. "I don't know."

We stayed there, locked in each other's eyes for a long moment, the world still and close around us.

"There are things I want to say, words on the tip of my tongue," he whispered. "But I can't let them out." His expression was so serious, so tortured, that I placed a palm to the side of his face, wishing to erase whatever was making him look that way.

"You don't have to say anything," I told him, though my heart was answering with different words entirely. "We don't have to name this or classify it. It can just be whatever it is. For as long as we want it."

But even as I spoke the words, I knew they were false. I'd never wanted anyone like Mateo. I'd never had anyone look at me the way he did, as if I was more than just the bombshell I pretended to be, as if he was more interested in what lay beneath. It was heady and terrifying. I only knew I wanted more.

He kissed me gently, ending the words between us for now, and I wrapped him in my arms, holding onto whatever we had for as long as I could.

Chapter 23
I'm the Map, I'm the Map...

MATEO

A rchie had been clear that we were all watching a movie tonight, so I'd arranged with Lily's grandmother for her to eat dinner there. Truthfully, I was in no hurry to leave the resort lately after work. Even passing glimpses of Annalee gave me a little thrill I hadn't experienced in so long they made every part of every day feel different, special.

I knew my fascination with her was something I should examine more closely, but it felt too good. I worried that if I

were to dissect it, analyze these feelings I had, this giddy anticipation of seeing her every day, I'd find a reason why it couldn't
exist, shouldn't exist. My life had been about maintenance for so
long, about the sheer work of existing each day with some
modicum of sanity intact—this was like an extended vacation
from misery. And though I worried it couldn't last, and that the
light frivolous fun between us would be no match for the serious
burdens of my real life, I wasn't willing to cast it off.

In fact, I'd come damn close to saying words that would only
serve to connect us more tightly. Words I'd only said to one
other person before. And no matter how amazing Annalee was,
could she really rival Poppy in my mind? In my heart? Could
the words I'd wanted to say be applied here as easily as they'd fit
the mother of my child?

Part of me worried that I didn't know Annalee well enough.
That I really didn't know her at all. But another part of me
argued that I knew more than enough. And reminded me that I
hadn't known Poppy well when we'd been in the midst of the
heady intoxication of the early feelings between us.

Was time spent directly related to enormity of feelings?

We'd cleaned up and left Annalee's room separately, and
now I stood at the edge of the theater, watching as she moved
down the aisle toward me. She smiled softly as she drew near,
and I was about to usher her to a seat next to where I was
planning to sit, away from the fighter pilot contingent in the
back, when Brainiac whistled loudly and then called,
"Monroe!"

Annalee's face changed suddenly, and she gave me a look
that I thought was an apology. But then she leaned close and
said, "Come on."

I followed her back up the aisle, and into the row of seats
where Brainiac sat with Will and Lucy, Aubrey and Wiley just
ahead of us. When Annalee sat, Brainiac's big hand dropped to

her knee, and something inside me clenched. I forced myself to remain still.

"How's things in the kitchen, Monroe? I'd imagine you're pretty steamed about it—a woman's place and all that?" he asked loudly.

Annalee laughed it off, but I hadn't really considered that particular irony. She'd told me at the cabin about avoiding the roles her mother and her family had tried to lay before her— beauty queen, wife, mother. And now Archie had her running the kitchen.

"You know, most famous chefs are men," she said lightly. "It's an honor to be in charge. And it gives me a lot of power, you know."

"Power, huh?" Brainiac said, but I could hear the respect he held for her in his voice. His hand was still on her knee, and I was struggling with the urge to remove it forcefully. She did not belong to me. She wasn't mine. But she wasn't his either.

"Power," she repeated. "If I'm running the kitchen, it's pretty easy to add a little something to the meal of anyone who's annoying me." She smiled sweetly at him as he faked a horrified gasp.

"Mateo, you're going to keep an eye on her, right?" he asked, leaning forward to look at me past Annalee.

Her gaze followed his, and my eyes locked with hers. I reminded myself that Brainiac was watching and waiting for an answer, and I forced myself to keep my voice light, my fists unclenched.

"Sure man. I'll make sure she doesn't poison you. But you better watch yourself. Don't piss her off."

He laughed. "I see you learned a lot about getting along with Monroe when you guys were stuck up there in the snow."

More than I was planning to share with him, that was certain.

"Hey everyone," Archie called from the back of the theater, pulling our attention and dousing the light chatter. "Thanks for coming. Aubrey and I are excited to host the first official movie showing of the new Kasper Ridge Resort. Apologies that we don't have the refreshments set up quite yet, but we ordered dinner in tonight, so we'll get that after the movie. For now, sit back and enjoy *The Map*. I think you'll see why we wanted to show it to you."

The lights flicked out, and the sound of an old movie projector clicking as it rolled forward filled the air. In the darkness, Annalee's hand found my thigh, tracing a line down it and disappearing. I reached out to capture it again, and we sat like that, holding hands out of sight of anyone around us, my heart swelling in my chest as her fingers traced soft circles against my skin.

The movie was old, made in the sixties, I thought. It followed two brothers in their search for a legendary treasure, and was kind of a buddy movie, kind of an adventure-heist film. They weren't cowboys, but they ended up on horseback in some canyon that could have been Colorado, and that was the first time the movie really showed the map they were following. They spread the tattered old document across the face of a rock, and the camera zoomed in. And Archie stopped the projector.

"There," he said, a note of triumph in his voice. "See that?"

We could all see the flickering image of a tattered map partially obscured by one of the actor's hands.

"It's the same," Archie said, his voice holding a reverence I didn't necessarily understand.

Aubrey stood and flipped open a laptop, an image on the screen of the map I'd seen the two of them with a few times. Their map was missing most of one side, but now that Aubrey held the laptop up near the big screen, I could see a resemblance.

"The markings are identical," she said, pointing to the little cross down in one corner and the dashed line that led away from it. On the screen, that dashed line kept going to the opposite corner of the map, and there were several other markings across the map face.

"We can finish the map. This is a clue," Archie said, excitement coloring his voice.

Aubrey hit a button on the laptop, and the missing portion of the map appeared on her screen along with the part they already had. "Now we just have to figure out how to read it."

"What do they do in the movie?" Will asked. "Do they find the treasure?"

"Wait," Lucy said, standing up and turning to face Archie. "We get to watch the rest of the movie, right? You're not gonna leave us hanging."

"You can watch it or I can just tell you how it ends."

Archie's suggestion was met with loud boos. He laughed and a few seconds later, the movie was rolling again.

In the end, the brothers did not find the treasure. Instead, they found some old house that their father had told them about —the place he'd grown up. And they decided to pursue a different kind of fortune, rebuilding the house and using the property to ranch, as their father's family had done. It was an interesting parallel to Archie and Aubrey and this resort, and though the map was definitely the intended discovery here, I wondered if there was anything else about the movie that their Uncle Marvin had meant to be impactful.

"Well that was a bummer," Annalee whispered, her soft breath tickling my ear as she squeezed my hand and released it.

I glanced at her leg as the lights came up, relieved to see that Brainiac hadn't kept his hand there through the whole film. I had known they were close, but an uncomfortable little stone of irritation had flared in me as he'd touched her. I wondered just how close they were and if there was history there. It was almost impossible for me to imagine him touching her, being with her, because if I let myself think of it, I thought it might literally drive me crazy.

The group wandered out to the lobby and toward the tables in the restaurant, but I couldn't stay for dinner.

"Hey, I've gotta get going," I told Annalee quietly, stepping away from the people heading in to eat.

"Sure," she said softly, her eyes meeting mine, then dropping. "See you tomorrow?"

"Yes," I said.

"I'm putting you to work," she said, her voice teasing. "So come prepared. Get a good night's sleep." The words weren't necessarily suggestive, but her tone was, and certain parts of me were very interested in the type of work she had in mind. In reality, we had a lot of prep work to do for the crowd of thirty guests that would be arriving in just a few days.

"I look forward to it," I told her. I leaned in, stopping myself at the last moment. "Shit. I almost kissed you goodbye," I whispered, backing away.

"I wouldn't have complained," she said, and her voice had dropped its playful tone.

This was hard. Whatever this was. And for a moment I wondered if we needed to keep it hidden. But the answer was obvious. Neither of us was ready for anything real. We'd established that already. And letting the others at the resort know about whatever was going on between us would only make it more real, and would definitely raise questions we weren't ready to answer.

We'd agreed. This was whatever it was, for as long as it lasted.

Only, was that enough for me?

"Bye," I said, rubbing a hand over my face as I walked away, tension draining from my body as the possibility of touching Annalee faded for the night. I needed to get my head on straight and spend more time thinking about taking care of my little girl, and less time considering how to make Annalee moan my name.

But, god, I loved it when she did.

Chapter 24
Douggie Masters Rides Again

ANNALEE

The next few days at the resort were the busiest I'd seen at Kasper Ridge. The newly installed phone system was ringing off the hook with assistants and agents checking details for their clients, the new computer bank had been installed and we'd all sat through a half-day training on how to operate the dashboard, and the cleaning crew we'd hired had been hard at work scrubbing the place from top to bottom.

Kasper Ridge Resort was beginning to look like an actual destination, not just a dusty old heap at the top of a mountain.

Monday's meeting had solidified last minute details, and I'd practiced the weekend's entire menu twice, with less help from Mateo than I'd hoped for, since he'd been tagged with going back up to the cabins with a crew to stock and clean the one we'd used for Douggie Masters.

Guests were going to begin arriving Friday, and Thursday morning had pretty much everyone at the resort spinning. Ghost had begun having us meet each morning to make sure we were all on track. At our meeting Thursday morning, an unexpected visitor joined Mateo at the table in the restaurant.

"New hire, Mateo?" Ghost asked, raising his eyebrows at the little girl sitting next to Mateo at the table. She was petite and bright-eyed, regarding Archie with a half-smile and only a little bit of wary uncertainty. A pig tail hung on each side of her pixie face, dark wavy hair that swung with each little tip of her head.

Mateo looked around and shrugged apologetically. "This is Lily. Normally her grandmother has her while I'm at work, but—"

"Grandma is on a boat," Lily explained, her blue eyes widening even further as she looked around the room. "A big one with a swimming pool on it."

"My mother-in-law is on a cruise," Mateo said, smiling at his daughter in a way that I was pretty sure was meant to tell her to pipe down. "So Lily's hanging out here, but I'll keep her out of sight. She won't get in the way."

Lily clearly didn't like the sound of that, and her little mouth pressed into a frown.

"He mentioned it to me," Aubrey said. "I told him we could set up one of the rooms in the staff wing so she can hang out and watch TV and stuff. Forgot to tell you, Arch."

"Sure," Archie said. "That's no problem." He grinned at the little girl who grinned right back at him.

I sat on Mateo's other side, and I was having a hard time reconciling the insanely hot guy I'd been sleeping with and fantasizing about constantly with the father beside me. He'd glanced at me a couple times, and I'd tried to look natural, but there was something about being confronted with his family that made me wary, uncomfortable.

We discussed guests' arrival plans, and spread the photos of our prominent guests along the center of the table, making sure everyone had names and affiliations memorized. That had been my idea, actually. This event could put us on the map if we handled it right, and the plan was for everything to be top notch.

Lily kept quiet as we talked, her big eyes following the conversation around the table. I found myself watching her more often than not, looking for traces of Mateo in those slight shoulders, the delicate jawline, her startling blue eyes. Lily's mother must have been beautiful. An unwanted pang of jealousy shot through me at the thought.

"Good thing there's no snow, because that ski lift isn't worth a fu—" Brainiac paused in his assessment of the ski lift, looking at Lily with a wrinkle forming between his eyes. "It's not worth a darned thing," he concluded, nodding. "Those parts are still on order, but I think I'm basically rebuilding the motor from scratch. Not a shock since it's gotta be fifty years old."

"That's pretty old," Lily said quietly, nodding at Brainiac.

"Careful, kid. Fifty's not that old," he quipped back with a wry smile. He wasn't even close to fifty, but he was older than the rest of us, and tiny bits of silver were beginning to show at his temples and sideburns. Brainiac and I had been close for as long as we'd known each other—maybe each of us had a part of us we tried to hide from the world at large. He knew more about me than most of the guys I'd flown with, and he held a special spot in my heart.

Lily smiled at my friend, and I was impressed that his gruff response didn't send her shrinking back into her seat, or into her dad at her side. She was tougher than she looked. I could relate to that.

When the meeting ended, Mateo caught my arm. "Annalee," he said as I turned to face him. My heart leapt as it always did when his green gaze met mine, but there was something else now too. I felt oddly nervous, glancing at the eager little face at his side. "I'd like to introduce you officially to Lily. She might be helping out a little bit in the kitchen today, if that's all right with you."

This was not a day to have distractions, I thought, but I also knew that Mateo was in a difficult position. And we were in good shape in terms of prep, which he knew.

"It's nice to meet you officially, Lily," I told her, leaning down slightly to peer into her face.

"You're very pretty," Lily said, matter-of-factly. "Daddy told me you were a kickbutt fighter pilot and that you could run circles around any of those guys in that meeting." Her pigtails swung as she nodded at her declaration, and I glanced up to see Mateo chewing on his bottom lip.

"Well," I said, looking back down at her. "I appreciate the compliment. And your daddy's right. Women can do anything men can do, you know. And often we do it better."

"I mean," Mateo grumbled.

"Right!" Lily trilled, grinning at me and then looking up at her dad.

"Like she wasn't already impossible enough," he muttered to me over her head. "Thanks a lot."

"She needs to understand that women don't have to get by on being pretty," I reminded him. "We can kick ass and take names just as well as we wear lipstick and high heels."

Lily giggled at my declaration, and I realized I'd probably crossed some kind of proper language in front of kids line, but Mateo didn't say anything. He smiled at me, those green eyes lit with something I recognized, and my body heated in response. In some strange way, seeing him with his daughter only made him sexier.

"We'd better go get things all prepared," I told them both. "People are going to want to eat tomorrow when they get here!"

"I like to eat," Lily said, leaving her father's side and coming to walk next to me as we headed to the kitchen.

"I find that most people do," I told her, surprised she seemed to think this was an earth-shaking revelation.

"I like cheese," she went on, undeterred by my easy acceptance of her enjoyment of food. "And goldfish crackers and Lucky Charms and chicken nuggets if they don't have sauce, and carrots if they're babies, and—"

"Lily." Mateo's voice was a low growl, but it had the desired effect and Lily stopped talking immediately. "Remember what we talked about."

Lily looked up at me as we came to a stop in the middle of the glowing industrial kitchen and stage-whispered, "I'm not supposed to ramble and annoy people."

Something about the way she said it, her little face in a smile that felt like it was a secret just for me, made me like her a bit more, and allowed me to loosen up just a tad. I smiled back at her. "It's okay."

Mateo got to work chopping vegetables that could be prepped ahead, and I set Lily over the sink with a scrub brush and about a million potatoes to scrub, figuring she didn't need any knives or peelers. The last thing I wanted was for the kid to lose a finger or something.

I worked on grouping things in the pantry and fridge for meals, and reviewing the notes I'd made for each course to make sure everything was going to be as smooth as possible when the added pressure of guests put my skills to the test. In the background, I listened to Lily and Mateo talk as they worked, and found myself smiling as I realized he had a secret soft, silly side I hadn't seen before.

In the afternoon, Mateo took Lily up to the suite to chill out and watch some television. When he returned, he stalked toward me, a fierce look in his eyes that would have scared me a little if I hadn't seen it before. He didn't say a word, just grabbed my hand and pulled me to the farthest corner of the kitchen, pressing my butt against the corner of the wall and pushing his knee between my legs as his arms caged me in.

"It's been torture," he said in a low voice that sent my nerves dancing. "Being with you all day and not being able to touch you."

His mouth found mine before I could answer and he kissed me like a man just home from a long deployment, like he was starving and I was the only thing that could feed him.

I melted into his arms and did my best to turn off the thoughts spooling though my mind. Seeing him with his daughter made everything more real. This wasn't just a crush. It wasn't a light little dalliance that didn't mean anything and could be dropped when we got bored. Mateo was a father, a family man. And involvement with him was involvement with that pigtailed little girl, whether I liked it or not.

Mateo and Lily represented everything I'd been avoiding my whole life. And somehow, I'd stepped right into it and was suddenly knee-deep in a longing I'd never expected to feel. But it didn't matter if I had images of the three of us becoming a family—that wasn't me. And a family was the one thing I knew, deep in my bones, I never wanted.

I kissed him back, but something inside me was screaming at me to pull away before I made any promises I couldn't keep.

Chapter 25
Don't be Grumpy and Brush Your Hair

MATEO

At the end of the day Thursday, Lily and I were met at the front door by Archie, who was standing in the lobby looking nervous. He'd been standing in front of the glass looking out on the turnabout in front of the resort, arms crossed over his chest and a grim look on his face.

"G'night Archie," I called. "We'll see you tomorrow morning." We planned to return bright and early to beat the first guest's arrival around ten.

"Yeah, good night," he replied, sounding lost in thought. But then he turned to face us. "Hey, Mateo."

"Yeah?"

"Why don't you guys just stay here this weekend? If Lily's coming back with you anyway, would it make sense to just sleep in that suite?"

"I mean..." Of course it made sense. I was going to be here long hours this weekend. Having a place to crash instead of a drive at the end of the day would be nice. But having Annalee nearby, just down the hall all night, would be a new level of torture.

"You don't want to be driving back and forth if you don't have to. No one's staying in those rooms anyway." Archie sounded like he'd already made up his mind.

"Can we, Daddy?" Lily bounced at my side, despite the fact she'd been half asleep a few moments ago. "That would be so fun!"

Fun wasn't the word that had shot into my mind at the thought of being so close to Annalee all night. "Yeah, I guess so," I said. "Thanks."

"Totally selfish offer," Archie said with a laugh. "I'm trying to stack all the odds in our favor this weekend."

"We're in good shape," I assured him, looking around the beautiful lobby, shined and glamorous in the low light from the chandeliers. "They're gonna love it here."

"I hope you're right," Archie said, following my gaze around the space as if he was just noticing it.

"Daddy is almost always right," Lily told him, sounding proud of me and making my heart clench inside my chest.

"Not always," I laughed.

"I said *almost* always."

Archie smiled at my daughter, and his shoulders lifted, as if he'd let go of some of the load he'd been carrying.

"Did you get the map put together?" I asked. "Figure anything out?"

The invisible bricks weighed him down again and he sighed. "It's even more impossible now that we have the whole map. We know where Lola's Gate is, so it should make sense from there. But it doesn't." He turned back to the windows, frowning at the world outside. "Of course it couldn't just be easy."

I wasn't sure what to say to that. I'd hoped that getting the map put together might be the resolution of this treasure hunt. We were all eager to see what Archie and Aubrey's uncle Marvin had left them. "Sorry, man. We'll figure it out."

"Yeah, hope so," Archie said.

Lily was drooping at my side again, and I took it as my cue to go. "Hey, we'll see you tomorrow," I said, tugging her to the doors.

"Yeah," Archie said. "Good night, guys."

That night after Lily was in bed, I laid in my own bed staring at the ceiling. I needed to get some sleep. It was going to be a long weekend. But my life felt a little like it belonged to someone else, and the feeling was unsettling. The interest I had for Annalee had everything else slightly off balance inside me, and the fact that I'd somehow migrated from contractor to sous chef was part of it. I was used to being behind the scenes, out of the way, busy with my hands and my body. Once we were working a job, there was always plenty of time for me to lose myself in the physicality of the work, and I'd gotten good at slipping into that exertion, turning off my head. But cooking—especially at Annalee's side—gave me little time to hide. I had to be on, to be listening and communicating, and it was as exhausting as it was exhilarating.

I'd been hiding in my job for years, I was realizing. Using it as a means to avoid my own thoughts and feelings. But now they were front and center all day long, and they seemed to take the shape of a curvy outspoken woman with eyes and lips that I couldn't banish from my mind. And right there next to that fierce interest, stood the familiar shadow of my guilt.

My phone chimed at my side.

Annalee: See you tomorrow. Get a good night's sleep. Things are about to get crazy!

I wanted to text Annalee back, and I held my phone over my face as I lay in bed, typing and then deleting a series of responses, none of which seemed to be right. Finally, I let out a frustrated sigh and plugged my phone in to charge, turning to my side and vowing to go to sleep.

Why was I in this situation? Why did I have to be so wrapped up in this woman? I hadn't gone looking for anything. I didn't need anyone. I'd been one of the lucky ones, after all. I'd had the love of my life already—Lily's mom. And I'd been faithful to her while she was alive, and faithful to her memory since she'd been gone. Until now, at least.

Guilt soured my stomach as I found my mind shifting to Annalee again, even as thoughts of Poppy floated in my memory. It wasn't as if I'd sought out this entanglement, and that was what had me tied up. I'd believed that someday I would feel ready, maybe. And that then, I'd go looking for someone new. Once I was sure it was time. But Annalee had wandered into my life—our lives—much too soon. And even though I didn't think it was the right time, the thought of losing her was painful.

My exhausted mind finally spun itself out and I slept, the morning arriving much too soon.

"Look how his hair is all sticking straight up," a little voice mock-whispered, practically in my ear, as consciousness pulled me toward wakefulness.

Another voice came, this one high and warbly. Lily's tiger. "He looks mad, too. Is he mad when he's asleep?"

"No Poppy," Lily said. I kept my eyes shut and didn't move,

trying to hold onto this moment a little longer. "He's not mad, but sometimes he's sad. He thinks about Mommy when he dreams."

A prick of grief twinged inside me. Lily had told me recently that she dreamed of Poppy too, only she'd been sad to admit that she couldn't really remember what she looked like. Of course she couldn't—she'd been only two when her mother died. We'd gone through the pictures on my phone then, and we'd both sniffled as Poppy's beautiful smile filled the screen.

"Maybe he looks mad because he's so hungry," I whispered, keeping my eyes shut.

Lily's giggle came high and sweet. "Poppy! He's hungry."

"What does he eat?" Poppy asked.

"Little girls and tiny tigers!" I growled, cracking an eye open and reach out to sweep Lily onto my bed as she giggled hysterically.

"No Daddy!" she laughed, squirming as I pulled her against me, tickling her lightly and pretending to eat her ear. "Don't eat us!"

She only struggled for a moment before settling against my body as I held her. She was warm and small, and for a few moments, every other worry I had in the world slid away, replaced by the wonder that this miraculous tiny person was mine. Mine to love and hold and laugh with, mine to raise.

"I love you, Lily," I whispered.

Suddenly the tiger was in my face. "What about me?" it demanded.

"I love you too, Poppy," I said, my voice cracking on my wife's name. "God, I love you guys." I squeezed my daughter tightly, letting her little girl scent flood my mind, chasing away everything else.

"We get to sleep at the hotel tonight, right?" Lily wiggled to turn in my arms so she could face me.

"If that's okay with you," I said.

Her eyes widened and she grinned. "I'm so excited!"

"Okay," I laughed. "Then we'll stay at the hotel. You remember that there will be a lot of other people there all weekend, right? Important people."

"I remember."

"So you're going to stay in the suite, right?"

"The whole time?" Lily's smile faltered.

"Not the whole time, but a lot of the time, okay?"

She sighed.

"I'll come up and check on you and we can eat together."

"And Annalee?" The question surprised me, and I wasn't sure what she was asking. Lily's eyebrows rose with hope and excitement.

"I'm sure you'll see her there. She lives there too."

"Can we eat with her?"

I swallowed hard and sat up, ready to get moving, to replace the churn of my mind with physical motion instead. "We'll see. She's going to be really busy this weekend."

Lily nodded, sitting cross-legged in the middle of my bed as I stood and stretched.

"Your hair is messy," she told me. "You should fix it before we see her."

I frowned at her. "Before we see Annalee?"

Lily nodded. "She's very pretty. You don't want to be messy or she might not fall in love with you."

I froze, surprise streaking through me. "Annalee's not going to fall in love with me, honey." I said the words slowly, hoping I could make Lily see that there was nothing to this, nothing she should be thinking about. Had we been so obvious that Lily had picked up on the chemistry between us? Or was it just that Annalee was the first woman my daughter had seen me with since her mother?

"She might," she sniffed. "She could if you practice not being grumpy and if you brush your hair."

I hated the bubble of hope that my daughter's words set loose within me. Because somewhere in the very back of my mind, hadn't I wondered if I could fall in love with Annalee? If I might not already be a little bit in love with her?

I sighed. None of this was right. None of these thoughts or feelings were supposed to be happening. I pressed my hand over the ring on my chest and took a deep breath. I needed to lock down my emotions or this weekend would be impossible to survive.

"Well either way, I need a shower," I told my daughter. "Can you grab a bowl of cereal while I get ready? And then we'll pack up and head over to the resort."

"Yay!" Lily said, bouncing off the bed and out toward the kitchen, thoughts of love and Annalee already set aside.

If only it was so easy for me.

Chapter 26
Your Official Babysitter is Here

ANNALEE

I was up uncomfortably early, starting bread for the day down in the big ovens in the kitchen. The resort was quiet still, no one else roaming about, and no guests had arrived yet. In a way it was nice, having the place to myself as the first faint rays of sun began to glide up over the treetops to filter down, lighting the landscape outside the windows with an ethereal glow. Still, I reminded myself why becoming a baker was not in the cards for me. I liked my beauty sleep, and while four a.m. might be something I could appreciate now and then, it wasn't anything I wanted to be awake for on a regular basis.

By the time there were others moving around the resort lobby, popping in and out of the kitchen for breakfast, I'd guzzled a pot of coffee and was practically hopping around the place. When Mateo showed up, adorable daughter in tow, I was almost giddy to see him, even though he hadn't answered my text last night. I figured he was tired and had turned in early—these long prep days had us all worn out.

"Good morning," I called to them from the front desk where Aubrey was using me as a practice guest, checking me into my room.

Mateo stopped and turned to face me, his face an inscrutable mask. What was he thinking? I didn't know the answer, but a hard little bullet of dread landed in my gut. Had I done something wrong?

"Hi Annalee!" Lily dropped her dad's hand and skipped across the lobby, wrapping herself around my legs in a hug. For a beat, I just stood there, unused to being accosted by small creatures. When she squeezed tighter, I dropped a hand to her little back, rubbing gently for a second and leaning down a bit.

"Good morning, Lily."

"Do you need any help in the kitchen today? I can scrub more potatoes if you want me to." Her grip loosened and her little chin lifted so she could look up at me, those bright blue eyes alight with hope and excitement.

"Not right away," I told her. "And you did so many potatoes yesterday, I think we're all set for the weekend. But I'll definitely let you know if a job pops up."

She let me go, frowning, and stepped back. "Okay. Daddy says I have to stay upstairs."

Mateo, who'd been standing back unmoving, finally stepped near. "There's a lot going on today, bear. I promise to come get you later so you can see all the people. But you stay put until then."

Lily frowned, but agreed, reaching for her daddy's hand again. "And then I'll come help Annalee."

Mateo lifted his eyes to mine, sending a shiver of lust through me. "Morning, Annalee."

"Hi," I said, my voice becoming a whisper.

"I'm going to get Lily settled upstairs and I'll see you in a bit, okay?" The words were all business, but I could see the dark want in his eyes.

"Mr. Simpson, can I make any dinner arrangements for you while you're here?" Aubrey interrupted whatever moment had been passing between us, her voice unnecessarily shrill.

Mateo looked confused, his forehead wrinkling as he turned to regard her.

"Uh, no thanks, ma'am," I answered. "All set for now."

"Great," Aubrey said. "I've got your room all set, the number is on the key envelope here. You let us know if you need anything, Mr. Simpson." Aubrey touched a few more keys on the screen in front of her and then handed me a little paper portfolio.

"You changed your name?" Mateo asked, his body closer now, just at my side. Heat flashed through me.

"I'm helping Aubrey practice. Just a little role playing," I said, making the mistake of looking into his face as I uttered the words "role playing." Suddenly I saw myself dressed up in a French maid's costume, straddling Mateo on my bed, and felt my face flush.

He might have imagined something similar, because he stepped back and cleared his throat loudly. "Okay. Well."

"See you in the kitchen," I told him, and he and Lily headed for the stairs, a small glittery pink backpack slung over one of his broad shoulders.

"Um, what's going on here?" Aubrey asked in a low voice,

leaning forward over the desk. She grinned at me and wiggled her eyebrows.

I leaned on the desk on my forearms, letting my head drop for a brief second, pulling myself back together. "Girl, I don't know."

"Something, though," Aubrey said, her voice almost teasing.

"Yeah, something." I pulled myself together, standing back up straight and smoothing the black pants I'd put on this morning. We were all wearing a uniform of sorts, black slacks and dark green Kasper Ridge Resort polo shirts.

"I knew it!" Aubrey laughed, but taking in my serious face, she dropped her grin. "Hey, if you need to talk..."

"It's all good," I said, coaxing a familiar false bravado into my voice. "We're good. Let's focus."

I turned to head back to the kitchen, glancing out the front doors to see a black town car pull into the drive out front. "Incoming!" I called loudly, and within a minute, Archie and Wiley both appeared from the bar, heading out to greet our first official guest. I ducked back into the kitchen, bracing myself for the busy weekend ahead and doing my best to pretend that Mateo's hot and cold behavior didn't bother me.

I got to work then, laying out a coffee and pastry station at the side of the lobby outside the restaurant entrance, and Mateo joined me to finish putting it together.

"Lily gonna be okay up there?"

"She has to be," he said. "Not a lot of choices. She's a good girl, she'll be fine."

"She seems great," I told him, not sure what kinds of things a person said about little girls to their fathers. This was an area where I had very little experience, so I'd decided to just treat Lily like a tiny adult. She was, after all, just a small human, so that was how I'd address her. For the first time, I wished I'd spent a little more time with my sister when her kids were little, but I'd been away back then. She got started so damned early.

"Doing my best," he said, heading back into the kitchen.

I followed him in, and together we launched into prep work for lunch, which would be our first official meal at the resort. I regretted that everything had to be served buffet style, since we didn't have waitstaff yet, but there were no complaints from the accumulating guests as they helped themselves to pasta, chicken, and salad from the table in the center of the restaurant.

The day streaked past us, more and more guests arriving until Aubrey reported that everyone we'd expected was present with the exception of one writer whose plane from Canada had been delayed. It was odd having the place bustling with activity after staying here so long together. We were used to a quiet hunkering emptiness inside the big resort, and it was as if the place had awoken, stretching its limbs and yawning to life, people populating every part of the hotel. There were lights and voices, movement and the clinking of glasses from the bar. It was nice, actually—a reminder of life outside our quiet haven up here, and more importantly, a signal that maybe this place might be successful.

There was a lull in the early afternoon when the lunch dishes had been handled and we'd gotten through the early prep for dinner, and I finally had a chance to sit down.

"I'm gonna check on Lily," Mateo said, lingering a few minutes at my side as if there was something else he wanted to say.

"Okay," I answered, feeling like I wanted to say something else too, but not sure what it would be. We'd worked together all morning, bustling around the kitchen and the restaurant, but beyond necessary words, we hadn't really spoken. "Hey," I tried, catching his hand before he walked away. "Is everything okay? I mean..." I gestured between us. "I'm not real good at subtext. If there's something I've done, it works best just to tell me." I swallowed hard, waiting for his answer.

Mateo turned his hand over in mine, catching my fingers between his, and he stared down at our intertwined skin for a moment. Then he inhaled sharply and looked up at me, his eyes darker than usual, full of something I couldn't identify. "Nothing's wrong," he said softly. "That's really the problem, if there is one."

I shook my head lightly. "Talking in riddles," I laughed, but my stomach was twisting with some knowledge my mind hadn't made sense of yet.

"It's just... I wasn't looking for this," he said, dropping my gaze. "For you. And I'm just not sure—"

"Hey," I said, feeling like I needed to reassure him. Whatever this relationship between us was, I didn't want him to cut it off. I didn't need him to marry me, but I didn't want him running away either. This felt too good. "Whatever it is for however long it lasts, remember? No pressure here. We're just enjoying each other." Even as I reminded him what we'd agreed, the words felt hollow in my mouth.

He sighed, then looked up into my face again. "Right. Yeah. Okay." Each word sounded slightly more certain.

"Okay?" I asked, hating myself a little for needing more assurance.

"Yeah," he said, and he leaned forward and caught my lips in a soft kiss that was far too brief. "Be right back." He dropped my fingers and turned, his broad back disappearing out the kitchen doors. I sighed in the silence, and dropped my head onto my arms on the counter before me. I was tired, and not just from running around the kitchen all morning.

I decided to take a quick walk outside, get some fresh air and clear my head before the dinner rush got rolling. I untied the apron I wore, dropping it onto the counter, and headed out into the lobby. Aubrey stood at the reception desk, looking as frazzled as I felt.

"Doing okay?" I asked her.

"Yeah," she shrugged. "I forgot how people all need things." Guests meandered through the lobby to the bar and toward the big double doors that led to the back patio.

"It's good though, right?"

She nodded, grinning. "It's amazing."

"I'm gonna go get a little air. I'll be out back if anyone needs anything and I'll head back in after twenty minutes or so."

"Totally," she agreed, her smile widening as a man approached us. She lifted a finger to keep me from heading out back and I turned to face the newcomer. "Annalee, I'd like to introduce Douggie Masters of *Out and Out There*. He arrived a few hours ago and has been looking forward to meeting you."

I turned to greet the man standing to my side. He was tall and broad, just as I'd imagined he would be after seeing his show. "It's lovely to meet you," I told him. "I'm Annalee Tyson. Heading things up in the kitchen this weekend."

"Charmed," Douggie said, giving me just the tips of his fingers to shake. "I've been dying to meet you," he said, his dark eyes glittering. "There's something so compelling about a female fighter pilot."

"Is there?" I asked, thinking about that. "A bunch of the other guys up here were fighter pilots too."

"I know," Douggie said, smiling at Aubrey. "But they're guys. I want to hear what it was like for you."

"What it was like?" This was forward and a little awkward, but it was hard not to be charmed by Douggie's smile and embracing manner.

He winked. "Looking like that, around all those men all the time. Did you have to prove yourself, did you have to try to be

183

better than them?" Douggie took my arm as he talked, leading me past the reception desk and out toward the back patio.

I looked up at him, persuaded to go along by his easy manner and welcoming smile. "Okay, I'll chat about it," I said. "But you have to promise that whatever you're featuring on *Out and Out There* is about the resort—I'm just here to help out."

"I love that you're confident enough to think I'd shift the entire focus of the show to be about kickass female fighter pilots making it in a man's world," he laughed. Then he leaned in close, "because I totally would."

We sank into a couple of Adirondack chairs positioned to look up at the ski mountain behind the resort.

"This place is going to be incredible when you get snow," he said stretching his arms over his head. "I wish my hubby could have come with."

"You'll just have to bring him back," I told him. "On a real vacation, not a working one."

Douggie grinned at me. "He'd love you," he said. "Okay, now tell me all the stories."

It took a few minutes, but Douggie's easy laugh and congenial personality coaxed me into opening up, and soon he was giggling as I told him about the time I'd had to "rescue" a few fellow pilots from a situation they'd gotten themselves into at a bar in South Korea by telling the proprietor that I was their babysitter, that the US Navy had begun appointing official sitters for some of the rowdier sailors abroad.

"He bought that?"

"I was in civilian clothes, so I guess so. First I told him I was an officer, and he didn't believe that, so I just played to his stereotypes."

"Girl, the things you must've put up with," Douggie sighed, patting my arm.

I grinned at him. "It was the time of my life. Can't imagine doing anything different."

"And now they've got you in the kitchen," he said, frowning comedically.

"Only temporarily."

"What are you going to do next? You staying on here?"

"I'm not sure," I told him honestly. "I'll do whatever Ghost needs for a while. We all kind of feel like we owe him that. He had a rough go at the end of his time in."

Douggie nodded sympathetically, and I wondered if he knew what I was referring to. We didn't talk openly about the mishap that had ended Ghost's flying days, but it had been in the papers at the time, of course.

"Well, just promise me you don't let anyone hold you back. You've got a fighting spirit. I can feel it." Douggie's eyes left my face, sliding to my side. "Oh, hello there. She yours?"

I turned to find Lily standing at the side of my chair, her little hands resting on the wooden arm at my side. She smiled shyly at me.

For a moment, my mind whirred, wondering what it would be like if Lily was my daughter. What if I'd chosen that path instead of the one I was on?

"No," I said, "but I know who she belongs to. Lily, this is Douggie Masters from *Out and Out There*."

"I know who you are," Lily said, all shyness gone in a flash. "I love your show. I want to be just like you when I grow up if I decide not to be a pilot or a contractor."

"Well, keeping your options open is always a good idea," Douggie said, beaming at her.

"Are you going up to the cabin in the backcountry soon? Where is your crew?" Lily looked around for the television crew, and I wondered too.

"No way, little miss. I film most of *Out and Out There*

myself. I do have one cameraman who always comes with, but he's off for tonight. And that's just in case there are any emergencies or if I'm battling a grizzly or something. Hard to film when you're fighting for your life." Douggie grinned.

"You've fought bears?" Lily's voice revealed her astonishment.

Douggie's smile didn't fade. "That was just an example. But I did fight off a particularly nasty raccoon one time. He was trying to steal my favorite slippers, which were drying outside my tent up in the Appalachians."

Lily's eyes widened, and she nodded her understanding. "Wow."

"Well, she. Is. Adorable," Douggie proclaimed. "And you're pretty cute too. You know, I've got a thread on an opportunity that might be perfect for you," he told me. "I'm gonna run in and freshen up before dinner. Big hike tomorrow!" He stood and waved as he turned and headed inside. I had no idea what he was referring to, and my mind spun with questions.

Lily climbed onto my lap on the chair, shocking me into stillness. I hadn't anticipated her decision to climb into the chair, but now that she was settled, I found I didn't mind. She smelled clean and a little bit like muffins, and her warm little body leaned back against me, infusing me with an unfamiliar longing.

"Aren't you supposed to be upstairs?" I asked her quietly.

"Needed to freshen up," she said, snuggling against me. Then she turned her head to look up at me. "I got bored and I could see you down here through the window."

We sat in content silence for a moment, and I tried not to envision what it would be like if Lily was my daughter, if I had this comforting little person in my arms regularly. I felt strangely warm and happy, like I was living someone else's life for a moment.

Quietly, Lily's voice floated up to me with a note of longing woven through it. "Daddy says my mommy used to hold me on her lap all the time."

I didn't have time to let that sink in, because a familiar masculine voice rolled across the space behind me, and Mateo didn't sound happy.

"There you are. I've looked everywhere for you!"

Chapter 27
This Hotel Room Sucks

MATEO

The kitchen was quiet between meals, and I'd taken the opportunity to check in with Lucy, make sure she didn't need anything. After all, though I'd been playing sous chef lately, the entire reason I was here was because Lucy Dale was my boss.

But renovation had been halted while guests were in the hotel, so even Lucy was busy doing other things.

"How's the cooking?" she asked, waiting in front of the bar, watching Wiley place drinks atop a tray. It seemed Lucy was playing cocktail waitress this weekend.

"It's fine," I said, suspecting she might be asking about something else, based on the way her eyebrows wiggled when she asked. "I think dinner tonight will be the real test, but we're ready to go. Taking a little break. Just wanted to make sure you're good, you don't need anything."

Lucy shook her head, and her long ponytail swung behind her. "I'm good."

"Want anything, man?" Wiley asked me, placing two glasses of wine on Lucy's tray.

"No thanks," I told him. I was already tired. Alcohol would definitely not help. "I'm gonna go check on Lily though. Could I get a root beer to take her?"

"Sure thing," Wiley said, moving with practiced ease behind the bar and filling a glass with ice and soda for me. "Here you go."

"Thanks," I said, taking the glass. "See you guys in a bit."

I headed up to the suite we were using this weekend, feeling a little bit guilty about having basically ensconced my daughter in a couple rooms for the whole weekend and not spending any time with her. But I hadn't had a lot of options, and hanging out in a hotel with every channel you could ever want on television was probably Lily's idea of luxury.

"Hey bear," I said, opening the heavy door to our rooms and stepping inside.

The television was playing in the bedroom, so I followed the cartoon voices through the door, expecting to see Lily lying on the bed. Only she wasn't there. I set the soda I carried on the dresser and moved to the bathroom.

"Lily?"

The door was open, and she wasn't inside. I turned, rushing to the other bedroom in the suite, and my stomach dropped as I realized it was empty too. One final bathroom check, and panic surged within me. Lily wasn't here.

"Shit!" I cursed, heading for the door again. Where could she be?

I stormed down the hallway, expecting to see her around every turn, my adrenaline pumping each time I found nothing. As I raced downstairs, I began imagining the worst. What if she'd left the resort? Had someone known she was in the room alone and taken her? The place was crawling with strangers today.

Guilt clawed its way up my throat. I should never have left her alone. Who did that? She was seven years old, for fuck's sake!

I scanned the lobby, ignoring guests who gave me questioning looks at my speed and clear concern, and made a tour of the restaurant. She wasn't in the kitchen, which I'd thought was the best bet, since she had a clear fondness for Annalee, but neither of them was there, the stainless steel counters stood long and cold, waiting for the dinner prep to begin.

"Oh god," I whispered. "Where are you, Lily?"

I practically sprinted through the movie theater and tried the locked doors of the non-operational arcade and bowling alley, my fear growing with every step.

Finally, I slammed through the big double doors in the lobby out to the back patio, which spanned the entire length of the resort and faced the ski mountain and backcountry beyond. She wouldn't have wandered away, would she? Lily was a mountain kid. She knew not to head off into the woods on her own.

I moved between the chairs spread around the open space, glancing up at the guests soaking in the enormous hot tub. We hadn't brought suits, so I was fairly certain she wouldn't be up there. I stood, swiveling my head to take in each one of the little groups of guests, and finally landed on a familiar figure in a lounge chair on the far side of the patio, a little girl—my little girl—in her lap.

I sprinted toward Annalee, relief and anger warring for prominence in my mind, and just as I stepped close, I heard Lily tell her that Poppy used to hold her in her lap too. As if she was comparing them. As if Annalee might be vying for the position of Lily's new mom.

Something inside me snapped, the fear and worry tightening into a fragile line finally broken by the guilt I'd been towing around with me since getting entangled with Annalee. What were we doing? We'd been trapped together for a weekend, that was all. I should have stayed away after that. I wasn't ready for anything else, and neither was my daughter.

"There you are. I've looked everywhere for you!"

I practically shouted at them, and they both stared at me, eyes wide with surprise. I glanced around, realized they weren't the only ones staring, and I quickly did my best to pull myself together. I couldn't ruin things for Archie just because I was the most irresponsible father on Earth.

Leaning in close to Annalee, I whispered, "What the hell are you doing? I had no idea where she was."

Annalee opened her mouth to speak, but I wasn't done. Every ounce of fear and guilt, every bit of worry that I'd been making all the wrong choices for my kid since the day my wife left me to raise her alone came out in a harsh whisper, cutting her off.

"You don't know what it's like to be responsible for someone else, to have to worry constantly about them. You can't just flit off with someone's child. She's not your plaything, just because your life is all adventure and fun. Some of us are trying to live actual lives, Annalee. Some of us are trying to be responsible adults."

Annalee's eyes burned and her mouth had pressed into a tight line, but I wasn't done. Tears had begun dripping down Lily's face.

"I think it's probably best if you stay away from my daughter," I finished, gathering Lily into my arms and standing up.

"Daddy, I'm sorry." Lily's voice was so small, so vulnerable, it only made me realize how irresponsible I'd been, how I'd been failing as a father while I'd been off chasing my libido all around this resort.

"We're going home," I told Lily. Clearly staying at the hotel had been the wrong choice. For both of us.

"What about dinner?" Annalee asked.

"I'll figure something out," I bit out, keeping my eyes away from her face. She was like a siren, and if I looked at her, I'd stay on this course, shirking my responsibilities in pursuit of something so beautiful it made me forget everything else. "But my family has to be my first priority."

I turned and took Lily inside then, gathered our things, and put her in the truck, heading home. She tried to explain a few times, but I couldn't talk, my mind was spinning in confusion. Should I be angry? Because I was, but it felt wrong, like the wrong choice for the occasion. It wasn't until we arrived at our own little house tucked back between the trees in a neighborhood off the main highway that I began to think a bit more clearly. Lily sobbed all the way home.

"Okay Lil," I said, turning to her as I shut off the engine. "I'm sorry for getting so mad. Tell me what happened."

My daughter wouldn't look at me. She kept her face buried in Poppy's fur and wailed.

Great. I'd failed yet again.

We went inside and I made a grilled cheese sandwich and put on *Frozen*, pulling Lily onto my lap with the food on the coffee table in front of us. She was still sniffling, but at least she let me hold her.

After a little while, she'd calmed down, and just about the time Elsa fled to the mountaintop in the movie, Lily turned to me. The look on her face was something so close to her mother's expression that my heart twisted inside my chest.

God, I missed Poppy. How was I supposed to do any of this alone?

"I got bored, Daddy. It wasn't Annalee's fault." My daughter was so good, so valiant, trying to keep someone she cared about out of trouble. I felt my anger soften.

"She shouldn't have taken you from your room without telling me." I needed to stay angry at Annalee, though part of me knew I might have acted a tiny bit irrationally.

"She didn't. I saw her on the patio talking to Douggie Masters and I went down to meet him." Lily clearly realized this was a poor decision, because she dropped her eyes and began toying with the fur on Poppy's tiger back as she spoke, her voice smaller.

"I told you not to leave the room."

"I know. I'm sorry, Daddy."

"Anything could have happened, honey. There were lots and lots of strangers around."

"I know."

There wasn't much else to say. I held my daughter close and comforted myself by dropping my nose to the soft top of her little head, taking in the familiar scent of her, feeling her weight in my lap. Eventually she scooted to the floor and ate her sandwich, and by the time the movie ended, she seemed to have recovered completely from the trauma of the afternoon.

That made one of us.

When Lily moved off my lap, I texted my best friend from Lucy's crew, Chris. We'd grown up together, and worked together often, doing construction with Lucy's company. He reluctantly agreed to come stay with Lily while I worked at the resort, and he arrived soon after the movie ended.

"Hey man, thanks for this." I shook his hand at the door as I let him in.

"Yeah, any time," he said, his eyes narrowing as he took in my face. "You, uh, you doing okay?"

"Just tired," I said, moving him toward the kitchen, out of Lily's earshot.

"Right," he said, clearly not buying it.

I sighed, rubbing a hand through my hair. "Actually, you have a minute?"

"I'm prepped for a long night of painting nails and singing 'Let It Go.' I'm pretty anxious to get to it, but I could spare a minute or two." He pulled out a chair at the little round table in the corner and I did the same.

"Yeah, she might give you some grief. She's disappointed about not staying at the resort. But I just wanted to talk to you...I screwed up, man." I wasn't big on talking, but Chris knew me better than anyone. I could talk to him.

"Pretty much a daily routine for me," Chris laughed. "What's the damage?"

"This is about Lily," I said, and his jovial smile faded. "I think I'm failing as a dad. I can't seem to be the guy I know Poppy would have wanted me to be."

He frowned at me for a moment before answering. "And who is that?"

"Responsible. Focused. She'd want me to make sure Lily had a good life."

"And you're doing all that. You're the most focused and responsible dude I know."

"Maybe I was. I've been... distracted." I thought back to my decision to shove my kid into a hotel room so I could follow around the object of my affections more persistently.

"Is this about the chick fighter pilot at the resort?"

I'd mentioned the weekend with Annalee at the cabin after

we'd returned when I'd gone out with the guys one night. I hadn't offered details, but they'd figured it out.

"Yeah."

"Honestly? It's about time you had a little fun, took something for yourself."

"Well I did, and now I need to focus on Lily again. It's not fair to her."

Chris stared at me for a minute and then dropped his eyes to the table, where his fingers were toying with the edge of a place-mat. "Look," he said softly. "Maybe I have no place to speak here. I'm not a dad, and I haven't been through the shit you have. But I gotta think that at some point, you have to move forward. You can't live the rest of your life trying to be a husband to someone who's gone."

I actually winced, as if he'd poked me.

"Lily doesn't want you to martyr yourself for her."

Was that what I was doing? I didn't think so. I was trying to protect her, take care of her. I just wanted to make sure she knew she had my full focus.

"You're a human being. You deserve a full life just as much as anyone. Lily would probably rather see you happy than have the most fucking responsible father on the planet."

"She's seven. She doesn't know what she wants. It's my job to look out for her."

"Yeah, it is. And who's looking out for you?"

I didn't have a good answer because I didn't like what my friend had to say. He wasn't a dad. He didn't know. "Yeah. I better get going. Thanks for this."

"Good chat," he said, rising. "You need me to stay over?"

"If you don't mind. I'll be back, but it'll be late."

"I've always loved your couch." Chris chuckled and left me alone in the kitchen. I heard him greeting Lily, laughing as she launched into conversation about something. Lily had known

Chris her whole life, I should have thought of calling him first instead of agreeing to stick her in that room at the resort.

I needed to go back and work. And face Annalee. And apologize.

I went into the bedroom and put on a clean shirt, splashed some water on my face and headed out, a confusing mix of sorrow and guilt flooding my bloodstream, washing away the anger I'd thought I was supposed to feel.

It was going to be a long night.

Chapter 28
Focus on the Food

ANNALEE

We needed to get started on dinner, and so far, I was on my own. I moved around the kitchen, prepping what I could and trying to figure out how I could run things on my own if Mateo didn't return in time for service.

I couldn't stop thinking about the way he'd left, the way he'd looked at me and told me to stay away from his daughter. I was clear-headed enough to see that his reaction was borne at least partly from fear—he was all she had, and for a long time it seemed like maybe she was all he'd had too. But that awareness didn't make it hurt less when his eyes had held me with that look of disappointment and anger. My skin flamed just remembering it, and anger mixed with shame inside me.

This.

This was exactly why I had never imagined myself around kids. Everything that went with that particular expectation of female life was mystical to me and I knew I didn't have the instincts most women seemed to pick up somewhere along the way.

Men, I understood. Heaven knew I'd been around enough of them. They were simple, for the most part.

Daddies, it turned out, were a different stock, and the incident with Lily today only demonstrated that I was better off sticking to my guns on this particular issue. Keep things light, remain unattached, and never, under any circumstances, get involved in anything resembling a family. My own early family life should have been evidence enough.

I had known better in the first place.

When Mateo pushed through the door to the kitchen just when I was pretty sure I was going to be on my own for the evening, relief and warmth were my first reactions. But then my rational side reminded all that giddy enthusiasm that we were most likely done. He'd lost faith in me, and I shouldn't have ever let myself get so close.

"Hey," he said, not meeting my eyes. "Just wanted to say sorry for blowing up."

"Um. Okay." I wanted him to look at me, but he wouldn't. Was he still angry at me, then? Or was he ashamed of himself? Why couldn't he meet my gaze?

"Where are things at?"

I stood still, watching him as I realized we weren't going to talk about it—not really. We were going to put everything behind us and go on as if nothing had ever passed between us. As if we'd never lain, heads close, in a darkened cabin and told each other things we didn't usually share. As if we'd never been anything at all.

"Guests are being seated now. We're working in two shifts, just like we planned."

"Good."

I hated this. Mateo was moving around me as if we were strangers. I knew it was for the best not to let things escalate between us—the simple fact of Lily's existence and my utter incompatibility with children wasn't going to change—but it hurt to feel the cold from him where there had been so much warmth just this morning.

"So that's it, then?" I heard myself ask, knowing damn well I should have left it alone.

He stopped moving and looked into my eyes for the first time since he'd arrived. The look in those green pools made my stomach twist and my hands long to reach for him, to comfort the pain I saw there.

"Yeah." It was more a breath than a word, as if it took effort to get it out. "Look, I had no business doing any of...what we were doing. I'm a dad, and that has to be my priority."

"Of course," I said, feeling suddenly like I was made of porcelain, as if I might shatter if said more.

"I'm sorry."

"Nothing to be sorry about." I turned, ready to busy my shaking hands. Dammit, why couldn't I just accept this smoothly, handle it like every other inconvenience I'd endured?

"I shouldn't have yelled at you."

"You should not have." At least we agreed on that.

"I was worried."

"Of course," I said again.

The single hottest encounter I'd ever been part of had suddenly turned into a frigid and dysfunctional workplace meeting.

I couldn't take it. I rushed off to the cooler at the far corner of the kitchen, forcing myself to go through the motions of pulling salads for the first course and lining them up for finishing and serving.

Aubrey, Fake Tom, and Ghost were all playing waitstaff for drinks and serving salads, while Lucy and Wiley stayed in the bar to handle drink orders and Brainiac manned the front desk. Most of the meal would be self-serve, and Mateo and I needed to cook and sauce the chicken, slice the prime rib, and finish the vegan curry and get it out to the dining room. That was our mission, and I knew how to put my worries in a compartment and seal it up tight until the mission was through.

We moved around each other, the tension in the kitchen generated more from within than from the stress of the meal service. When both shifts of diners had been fed, Will and Aubrey came in to help clean up after bussing the dining room.

"That went great!" Aubrey was bouncing, as usual, but she stopped after a look between me and Mateo. He'd remained silent throughout the service, and tension was practically zipping off him like static electricity.

"Nice work, guys," Fake Tom agreed, clearly more willing to ignore the icy environment in the kitchen.

"Thanks," I said, giving them each a smile. Fake Tom held my eyes a long moment, and I saw the question there, but we'd never been close enough that I would tell him about the confusion and pain stirring around inside me right now.

"Everything okay?" Aubrey asked.

"Yeah," Mateo answered. "Great."

"You might want to grab a dictionary and look that word up," she said, partially under her breath.

Fake Tom chuckled. "Let's get going. My days as a dishwasher are numbered. It's not something I want to drag out."

"You just have to rinse them. The new dishwasher we put

in should do the rest," I told him as he and Aubrey moved back to the industrial sink and counter we'd put in a few weeks back.

Mateo was cleaning up the areas we'd used in the kitchen, covering food and putting it away while I began prepping berries and batters for breakfast.

"Five?" I asked him, making sure he'd be here at the time we agreed upon. It seemed clear he was no longer planning to use the suite upstairs, since he'd taken Lily home.

He didn't look at me, taking off his apron and hanging it up. "See you at five." He turned to leave and something inside me snapped, seeing those familiar broad shoulders sagging, feeling the magnetic pull between us.

I followed him to the lobby, and trailed him toward his truck, keeping enough distance not to make any kind of a scene for the few guests lingering in the bar and near the reception desk.

In the cool darkness outside, I found my voice. "Hey."

Mateo turned, and we faced each other in the dim light from the resort, the stars overhead glimmering between the tree-tops and making the woods look otherworldly, foreboding. "Annalee." It was a plea of some kind, only I wasn't willing to let it all go so easily.

"I'm sorry about earlier," I told him. "Only, I don't know what I'm apologizing for really. Lily came down and found me. I didn't go looking for her. Trust me, a kid is the last thing I've ever wanted in my life—I didn't seek her out. But I didn't think I should tell her to beat it, either. She's a good kid."

He absorbed my words, his face shifting slightly, his mouth opening and then closing firmly again. "Right."

"Right?" My confusion and hurt were sharpening into anger.

"Listen," he said. "It's clear that we just let things go a little too far. I lost sight of my priorities, and things got messy. But it's not gonna happen again."

"So we're done here?" I was angry, but I wanted something more from him. I wanted him to acknowledge that whatever we'd had, whatever we'd been, it was more than a crush. It was more than a light little dalliance. It had felt like so much more.

To me, at least.

"We have to be," he said, and his voice revealed that he felt it too. "I owe my daughter my full attention. I'm all she has. Until she's old enough to take care of herself, she has to be my primary focus. I promised Poppy."

"Your wife?" I asked softly. Was I competing with a dead woman? I realized with a sinking certainty that this was how it would always be with him. I'd never win in a competition against someone who'd died young and perfect. I was real, and I was messy, and clearly, Mateo wasn't looking for that.

He sighed, those glorious shoulders sagging even lower. As angry as I was, I wanted to reach for him, to hold him, but the pain growing inside me wouldn't allow it. I had my pride.

"My wife made me promise her I'd keep Lily safe. When she was dying."

God. What did you say to that? But Mateo wasn't done. He rubbed a hand over his face, and went on, moving to lean against his truck as if he needed the support of the solid steel behind him.

"There're things I haven't told you. About Poppy. About Lily. And if I tell you, then I think you'll understand why this can't be more than it already was."

"Go on then." I steeled myself, crossing my arms around me and hugging myself, as if I could make a shield, protect myself from whatever was coming.

"Poppy died because of me. I wanted kids, and she wanted to give them to me. We dreamed about a family - especially me.

And we had all these talks about what it would be like, about how our house would be full and warm.

"And then we found out she couldn't. That trying might kill her. And I tried so hard not to want it anymore... but I did want it. And so when she said we should try, I agreed. And so it's all my fault. I wasn't strong enough to look past what I wanted to do what was right for her.

"And I'm doing the exact same thing again. With you."

My blood iced as the horror of his words—of his memories— settled into me. "Mateo, that wasn't your fault," I whispered.

"We would have been fine together without kids. But I can't regret Lily, either. It's just..." his voice slipped, and I could hear the exhaustion and sheer impossibility of his grief pushing against his words.

"You can't think like that."

He took a deep breath, straightened up. "That's it though. That's the reality of the situation, and that's why I owe Lily my focus. I took her mother from her, and I'm all she has. It's my job to be there for her. Always."

"You didn't kill Poppy." It felt wrong, saying his wife's name, but I knew he needed someone to tell him this.

"I have to go." He turned and climbed into the truck, leaving me standing beneath the cold stars in the parking lot as he drove slowly away.

What was I doing here? How had I gotten in so deep with a man I could never, ever have? I'd known since I was a kid that I would be a terrible mother, and that was why my life had been planned in a way that would never allow for kids. I didn't seek a family, I didn't plan one. And somehow, I'd managed to stumble into one and do my level best to tear it apart.

I let my eyes drop shut and took a deep breath of the cool mountain air. I could feel my time in Kasper Ridge slipping away. I needed to move on. To find my next adventure.

Inside the resort, the bar was picking up steam, and though part of me wanted to be alone, I forced myself into the warm paneled room where guests mingled with Ghost, Brainiac and Fake Tom, as Wiley, Aubrey, and Lucy served drinks behind the bar. There was a stool open at the end, and I slid onto it, oblivious to much of what was going on around me.

The bar was an intimate space that was probably the most authentic remnant of Marvin Kasper's days as proprietor of Kasper Ridge. The walls were lined with pictures of him rubbing elbows with everyone from movie stars to politicians and athletes. The guests milled along the walls, taking in the photographs, and chatting each other up, but it all faded to a steady hum in my mind.

"Whiskey neat," I told Lucy when she stepped close, eyebrows raised. I didn't want her to ask about Mateo, and I suspected the bar was too busy for her to have time for idle chit chat anyway. I wanted to drink my whiskey in peace and then go up to my quiet room to formulate my next plan.

"There you are." Douggie Masters turned in the stool next to me, a warm smile on his face.

"Hey," I said, coaxing some false brightness into my voice. "Ready for your big hike tomorrow?"

"I am," he said. "Though if I'm honest, it's tempting just to stay here and enjoy the resort. This place is amazing. I can't wait come back and ski."

"You definitely should," I told him. Of course there was no guarantee we'd have the lifts operating this season. I wondered what kind of progress Brainiac was making there. I wondered if I'd even be here long enough to see it.

"I had a chat today with my agent," he said, his eyebrows dancing as his eyes shone.

"Oh?" I asked, wondering why he'd mentioned this to me.

"About the opportunity I mentioned to you earlier?"

"Oh, right."

"It's an amazing concept, a travel show called 'From Standard to Stellar.' Or something. I actually think that name is a horror, but anyway. Basically, you'd go stay at hotels and resorts around the world and sample all the amenities. Then, for the big reveal, you'd take the owners or manager or whoever through a plan to upgrade the whole experience. Like, seaside patio? Well, that's nice, but what about overwater dining? You get it?"

"Yeah, that will be great," I agreed.

"So you'll chat with my agent?" Douggie's eyes were lit with excitement.

"Wait, what?" I wasn't tracking.

"You'd be perfect for it. Coming off the renovation of the Kasper Ridge Resort, former fighter pilot and all-around kickass female... people would eat it up."

"You think I'd be the host?"

"If you want it," he said, and it was like a doorway opened up, an escape hatch.

"Yeah," I said, the idea spinning in my mind. Constant travel—new places, new people. It'd be perfect. I ignored the kernel of sadness that pressed against tender spots inside me when I thought about leaving Mateo—and Lily—behind. "I'd be really interested."

"Yes, you would," Douggie said, grinning. "Another drink for the future star!" he called out, earning me a questioning look from Lucy, who poured another finger of Half Cat into my glass.

"I'll set it up before I go tomorrow morning. Where can I find you?"

I gave Douggie my cell phone number, and told him I'd be in the kitchen bright and early.

"Doesn't hurt that you're a smoke show, of course," he said as we talked about some of the ins and outs of hosting a show like his. I tried to ignore this comment and the way it made me feel like maybe this was actually a step backwards. Hadn't I just decided that trading on my looks was a thing of the past? I was tired, and confused, so I let it slide.

"Thanks for the chance," I told Douggie, rising as I finished my whiskey.

"Of course," he said. "I'll see you in the morning, doll."

"Good night."

I wandered out of the bar and up to my room, the warm buzz of the whiskey and of Douggie's belief in me soothing some of the aching hurt of Mateo's rejection. I'd been fine before him. Clearly, I'd be fine after him. It was just the in-between part that was going to hurt.

Chapter 29
Ciphers and Sorrows

MATEO

Sleep was one more thing I couldn't seem to get right that night. I tiptoed past Chris, snoring on my couch with one arm flung over his head, and stuck my head into Lily's room. Her breathing was deep and even, her nightlight casting a soft pink glow against her beautiful face. She looked a lot like Poppy when she slept—dark lashes on fair skin, an expression on her lips that looked like a cross between an angel and a very mischievous little girl.

The rest of the night was spent in fitful bouts of almost

dreams, many of which featured Annalee or Poppy, and a couple where they both appeared, neither one solid enough to touch or talk to, both of them edging into the periphery of my awareness before I could resolve anything at all.

And morning came in the form of my alarm blasting out of my phone at four fifteen.

I stumbled out of bed, knocking into the dresser and cursing loudly, my head as dark as the world outside, where, for all intents and purposes, it was still the middle of the night.

When I finished my shower and moved out into the living room, Chris's voice came in a low whine.

"You're fucking kidding me, right? It's Saturday, man."

"Sorry. Thought I mentioned this. I have to be over there at five. Gotta get Lily ready."

"You're gonna wake her up now?" Chris sounded offended on Lily's behalf.

"No choice." The last thing I wanted was for Lily to have to spend another day alone at the resort in the room, but until Julia returned from her cruise, this was the only option I had. I was sure Chris had had more than enough of Disney princesses and mac and cheese.

"Let her sleep. I'll bring her over at a reasonable hour." Chris rolled over on the couch, pulling the pillow over his head when I flicked on the kitchen lights to make coffee.

"You sure?" I asked.

"Yes, now go away." Chris was not a morning person.

I finished filling my travel mug and switched the light off. "Thanks man."

"Please go away."

That was something, I figured. At least Lily didn't have to get dragged out of bed before five today. But that one bright turn of fate didn't do much to power out the darker feelings spreading to every recess inside me.

The conversation I'd had with Annalee by the truck haunted me.

You didn't kill Poppy.

She didn't know. She hadn't known me then, and she didn't know my wife. It was easy to say that, but she had no idea how badly I'd wanted to be a father, no way to understand the kinds of conversations I'd had with my wife. Conversations that had led directly to her death.

Why couldn't I have been happy with what we had? We were amazing together. Perfect. But I'd had this idea that because we were so perfect, because everything was so good, we could handle anything.

But you can't cheat death.

I don't know if I didn't take Poppy's condition seriously enough—or if she didn't. The doctors were clear, but they'd given her just enough hope to believe she could have it all—that with close supervision, her condition would allow us to have a baby. And it did.

But no one can have everything for long.

So I had basically made a choice without really knowing I was making a choice. And now I owed my daughter every ounce of my energy as a penance for taking her mother away from her. Away from me.

You didn't kill Poppy.

Didn't I, though?

And so pushing Annalee away was the only real option. Lily deserved all of my attention, and Annalee was a huge distraction. One that made my body ache and my heart thud in my chest every time I saw her. A distraction that made me feel like I'd severed a limb or given away a critical organ now that I'd decided we were through. But a distraction from what I needed to focus on, all the same.

I knew I had done the right thing, no matter how it felt now.

The sun remained below the treeline as I parked and headed inside the resort, steeling myself for a challenging day.

I pushed into the kitchen—all bright light and steely shine in comparison to the calm darkness of the lobby. Soft pop music played, and I could hear the sink running at the far side of the room, so I followed the sound. But as soon as I found Annalee, I wished I hadn't.

She stood at the sink with her back to me in only her light blue bra and black work pants, rinsing something out of her shirt beneath the water. The sight of her skin twisted up my stomach, begging me to step closer, to touch that soft silky expanse, and my mind practically staged a revolt.

I must have made some kind of noise, because she startled and turned to face me with a little "Oh." And then she was standing before me, her perfect breasts held in the soft satin fabric of her bra, her face shifting from surprise to something that looked a lot like disappointment.

I took a step back, ripping my eyes away as my heart thundered in my ears. "Sorry, I—"

"No, my fault. It isn't like I wasn't expecting you. I exploded coffee grounds all over my shirt though, and wanted to get them out right away."

"Yeah, of course, I just..." I was having real difficulty with words.

"Can you finish getting the pot going?" she suggested, and I strode across the space to the huge coffee pot, grateful for something to focus on besides how badly I wanted to touch Annalee, to taste her lips again, to feel those perfect breasts in my palms.

When I turned back around, she was dressed, dabbing at the front of her shirt with a towel.

"I... uh..." My mouth started working before my brain was even close to engaged.

"Yeah," she said, cutting me off. "Let's just get through this. Muffin batter over there." She pointed past me to where huge trays waited for paper cups and batter.

I got to work, and the morning dissolved into a frenzy of activity. Muffins, bread, egg casserole and fruit flew out of the kitchen in a seemingly never-ending parade and I marveled at how much these influencers seemed to eat. A few special requests floated back to us too, via Aubrey or Lucy—things like avocado toast and smoothies with protein powder—and Annalee was prepared.

She was always prepared. And so fucking sexy it hurt to look at her. And she was definitely not for me. No matter how much I wanted her to be mine. My path was set.

We were just finishing cleaning up when her phone chimed, and she pulled it from her pocket and let out a strange little, "oh" as she glanced at the screen.

I didn't mean to eavesdrop—not really. But I was prepping sandwiches for lunch, and she took the call on the far side of the kitchen.

"This is Annalee Tyson, yes." And then, "He told me last night. That's really exciting." A pause. Then: "I think I am ready for a new adventure, yes. Can I send you a photo or something? What do you need?" Another pause. "Did you say Paris?"

What the hell was she talking about? I gave up the pretense of not listening and stilled my hands in their tomato slicing to hear better as something like jealousy threaded itself through me.

"I'm really flattered, and of course the meeting will work. I'll figure it out." Another pause. "My passport is current."

I turned at that and watched the smile light her face as she nodded into her phone. "I'll see you next week then. In Paris!"

Annalee's eyes lifted to mine as she ended the call and pushed her phone back into her pocket. For a moment, neither of us spoke, but I felt heat rising in my cheeks. I wanted to ask questions. I wanted to stop her. She couldn't go to Paris. What about Kasper Ridge? The resort?

A tiny voice inside cried, "what about us?" but even as I acknowledged it I realized I had done this. I'd pushed her away, so of course she could go. She could do whatever she wanted to.

"Guess you'll be rid of me soon," she said.

The darkness that had plagued me all morning grew thicker, suffocating. "Why's that?" I managed.

"Douggie hooked me up with his agent. They're considering me for a show, if you can believe it. I'm meeting him next week. In Paris!"

I swallowed hard, not even sure I could find my voice as sadness swamped me. "I heard."

She looked happy, but there was something in her voice, or maybe it was her posture, that made me wonder if her excitement was genuine.

"That's what you want?" I asked.

She straightened up, pushing a tendril of hair off her face and back toward the bun she'd captured most of her waves in. "It's the next thing, I guess. That's how I live. Jumping on opportunities that come my way. I'll never be bored!" Her bright smile was like a knife twisting inside me. I didn't want her to leave.

But I couldn't keep her here. I had nothing to offer her.

"That sounds great," I said, and the lie was clear on my voice. I dropped the knife, needing to get away for a moment, to clear out whatever turmoil was kicking up inside me. "I'm just. I'm gonna..." I threw these words behind me as I bolted out into the lobby, feeling more than a little out of control.

What the fuck?

I stood against the wall in the lobby for a minute, doing my best to get my thoughts together when I heard my daughter's high merry laugh coming from the bar. I followed it.

Lily and Chris sat at the bar, Wiley laughing with them on the other side. Each had a steaming mug before them, and Archie was at the other end of the bar helping some guests. Lily's puzzle book was spread on the bar between them. She'd been obsessed with it lately.

"Hey," I said, doing my best to sound normal despite the revolt being staged against my will inside me.

"Daddy!" Lily slipped off her stool and threw herself at me. I dropped to squeeze her tight and felt my whirling emotions slow. "Wiley gave us hot chocolate, and he put four marshmallows!"

"Four, huh?" I caught Wiley's eyes over her head, and he looked slightly guilty. "That was pretty nice of him."

"Yeah. I remembered to say thank you, too."

"Good girl." I stood and slid onto the stool next to Chris as Lily hopped back onto hers.

He turned and gave me a look over his mug of coffee. "You look like doo doo, man."

Lily snickered at this.

"Long shifts. This kitchen work is no joke. There's a reason I went into construction."

"Oh yeah," Chris agreed, mockery clear in his tone. "No long hours or hard work there."

I blew out a breath, not in the mood to trade sarcastic barbs with him. "Thanks for bringing her over."

"No worries."

"Coffee?" Wiley asked. "Or hot chocolate with four marshmallows?"

"Nah, I'm good." I didn't think more caffeine would help my already turbulent emotions.

Archie wandered over and stopped next to Wiley. "So?" he asked.

Wiley fished something out of his pocket and spread it flat on the bar. The map. Always with the damned map.

"I've compared it to every map I've been able to find of the area. If we're sure this is supposed to be the lodge, then I have no idea. There's nothing even close." He pointed a finger at the mark that looked like a house in the center of the map.

"We're not sure of anything." Archie sounded as mixed up and tired as I felt.

"The mysterious map, huh?" Chris asked. Pretty much everyone on the mountain had heard about it at this point, and half the town was involved in speculation over what Marvin Kasper's mysterious treasure hunt would lead to. The other half was pretty sure he'd just been a crazy old man. I wasn't sure where I stood at this point. I didn't care.

"Yeah, but the more I look at it, the more mysterious it becomes. We're making no headway." Archie leaned onto his elbows, dropping his head.

Lily was squinting at the map, concentrating hard. I was about to ask Archie who he'd shown it to around town, if he'd recruited any of the old timers, when my daughter spoke. "I don't think this is a map."

"Um." I laughed. My seven-year-old was going to solve the treasure hunt.

"You don't, huh?" Archie asked, looking at her with clear interest. "Well, what is it then? Any idea?"

Lily turned her attention to the workbook spread on the bar and began flipping pages. She stopped at one and turned the book around to face Archie. "I think it's one of these."

The page Lily opened to, the one we were all staring at now

in varying states of awe, was a simple cipher. She'd already solved the one in her book but looking at the symbols in the book next to the ones on random places on the map made it pretty clear she could be right.

"A code," Wiley said, amazement in his voice. "Dude, these are like hieroglyphics. It's a code!"

Archie was still looking back and forth between Lily's book and the map, while Lily went back to fishing marshmallows out of her hot chocolate, clearly not as fascinated as everyone else.

"Your daughter's a freaking genius, man." Chris slapped me on the back.

She was. I felt pride swell within me. She was amazing. She was everything.

"Now you just need the key," Lily said, twirling her spoon around over her mug.

Archie sighed. "Right. The key."

"Or," Lily said, capturing everyone's attention again. "You can look for repeating symbols because those are probably common letters."

The map had symbols scattered over it, with lines that we'd thought were some kind of path connecting them.

"What if the lines show which symbols make up words or sentences?" I asked.

Wiley nodded, pulling a pad of paper out from behind the bar and doing his best to copy the symbols into sequences dictated by the lines on the map. "So maybe there's sixteen words here?"

"Holy shi—" Archie caught himself. "Shirt balls. Lily, you can have all the marshmallows you want. Don't suppose you can solve this for us?" He pushed the paper in front of her, and my daughter peered at it.

"I don't have the key," she said lightly. "My book always gives you at least part of the key." She pointed to the book, where a few of the letters in the key were pre-printed in dark ink. The rest were scrawled in Lily's handwriting.

"You sure she's only seven, man?" Archie asked me, grinning.

I lifted a shoulder. "Her grandmother was a teacher, so she does a lot of workbooks when they hang out together. She's been reading since she was four."

Lily grinned, clearly pleased that she was the subject of our attention. "I can do times tables too."

"Yes, you're a prodigy," I said, hoping to defuse the adulation. Lily knew she was smart, she didn't need to get arrogant about it.

"Well," Archie said. "We may come back for some help on this, if that's okay with you."

Lily lifted a shoulder and made a non-committal sound as if she'd try to fit this into her busy schedule.

"Come on, you. I need to go finish lunch prep, and you have a full day of cartoon watching ahead. I made you a peanut butter and jelly to take up to the room. Thanks, Chris. I owe you, man."

"What's your plan for tonight?" Chris asked, sliding off the stool.

"I'll just let her fall asleep upstairs and I'll grab her when I'm done." I wanted Lily in her own bed, back at our house. This weekend couldn't end soon enough.

He nodded. "Call if you need me. I was headed to the Moose with Tony, but it's not a big deal."

"Have a good night. You're off duty," I told him. "Let's go, bear." I took Lily's hand, and together we headed upstairs to get her settled.

"I promise to stay in the room, Daddy." Lily's little voice sounded guilty, apologetic, as if she knew how much turmoil finding her downstairs the day before had caused. But really, none of that had been her fault. It was all mine.

"Good girl." I settled my daughter and then went back down to the kitchen, steeling myself to face the woman who turned me inside out without even trying.

Chapter 30
Onions and Agony

ANNALEE

My head was a mess. As I put together a huge pot of pasta sauce and pulled garlic bread from the freezer, I barely registered what I was doing. Mateo stayed on the other side of the kitchen, chopping and tossing vegetables for the salad and layering the dessert trifle. He hadn't spoken to me since he had come back in, and I told myself it was for the best.

I needed to get through this weekend, hopefully set Ghost up in the best way possible coming off this event, and then get on a flight to Paris. It was exciting—a huge opportunity. It was my life taking yet another unexpected turn, one I could only consider because I'd stuck to my guns all these years and remained independent. *Free.*

But I didn't have that same feeling I'd had before when a new adventure presented itself. Like when I'd come up to Kasper Ridge, for example. I'd been furloughed from my position flying for the airlines, something I'd enjoyed but hadn't felt like I needed to do forever. That was lucky since the economy and the industry were less than a sure thing. I felt for those guys who'd planned to settle in there and stay until they could retire —they'd had to scramble when things fell apart. But for me, it was just another nudge from the universe that meant it was time to open up my aperture and let the next opportunity in. And it had come. Ghost called, invited me to the resort, and here I was.

But I couldn't stay here. And Douggie's agent had opened the next door just when it was becoming clear I needed it. How could that be anything other than a sign?

When lunch ended, I cleaned up and began dinner prep, doing my best to ignore the handsome hulk of man with all the intense brooding energy at the other end of the kitchen. He'd been emanating misery since he'd come in, and I was struggling with my reactions to him. I didn't like seeing him upset—of course I didn't. But I knew his mood had to do with me, and he had been the one to put an end to everything between us. He made the bed and now he refused to fuck me in it. Not my problem, I decided.

"Hey." His voice interrupted my efforts to get good and mad so that I didn't want so desperately to kiss him. I jumped and turned to face him, doing my best to avoid those bottomless green eyes.

"Hey. Yeah. Oh." *Articulate, Annalee. Articulate.* "What?"

He paused, dropping my gaze. "The, ah, those onions. The

prep note you left over there for dinner says chop. How big? And all of them?"

"Quarter inch dice. All of them." I gripped the steel counter with a death grip, the only way to keep myself from stepping closer to him, from begging him to see that there was something here, that walking away from this wasn't the right choice, for either of us. I knew if he'd given me even a glimmer of hope, I wouldn't get on that plane.

But he just nodded and spun, heading back to the side of the kitchen that seemed to have become "his" since we'd stopped doing whatever it was we were doing.

I finished prepping dinner, layering the lasagna and sliding the big pans into the refrigerator until it was time to bake them.

And then I ran away. Being around Mateo was like pressing my face to the window at the bike shop, knowing there was no chance of ever getting that beautiful bike with the streamers coming out of the handlebars. But knowing that never stopped me from wanting it with all my heart.

I spent a little time in my room, packing and organizing my things, but after a while the walls felt like they were closing in, and I was struggling to keep my mind in check. I needed distraction. Some fresh air.

The lobby wasn't crowded at this time of day, but the back patio was packed. Aubrey and Lucy were running drinks from the bar out to the twosomes and threesomes of people gathered on chairs, enjoying the perfect late-summer weather. I was glad to see the sun shining, and thought for a moment of Douggie up in the cabin I'd shared with Mateo. It would be a whole different place than the one we'd sheltered in. Without the snow to muffle the world, to camouflage it, Douggie certainly wasn't at risk for falling prey to any fantasies about what might or might not be.

I was projecting.

"Need help?" I asked Aubrey as she headed toward me with an empty tray.

She grinned, bouncing as usual, and grabbed my arm, pulling me beneath the eaves of the building and away from the guests. "Hey you. Just in case no one has thanked you yet, thank you. This whole weekend was your brainchild, and it's going so well!" This last part ended on a squeal with more bouncing.

It was. And I was glad. "Good," I said, pushing myself to match her enthusiasm.

"Archie and I were talking about the stuff you might do as the official events director here. Once we get through this week-end, we have a million ideas to throw at you."

After the weekend. I swallowed. "Yeah, totally. If nothing else, I can help you outline a calendar."

Aubrey's eyebrows drew down over her bright eyes and she stopped bouncing. "If nothing else," she repeated.

"I have an opportunity," I said, feeling like I was betraying my friends somehow, doing something dishonest. I told her about Douggie, about his agent and the interview in Paris. "I might not get it," I said.

"Of course you will," Aubrey told me, and her smile was back, but only at half wattage. "If that's really what you want."

"It is." I said the words, and waited for the certainty to bloom inside me as a result. But it did not. I didn't know what I wanted. For the first time I could remember, my heart didn't feel like it was leading me as it always had. "It's a fantastic opportunity."

"Sounds like it," Aubrey said. "Here, come help Wiley in the bar if you have a few extra minutes. These influencers drink like merpeople."

"Are merpeople big drinkers?" I asked, forcing myself to make small talk, to be charming, to be Monroe.

"Fish just sounded cliché," Aubrey said. "If fish drink a lot though, I'm sure mermaids are total lushes."

"Probably right." We stepped into the bar, which was just as packed at the patio had been. A bright peal of laughter came from the far end where a few women stood in a group close to the wall. One of them raised her arms, probably illustrating whatever she was talking about, and one of her hands knocked a framed photo from the wall. I watched as it fell to the floor with a crash, the sound of shattering glass halting the noise inside the space for a moment.

"I'm so sorry!" the woman cried, jumping up to pick up the frame.

"No big deal," Wiley said, sounding as friendly and welcoming as ever. "Don't touch it, okay? I'd hate for you to get cut. I'll just take care of that." He made his way over and picked up the glassless frame, setting it on the bar, as Lucy joined him with a broom and dustpan.

"I really am so sorry," the woman said, looking upset.

"It's not a problem," Wiley assured her. "Happens all the time." He gave her his dimpled grin, and she seemed to relax, sitting back down with her friends as Lucy disappeared behind the bar again.

Aubrey went over to pick up the photo and carried it behind the bar. I stood across from her, my mind in a million places.

"Holy shit," she said, snagging my attention again.

"What's wrong?" I asked.

Wiley came to lean over her, his eyes following her widened gaze to the back of the picture that lay on the bar in front of her. The back of the frame was covered in brown paper, the hanging wire screwed in at each side, but that wasn't what she was looking at.

"Look," she breathed, pointing at a symbol drawn in black marker on the paper. "This is on the map, isn't it?"

We all looked more closely at the symbol, which resembled a roughly drawn house, with a square and a triangle set atop it. It was the symbol in the middle of the map, the one we'd thought was the hotel.

"Definitely," Wiley said.

"What does it mean?" I asked, voicing the question we were certainly all thinking. We took turns flipping the glassless photo and examining it carefully. It was a black and white image of a baseball player, or at least of a guy holding a baseball and standing at Marvin's side, grinning. The photo had clearly been taken here in the bar, since we could see other photos on the walls behind them.

"Excuse me," a voice said from the doorway. "I'm sitting outside and I ordered a drink a while ago?"

"Yep!" Aubrey called, her voice bright. "Be right out!"

She looked between Lucy, Wiley, and me. "We'll get back to this tonight after dinner service. Archie needs to see it."

"Okay." Wiley slid the picture beneath the bar, and we spent the rest of the day rushing around, doing our best to meet the many needs of our important guests.

Evening found me back in the kitchen, drowning in the thick tension surrounding Mateo every time I turned around. He had the sexy brooding thing down to an art form, and it took everything I had not to wrap myself around him—even though I knew he probably didn't want me to. We were done.

But toward the end of service, when there was a lull and we both had a moment to breathe, I found myself at his side, each of us leaning against the steel counter for a beat, catching our breaths.

"This is insane," he said in a low voice. "We're gonna need a full staff before any more guests come in."

"Definitely."

"And you should look for sous chefs with actual experience, probably," he said.

"You have experience. Just not in the kitchen."

"Right." He chuckled. I wasn't looking at him, but I could see him in my peripheral vision, and feel his heat at my side. I didn't want to break the spell, because I knew he'd move away from me, and this was the closest I'd been to him all day. It wasn't much, but I couldn't help wanting it, craving him.

Mateo rubbed a hand through his hair, then dropped it back to the counter behind him—directly on top of mine. "Oh," he said in a whisper. "Sorry."

As he went to pull away, my hand caught his. I didn't think about it, didn't plan it, but I held him there, still not looking at him. We stood that way, leaning against the counter, side by side, our fingers twined together. I let my eyes drop shut, my breath coming fast, as the heat from his hand traveled up my arm, and my stomach twisted.

What was it about him? I couldn't get enough. Would I ever stop wanting him to touch me? Needing him to see me?

"Annalee," he whispered again. "I—"

I spun, moving myself to face him. He was slouching against the counter, so when I stepped between his powerful thighs, we were face to face. It was like approaching a tiger or staring down an oncoming train—I knew I shouldn't do it, knew there was danger here, but I was driven by something deeper than logic, and there was more here between us. I needed to understand it.

He dropped my hand to grasp my waist, both his hands gripping me possessively, fingers digging into my flesh. My hands found his forearms, my fingers resting against the corded muscle.

I stepped nearer, the heat between us an inferno I was willing to suffer, desperate to let consume me. We were centimeters away from one another, each of us breathing hard as our eyes met and held.

The world spun. The kitchen disappeared, and a buzz filled my ears as I lost myself in those eyes—familiar and yet completely unknowable. Who was this man? Why couldn't I walk away?

He didn't speak, didn't move. I knew he was breathing, but what I wanted was to know what he was thinking—what he really thought. Then his eyes dropped shut, and he exhaled a long mournful breath as his forehead touched mine.

I let my breath go too, closing my eyes and letting the heat between us dissipate as the sounds of the hotel around us came back and the fingers at my waist slowly, slowly lessened their grip. The moment died.

"I'll go get started with batters for tomorrow," I said, pulling myself away, forcing my eyes to stay down, away from the man I was certain I'd fallen in love with. "Almost done here, and then you can get back to your life," I told him, walking away on shaking legs.

Everything felt wrong. My life was no different than it had always been—my grand adventure continued. Why the hell did everything feel so wrong?

Chapter 31
Breakfast with Bears

MATEO

Guests began leaving the following day. Most of them departed with promises of fame for the Kasper Ridge Resort, giving Archie and Aubrey assurances of sold-out weeks come winter, and glowing reviews. The phone up front had already begun ringing incessantly, the result of influencers posting throughout the weekend about the exclusive new resort opening soon in the Rockies.

In some ways, the knowledge that Kasper Ridge might make it was a relief. We'd have to push hard on finishing construction, but I was happy for the Kaspers.

Douggie Masters returned from the cabin out back, practically giddy about the adventure he'd had.

"A bear actually lumbered out of the forest while I was sitting on the front steps enjoying my dinner!" He clapped his hands as he told us about it. "At first, I thought he was going to wander right on by, but then he turned his big shaggy head and made a beeline for me."

We were at the entrance to the bar when he told this story, and everyone in the small group of staff turned to look up at Rufus, the old stuffed bear that stood on a platform above the space, looking down.

"It was a little terrifying, but the cabin up there is sturdily built," Douggie went on. "I took my stew and my cameraman inside, and that big 'ol bear grumbled around out there for a while. At one point, he stood up and stared at me through the window!"

"That sounds kind of scary," Aubrey said, hanging on Douggie's every word.

"Darlin' that's what makes for great television!" Douggie laughed and gave her a quick hug, shaking Archie's hand. "Thanks for a fantastic time. The show should air in a few weeks. I'll give you a call."

"Thanks again," Archie said, exchanging his usual haunted look for a wide smile.

Douggie looked around and his eyes landed on me. "Where's your lady?"

"Uh. Lady?" All eyes moved to me. The rest of the crew had certainly noticed the tension between Annalee and me, but no one had asked anything directly.

"The beautiful Annalee," Douggie went on. "I need to say goodbye."

"Did you look in the kitchen?" Aubrey asked, and when Douggie turned that way and headed off, I could have hugged her for pulling the attention from me. But as soon as Douggie was gone and Archie had moved to say goodbye to another guest, she stepped close. "What is going on with you guys, anyway?"

I shook my head. I didn't want to discuss it, and there was nothing to discuss now anyway. Whatever had been was over. The moment we'd shared in the kitchen the night before had haunted my dreams, and a deep sense of longing and regret plagued me. Aubrey's questions didn't help. "Nothing," I told her.

"Bullshit," she said, her chin jutting out in front of her. "There is something, and you're an idiot if you let it go."

"Thanks," I said, amused at her straight-talking nature, even through the irritation I felt at her inserting herself. "But she's leaving anyway, so even if I thought there was something..."

Aubrey sighed, as if I was almost too stupid to live. "Right. So that'll just be it then?"

"I sense this might be a rhetorical question."

"You're just going to let her go?"

"She's a grown woman. She makes her own decisions." The words felt flimsy coming out. I was going to offer something else when Annalee's light laughter pealed out of the doorway to the restaurant, and we both turned to see her hugging Douggie goodbye.

"You're gonna kill it, girl," he called to her as he wheeled his suitcase toward the front doors. "Thanks again," he said, his eyes finding us as he headed out.

Annalee stood for a long moment watching him go, and then her eyes swung to mine and held them. As our gazes met, a painful sense of longing flooded me, and in some strange way it was a sensation similar to that when Poppy had died—a desire for the impossible, for things that were already past.

"Moron," Aubrey muttered at my side, ignoring my narrow-eyed gaze. "Don't go anywhere, okay? We're wrapping up the weekend in the bar at six once everyone is gone. Lessons learned, and all that."

"Got it." I thought about my daughter, up in the room. She'd be heartbroken if she didn't get to say goodbye to her idol, Douggie. I moved quickly and caught him before he walked out the front door.

"Would you be able to hang out for five more minutes?" I asked him. "My daughter Lily would love to say goodbye. She loves your show, man."

Douggie's smile widened and he glanced at the expensive watch on his wrist. "Of course, but it's gotta be quick!"

"Thanks." I rushed to the front desk and Brainiac dialed the room Lily was waiting in, handing me the phone.

"Hello?" Her little voice came on the line, sounding a little worried.

"Hey bear, it's me. Want to come down to the lobby and tell Douggie goodbye?"

"Ooh! Yes! Is it okay if I leave the room though?"

"I'm asking you to. I'm waiting for you down here. Just take the elevator, okay?"

"Be right there!" Lily must have forgotten to hang up the phone because I could hear the television in the background and the sound of the door to the suite opening and closing. I handed the receiver back to Brainiac, who watched me with an expression that wasn't quite friendly.

"Thanks."

Lily appeared a moment later, and rushed to my side. "Did he leave?"

"He's waiting for you." I walked her to where Douggie stood near the doors with his luggage and his phone in his hand. He looked up as we approached.

"There she is. I wanted to tell you goodbye, Miss Lily."

"Goodbye Douggie. I'm so happy I got to meet you."

"Well, the pleasure was all mine. I hope to see you when I come back in the winter time," he said, dropping to squat so he could speak to her face to face. "I didn't tell you this, but I have a little girl at home too, and if my husband comes with me to ski, we'll definitely bring her along. Maybe you guys could be friends."

Lily clapped her hands. "Yes!" Then she looked uncertain. "How old is she?"

"She's only three, so you'd definitely be the older, wiser friend."

Lily nodded, thinking about that. "I would like that."

"We'll see you then!" Douggie reached a hand out for her to shake, and Lily did her best to shake properly, though I thought that was probably the first time she'd ever shaken hands.

"Bye, Douggie," she called as the man gathered his things and headed outside.

By that evening, the resort was almost back to the way it'd been for months before the influencer weekend, quiet, empty, a little ghostly. But the echoes of laughter and the recent atmosphere of giddy excitement lingered too.

Everyone sat in the bar, where we'd pulled a couple of the little tables together. Lily sat at my side, her puzzle book in front of her, but her eyes following the conversation bouncing around the table.

"That went better than I could have ever hoped," Archie told us. "Between the re-bookings we already have and the phone calls and web queries pouring in, we're going to have a full season."

"And people don't care that we don't know whether there will actually be skiing?" Aubrey asked him.

"People are asking, for sure. But I've been honest about it."

All eyes turned to Brainiac, waiting for progress on the lift that would determine whether there'd be skiing at the official start of the season.

"Supply chain issues," he said. "I'm working on it, but like I told you before, plan B pretty much involves rebuilding the thing from scratch, which I've been working on. The motor is simple enough, but the thing has to pass inspection, and this is kind of a new field for me."

"Think it'll be done in time?" Archie managed to make it a question rather than a demand.

"I think there's a good chance it could be. But for now, people better be coming for the excellent hospitality and great accommodations. Not the skiing." Brainiac crossed his arms over his chest, clearly done speaking. The guy was a bit of an enigma, and I'd never really gotten close enough to figure him out.

"So we're going to need someone to run the restaurant," Archie was saying now. "If you're really dead set on becoming a star, Monroe."

"They didn't call me Monroe for nothing," Annalee joked. "It's my big shot."

I glanced up at her across the table, my heart lurching as our gazes met. She was smiling, but the glee on her face didn't reach her eyes. I tore my focus away, looking at the marred wooden surface of the old bar table instead.

"When do you go?" Aubrey asked.

"I've got a flight out of Denver tomorrow," she said. "And if all goes well, I'll be headed to London from Paris. Don't worry though, I've got a replacement coming in."

My stomach twisted.

"You're going to be famous?" Lily asked, her little voice squeaking at the end of the question.

"No," Annalee laughed, warmth filling her voice as she spoke to my daughter. "They're just kidding around. But I might be on a show."

"We'll watch it all the time, right Dad?" Lily grabbed my arm, forcing the eyes around the table to me.

"Uh, yeah. Of course." The words sounded garbled to my own ears. I hated the thought of her leaving, but I didn't know what to do. I'd already made my position clear to her. Only, it was beginning to feel much less clear to me.

"Mateo, if you're interested, we could use some continuity in the kitchen," Archie said.

I managed a laugh. "I don't think I'm a good fit there. It was fun for a weekend, but I think construction is where I belong." I glanced up at Lucy, who flashed a supportive smile.

"Good to hear," she said. "Will's gonna need a foreman for the construction of the outpost at the top of the lifts."

I raised an eyebrow at her.

"Cruz Construction won the contract," she said, shrugging as if this hadn't probably been a foregone conclusion.

"Sure," I said, part of me wishing I could just go back to my life before this resort sprang back to being, before I had begun to want things that I hadn't even considered possible before.

We recapped the weekend, the group laughing and making notes as we shared insights about what had gone well and what we could do better.

"I've begun official bookings the second week in November," Archie told us. "So we have until then to get winter season ready to go and hire in a real staff."

"Two months," Aubrey said, her voice contemplative. "Think that's enough?"

"It'll have to be," Wiley said. "We can do it. Look what we've already accomplished."

There was agreement around the table, and before long, the discussion turned back to the topic that shadowed everything else at the resort—the hunt.

Archie showed us all the symbol on the back of the photo from the wall and laid the map out on the table again. He also put out a copy of the poem his uncle had left, and the key they'd used to open the old gate at the park. "This is what we've got now," he said. "In addition to the little note Rufus gave us: 'Rufus was named for Rudy *the traitor* Fusterburg. May he rot in hell.' And thanks to Lily, I think it's clear that the map isn't a map at all. It's a message of some kind."

"And this," Aubrey said, holding up the photo, "might be the key."

Lily was listening carefully, her eyes narrowed at the symbol on the back of the photograph. "But what letter is that?" she asked Aubrey.

"We don't know," Aubrey admitted. "And that's what we were hoping everyone could help figure out."

Lily frowned and shook her head. "You need more. One letter won't help us." Lily stood and went to the wall, crowded with photographs. "Did you look at the rest?" She gave me a questioning look as she reached for a frame. It wasn't my place to give her permission to disassemble the bar, however.

"Go ahead," Archie called.

Lily pulled a photograph off the wall and turned it over. "Nope," she said.

But we were all standing then, each of us removing a frame. For a few minutes the bar was filled with nothing but the sound of us taking down photographs, until Annalee called, "Got one!"

She turned over the photo on the table to reveal a second symbol. This one also matched the map.

"Shit, this is it!" Archie cried. Lily's head whipped to me, clearly wondering if I was going to reprimand Archie for his profanity, but there was too much excitement in the bar for anyone else to notice.

Soon, almost all the photos had been taken down, and we had seven of the symbols on the table in front of us.

"There are sixteen symbols," Aubrey said. "So we need nine more." Everyone stood on the tables to reach the highest photos while Lily frowned at the map.

"There are probably only five more," she called out. "Because some of these symbols are the same."

While the adults scrambled to find the rest of the symbols, Lily looked between the map and the poem Archie had placed next to it. There were intermittent shouts of "got one!" And "here" as the crew found the rest of the photos and laid them out along the bar.

"Daddy," Lily whispered at my side. "I think I know how to figure it out. Part of it."

I smiled at my brilliant daughter. "You can tell them. You've been right so far."

She nodded at me, a tiny smile playing on her beautiful face. When most of the group was staring down at the line of symbols, Lily's little voice rose. "Now you have to figure out what they mean, and I think they aren't letters. They're words. So you need to know what words they are," she said. She picked up her puzzle book and pointed to the key on her own code. "But I think I know what order they will go in."

"You do?" Aubrey asked, sounding amazed. "How?"

"The poem," Lily said. "It has the same number of words and the same number of repeated words as the map."

Now Aubrey came over to the table to check Lily's math. "It does," she agreed. "But we still don't know what word each symbol stands for."

We spent a little time setting the repeated words aside, trying to understand what they might be, while Archie and Brainiac pored over the photos on the front, trying to find clues.

"What if we take them out of the frames?" Brainiac asked Archie.

"Yeah, why not?" They slid the photograph from the broken frame, and Brainiac bent low, peering at the parts of the photo that had been obscured by the thick wooden frame.

"That's it," he murmured. "Look."

We all gathered around, and he pointed at a word scratched into the photograph at the very bottom, a spot that had been covered by the frame.

HEART

"Heart?" Aubrey asked. "That's not a word in the poem!" She blew out a frustrated sigh as we began sliding photographs out of frames all along the bar, calling out words when we found them.

"Dispute!"

"Copyright!"

"Studio!"

"Lola!"

Excitement built as we discovered the words, and Annalee and Lily had sat down at the table to write each one down as it was called out. Seeing them working side by side made my heart twist inside me. Why couldn't things be different?

"Put these ones twice since they're the repeated symbols," Lily instructed, pointing at the words "heart, bear, Lola, and rights."

"This is beginning to seem like some kind of legal thing," Aubrey said, stepping to look over Annalee's shoulder.

"Now we just have to put the words in order," Lily said.

Annalee frowned down at the paper in front of her. "How do we know what order?"

"It has to be the poem, like Lily said," Aubrey said, and Lily nodded.

We all stared down at the words of the poem for a long moment.

"Ticking clock," Archie said slowly. "So which words start with those letters? T and C?"

"The," Lily said, pointing to the word Annalee had written. "And this one. Copy...right?"

Annalee began writing on a clean sheet of paper: *The copyright.*

Soon, we had a list of words written, and we all stared down at them. Finally, Annalee cleared her throat and read loudly, "The copyright, Lola dispute, rights writer, Lola greed. Bear bear? Heart heart? The key, rights studio."

Silence filled the bar.

"Well that makes no fucking sense whatsoever," Aubrey said, sinking into a chair. "Sorry," she said, her eyes flitting to my seven-year-old.

"I've heard it before. Daddy gets mad when the lids are sticky on the pickle jar," she explained.

Annalee chuckled, and I glanced at her, our eyes locking over the table and my heart thumping inside me.

"You really gonna let her go?" Brainiac was at my side, leaning in close as the others debated the meaning of the code we'd found.

"Not my place to stop her," I said. "And it's what she wants." She'd made it clear.

"Think so?" he asked, frowning at me.

"I have the sense you're eternally disappointed with me, man. I don't know what to tell you. And honestly, I don't owe you an explanation—I don't even know your fucking name." The long weekend was taking its toll, and I had little patience for this grumpy professor guy poking into my business.

"It's Harrison. And I'm a little protective of our girl there."

Clearly.

"We've been through it all, there's nothing there," I said, exhausted.

"You're wrong. Figure it out."

I glared at him. The last thing I wanted was to be told what to do by some guy from Annalee's past.

But his look softened, and his hand wrapped my bicep, turning me away from the little group at the table. "Look, she's been through some things, maybe she told you."

"A bit."

"So you know she thinks she has to do everything herself. She doesn't want to depend on anyone."

That seemed true.

"But she should. She deserves to be able to depend on someone besides herself. Are you that guy?"

"I've got a kid," I muttered, my old defense feeling thin.

"Yeah," Brainiac said, steering me around again and pointing my focus to where Lily sat in Annalee's lap, whispering in the woman's ear. Annalee's beautiful face was aglow as her hand stroked my daughter's little back, and for a moment, it felt like I'd been socked in the stomach. "Figure it out," he said again, though I barely heard him over the rushing in my ears. "You're running out of time."

Chapter 32
Enough of a Good Thing

ANNALEE

It didn't feel right to leave Ghost high and dry in terms of event planning, so I made a few calls before I headed to the airport, and early Monday morning I stood in the morning chill to watch a Town Car pull into the circular drive.

The loud "whoop" could be heard even before the car door cracked open, and seconds later, I was wrapped in a bear hug like none other.

"Monroe!" My old friend bellowed.

"Sass!" I cried in return, but my voice was muffled in my enormous friend's shirt. Sasquatch was huge—he'd pushed every size limit for the cockpit back when we were flying, and was always on the bloody edge for weight. But the guy wasn't fat —he was pure muscle, and as he stepped back to grin at me, my heart surged with warmth for my old squadron mate.

"This place is insane," he said, grinning as he looked around. "I almost lost my lunch on the way up—all those twists and turns—but it was worth it."

"Sass, pilots don't get carsick."

"As far as you know," he shot back. "You sure you wanna leave this place? What in the world for?"

At that moment, Mateo's truck pulled past the turnaround, heading for the employee lot, and I swallowed hard, my eyes tracking it.

Sasquatch followed my line of sight. My friend squinted as he watched Mateo climb down from the cab, his broad back covered in a red and blue flannel shirt, and his muscular legs wrapped in denim. "What, that guy?" Sass was loud, but thankfully Mateo was too far away to hear him. "What's going on, Monroe? You were always bulletproof when it came to dudes."

"Not that one," I muttered.

"Not even gonna introduce me?" asked the guy who slid out of the car to stand at Sasquatch's side. I didn't recognize him, though he looked familiar. He was smaller than my friend, though most people were, and he had a stocky strength about him. A sweep of inky hair covered his forehead, and bright blue eyes danced above a playful smile. Where did I know him from?

"Hi," I said, sticking out my hand. "I'm Annalee Tyson. I flew with Sasquatch here back in the day."

"She's the reason we're here," Sasquatch told the stranger. "Well, part of it. The other part is Ghost. If Monroe's tagging out on babysitting, we're tagging in."

The handsome man in front of me looked confused, but seemed to realize Sasquatch was not going to remember his manners any time soon. "I'm Antonio Costa," he said, shaking my hand with a firm grip.

Mateo wandered by then, glancing our way as he shouldered a tiny pink backpack covered in sequins, Lily at his side. He frowned at me, but made no move to stop.

"Mateo, Lily," I called. "Let me introduce you. This is Sasquatch and Antonio. Sass is going to take over events for me. He's an old squadron mate. And Antonio—"

"Played for the Sharks," Mateo said, shaking hands with both men, but grinning at Antonio. "Used to watch you guys religiously."

"Thought you'd be more of a Rapids fan up this way," Antonio said, his handsome face pulling into a grin.

Mateo lifted a shoulder. "Never have been good at doing what people expect, I guess." He glanced at me. "This is my daughter Lily."

Lily stared up at the men, suddenly shy, and then she wrapped her arms around my legs. "You're not really leaving, are you, Annalee?"

My heart threatened to split into shards as the little girl squeezed tight, and I swallowed hard, fighting tears suddenly. I squatted down so I could look her in the eye. "I am," I told her. "In fact, this is my ride, right here."

Sasquatch glanced behind me to where my bags stood against the hotel wall. "Those yours?"

"Yeah, thanks." He loaded up the trunk of the Town Car while Mateo and Antonio made small talk, and I gave Lily a hug, my heart shredding the whole time. "Bye Lily. I'll miss you," I told her. "Be good and help Ghost figure out where this treasure is, will you?"

"Don't go," Lily said, her voice muffled as her little arms nearly choked me.

"I have to go, honey." I extricated myself and stood, fighting emotion as I stepped toward the car where Sasquatch stood, the trunk's open lid blocking Mateo's view of us.

"What's the deal with that guy?" Sass asked.

"Nothing worth mentioning." I squeezed his arm. "Thanks for coming on such short notice. Ghost is going to be so happy to see you. Sorry I can't stay longer to help get you situated, but you can call me as you get settled in and I'll explain where I left things."

Sass smiled at me. "Wish you were gonna be around a little longer."

"This is where the universe is taking me," I said, but the words felt tinny and wrong on my tongue. Was the universe opening this door, or had I gone looking for it?

"What's all this?" Ghost's voice boomed from the front of the resort, and I turned to see him grinning at Sasquatch. "Hey man!"

They did the bro-hug thing, and Ghost looked at me questioningly, but I felt like I'd done the right thing.

"Replacement," I told him. "Sass has been running events for professional soccer for a while now. He was between things, so I called him to come up here."

"And you brought a soccer star with you," Ghost said, spotting Antonio.

"Retired," Antonio said, his voice carrying a note of humility that made me respect him immediately. "I tagged along, hope that's okay. Antonio."

"The more, the merrier," Ghost told him. "We're just starting to put together the crew to open in November. We can use all the help we can get."

The men stood in a knot on the front sidewalk talking, and Lily approached me once more.

"Please don't go," she said, her little eyes shining as she

looked up at me. I couldn't take much more of this. Tears stood in Lily's eyes, and I was about to lose it myself.

"I'll send you some letters, how's that?"

She shook her head. "I'd rather if you just stayed here. Daddy will miss you too. And Poppy." She held up the stuffed tiger she carried.

"I'll miss you too, but I promise we'll see each other again, okay?" The words were out before I even realized I had no idea what the future would hold. I shouldn't have made an empty promise to this little girl, but I didn't know what else to do.

Her pigtails swayed as she continued shaking her little head back and forth. My heart felt like it was tearing itself into little pieces inside my chest. I had to get out of here. I patted Lily's head, knowing another hug would probably kill me, and then stepped away.

"Stay on the curb, okay?" I told Lily, making sure she wouldn't be in the way of the Town Car. I stood up, closed the trunk and slid into the back seat, pulling the door shut behind me. I rolled down the window and called to the group assembled there, "See you later, guys! Good luck!" I purposely avoided Mateo's gaze, knowing I'd see it in every dream I had for the rest of my life if I let myself look.

"Let's go," I said to the driver, and a moment later, we were pulling away from the curb. The men all stopped talking, turning to watch the car go, and I forced myself not to stare at Mateo, not to wonder if this was the last time I'd see him.

"You heading to the private airfield?" The driver asked. He'd picked up Sass at the little airport situated just up the road from the resort. Now that I'd met Antonio, I understood how Sass had managed to get a ride up here on a private jet.

"No," I answered. "Denver International. Hope that's okay. I thought you knew."

"That's what I thought," the man said. "Just making sure."

That was the only exchange we had, and the next four and a half hours were spent watching the scenery flash past the windows as I followed the path my life was taking me, away from the man I should never have let myself love. With each mile, the hole inside me gaped further open, the ragged edges painful and sore.

I was doing the right thing. My mind was sure of it, even if my heart seemed determined to moon over images of Mateo and Lily, forcing me to think about things I had no business considering. I couldn't have stayed. He made it clear he wasn't looking for a replacement for his dead wife, and I was not looking for a family. He'd sent me away. Hadn't he?

Chapter 33
That's a Sasquatch

MATEO

The new presence of a hulking giant of a man and a soccer star didn't begin to make up for Annalee's absence. I walked the men inside, my daughter sulking behind us, and I did my best to ignore the disappointment and pain I felt at Annalee's departure. She hadn't really even said goodbye.

Lily was a mess, and in some ways it helped me to have her to console, since I wasn't willing to let myself fall apart. But I wanted to. As soon as the car was gone, I was certain I'd made a mistake.

Why did it always take me losing things to understand their value?

"You gonna be okay?" Archie asked me, pulling me aside as Brainiac and Will greeted their old flying buddy and met Antonio. He glanced at the chair at the side of the lobby where my daughter was sobbing into her stuffed tiger.

"I'll be fine," I managed to say, biting the words out.

"You're a shit actor," Archie said.

I shook my head and raised my palms. "Maybe I should have asked her to stay. I don't know. It's too late now."

Brainiac glanced over and frowned at us, then broke away from the group and strode to my side. "You let her go, huh?"

"Didn't have a choice," I said, knowing it wasn't quite true.

The older man stared at me a long second, and I felt my patience at his evaluation sliding away. "What?" I growled.

"I'm trying to decide if I should help you or just let you suffer your own stupidity."

Archie turned to stare at him. "What's up your ass this morning?"

"This moron is in love with Monroe. And he's the first guy I've ever seen her lose her shit over. But they're both too stubborn to do anything about it," Brainiac explained.

"So you just let her leave?" Archie asked me.

Lily was suddenly back at my side, staring up at them. "Can you make her come back?" Her tear-stained face made my broken heart shatter even more completely.

"Shit," I muttered, turning to go be miserable somewhere, taking Lily's hand.

"Hang on," Brainiac said, catching my arm. "Do you love her, man?"

I glanced at my daughter, and at the two strangers who were watching this scene like it was a remake of *Dynasty*, their eyes big and interested.

What the hell did I have to lose now? She was already gone. "Yeah," I said. "I did. I do."

Lily wrapped her arms around my thigh and squeezed as I admitted what was in my heart for the first time.

"Then don't let her go," the guy they called Sasquatch said in a booming voice.

"Trust me," Will said. "You have to stop her from leaving." Great. Annalee had timed her departure with the Monday morning meeting, so everyone was here to offer their opinions.

I pointed to the front of the resort. "News flash. She already left." Lily squeezed my leg tighter.

Brainiac frowned at me again. "I'm having serious reservations about this. I'm not sure you're that smart."

Archie elbowed him. "No one's as smart as you, asshole. You have a solution here?"

Brainiac turned to address Antonio and Sasquatch. "How'd you guys get up here? Denver International?"

"Private jet, my man," Sasquatch proclaimed, looking gleeful. "Private airfield just up the road."

"Jet still there, you think?" Brainiac asked.

"The pilot said he was going to spend the night," Antonio supplied. "So, yes."

"Give him a call," Brainiac said. He turned to me. "Get yourself together. We're going for a ride."

I shook my head at him, uncertain quite what was happening, but I knew I couldn't let Annalee leave. Still, things were moving too fast, I needed a moment. "Give me a minute?" I asked, glancing between Aubrey and Lily, catching the woman's eye as I practically sprinted to the men's' room at the side of the lobby. I glanced back to see Aubrey take Lily's hand.

I needed to be alone for a minute.

I braced my hands on the sink and stared into the mirror. What was I doing? Would following Annalee have any purpose, or would it just prolong the inevitable? Did she want me to stop her? What about the promise I'd made to Poppy?

For long minutes, I stared at myself in the mirror, all the broken pieces of my heart rearranging themselves within me.

I couldn't go on like this, I realized. I couldn't keep trying to be everything for Lily when I wasn't even whole for myself. I'd let myself fall in love, I realized, and though it felt like it had caused the world to upend itself and made everything worse, maybe that wasn't the truth. Maybe that was only my fear.

Because if I'd lost Poppy, I could lose someone else, and that reality was too painful to consider. But wasn't this basically the same thing? Only I was choosing to let Annalee go? Letting my daughter suffer the loss too?

A deep whoosh of air escaped me as I understood that I hadn't prevented any pain for either of us, and instead was causing it. Making it worse.

I lifted a hand to my chest and pressed against the ring lying there, its solidity reassuring amidst the confusing swirl of thoughts in my head. Then I slid my hand to the back of my neck, lifting the chain and pulling it off over my head. For a long moment I stared at the gold band in my hand. Then I lifted it to my lips and slid it into my pocket.

One more deep breath, and I turned back to the lobby. I would not lose someone else I loved. Someone my daughter loved. Not if I had a choice in the matter.

Soon, I was riding in the back of a Suburban, the entire vehicle stuffed with men and Lily sitting at my side. "What's happening?" she asked me.

"I'm not totally sure, but I think I'm going to have to follow Annalee." I said.

"How? She already left." Lily looked around her as we headed up the highway, away from the resort.

Brainiac had a conversation I couldn't quite hear on his cell phone, and by the time we were pulling into the tiny airport, it was pretty clear this plan involved a small plane. Goose bumps swarmed my skin and my throat threatened to close up.

"Ready to get the girl?" Brainiac asked me, heading for the airport office.

I followed him, uncertainty swamping me and the old familiar panic that resulted from the concept of air travel creeping up my spine. "Can you, uh, give me some idea of the plan here?"

"She got a head start on us, so we can't drive after her. We'll never catch her. Gotta fly." He had a brief exchange with the woman behind the counter, who made a quick phone call to verify. Then I watched in fascination and horror as he filed a flight plan, showed her his credentials, and walked away with the keys to an airplane.

"So you'll go get her and bring her back here?" I asked hopefully. Lily had been bouncing along at my side this whole time, and she was clapping her hands gleefully now that she understood what was happening.

"I think it'll work better if you come with," Brainiac didn't even look at me as we approached the little plane. It wasn't the smallest plane I could imagine, but it was close.

"I can't fly," I told him, terror threatening to climb my throat.

"That's what the plane is for," Brainiac told me, glancing my way and shaking his head. As he took in my face though, his dismissive look shifted. "You're scared of flying, man?" Clearly the pale skin, sweating, and trembling had given me away.

"Yeah," I managed.

"It's the only thing Daddy is afraid of," Lily told him.

"Ever been in a plane?" Brainiac asked.

"Few times." I heard the shake in my voice, and wished I

could do something to banish it, but I was close to emotional bankruptcy after everything that had already happened.

Brainiac seemed to think about this for a moment, looking between me and Lily. "Would you be better or worse if she comes with?" He asked, pointing at my daughter.

"She's not coming," I said. I'd risk my own life, but I wouldn't risk hers.

Brainiac nodded as Lily protested loudly.

We walked her back over to where Sasquatch, Archie, Will, and Antonio stood. "Keep an eye on this one," Brainiac said, pointing at Lily. "We'll be back in a couple hours."

"Um," I said, my head spinning and my stomach close to revolt. Panic was threatening, but my heart was pushing me to master it. Brainiac was going to give me a chance to tell Annalee what I really felt. To ask her to stay.

Even through the swirling adrenaline and the threat of impending vomit, I could feel the certainty inside myself when I thought about standing before her once more, telling her how much I loved her, asking her to give us a chance.

"You can do it, Daddy," Lily told me, squeezing my hand tightly.

"You can, man," Sasquatch said. "Go get her."

"You guys okay watching Lily?" I asked Archie.

"Of course," he said.

"We've got her," Will assured me.

"Daddy, go!" Lily cried.

"Ready?" Brainiac asked me, moving toward the plane again.

I blew out a shaky breath, trying to steady myself. "Yeah. Okay." I followed Brainiac to the plane, and we decided I'd be better off in the copilot's seat than I would be in the back all alone.

He walked me verbally through everything he did to check

that the plane was ready to fly, but aside from a few things like "full battery start" and "fuel," my brain was putting up too much of a fight for me to follow. Lights blinked all around us across the dashboard, and Brainiac confidently flicked switches, touched panels, and communicated with the airport as I worked on not passing out. Soon the tiny plane was roaring to life, shaking and shuddering as it rolled down the narrow runway at increasingly terrifying speeds. A few minutes later, the wheels had left the ground, and the Rocky Mountains dropped away from the windshield in a sickening slide that had me gripping the edges of my seat.

"You're doing great," Brainiac told me, glancing over at me.

I stared out the windows at the incredible views below—trees and mountains stretching out as far as I could see. As we moved smoothly through the air, I actually felt myself relaxing, my mind focused on the sheer wonder and beauty around me. This was the part of flying I'd forgotten. "This is incredible," I said, feeling my worry fade slightly, replaced with awe.

"Just needed to get back on the horse, I think," Brainiac said, nodding at me.

We flew in silence for a few minutes, and my mind relaxed enough to begin ticking into action again as I realized I was going to have to come up with something to say to Annalee.

"Got any tips?" I asked the man at my side. I wasn't a huge fan of this man, but he knew Annalee better than anyone else.

"Pull back, you go higher, push down, you go lower. Pretty much all there is to it." He smiled at me.

"Not for flying a plane. For talking to Annalee. You guys seem... close." I almost choked on the word. I didn't like thinking about them together.

"Whatever you're thinking," he said, "it was never like that. Not even once."

I wished I didn't feel so much relief at his words. What

difference did it make whether they'd been together? He wasn't staking any claims now.

"She's smart, so you can't bullshit her," he said, his words drawn out like he was thinking carefully about the question. "And she's good at protecting herself. But I've seen the way she looks at you. She's not playing."

"Neither am I," I said, suddenly feeling much surer about everything. I was doing this. I was in a plane, on my way to stop the woman I loved from walking away. She might still go, she might still decide to leave, but at least I would have tried. It would be up to her, not tied to my fear or guilt.

We passed out of the mountains, heading up the front range toward Denver, and nerves began to replace the sick feeling I'd had when we first started our flight.

"How the hell am I going to find her at the airport?" I asked, looking at Brainiac. I hadn't considered the logistics of it all. Airports were pretty locked down. I couldn't just wander around looking for her.

"Let me make a couple calls," he said. "I've got some buddies at most of the airlines at this point, and a couple in control."

"I'd rather if you just focused—"

Brainiac was already talking into the radio, so I just sat back and watched the airport get bigger in the front windshield. By the time we landed, my knuckles white and my heart in my mouth, he seemed to have a plan.

"Called in a couple favors for you," he told me as we taxied to a stop in front of a hangar at the far end of the commercial runways.

"You barely know me," I said, feeling grateful.

"I know her, though. And if you're going to make her happy, it's more than worth it." He clapped me on the back. "Come on," Brainiac headed off across the tarmac, and while I'd never wandered around the back side of an airport before, he seemed to know where he was going.

"I'll try," I said, mystified at the ease with which this guy seemed to navigate the world. I did my best to keep up, hoping it wasn't already too late.

Chapter 34
Getting an Upgrade

ANNALEE

It was a long car ride to Denver International, and I spent almost half of it on the edge of my seat, close to telling the driver to turn around. Each mile I put between myself and the resort, or more specifically, between me and Mateo, built the mounting certainty within me that I was doing the wrong thing.

But he really hadn't offered me a choice, had he? Could you force someone to admit something they weren't ready for?

Eventually, I sat back in the seat, sinking into defeat and forcing my mind ahead.

To Paris.

To the next adventure.

My mother called as I struggled and I nearly didn't answer, but I hadn't talked to her in a while, and I needed some distraction. Maybe the conversation would leave me annoyed and riled about something other than Mateo.

"Hey Mama."

"Hey, little girl. How are you doing up there in the mountains?"

"The mountains were great, Mama. But I'm leaving."

She made a little noise of confusion. "You just got there. Your daddy and I were trying to plan a trip to come say hello, to see the place."

"Well, you don't need to bother now. You might get to see me soon in your own living room."

Her excited squeal made me realize I'd phrased this the completely wrong way. "You're coming home?"

"No, sorry. Didn't mean to make you think that. I'm headed to Europe to talk to a producer about a television show. A travel show."

"You're gonna be on TV?" Mom was clearly impressed by this. Television was one career path for pageant girls, at least those that didn't immediately get knocked up and tied down.

"It's not a sure thing."

"Honey, forgive me saying, but you don't sound excited about it."

"I'm excited."

"Hope they don't need any real good acting on this TV show, sugar."

I sighed. "I'm just tired is all."

"Because you never stay in one place long enough, that's why."

She might have had a point.

"Tell me why you're running away now." Mom sounded suddenly as tired as I felt.

I shook my head. I was not running. "What do you mean? I got an opportunity that was too good to pass up."

"Annalee, honey. Don't you ever get tired of moving aroud all the time?"

"Of course."

"Then why don't you stop?"

"I don't want to miss out, Mama. I don't want to get stuck in one place, find myself tied down and miserable."

"Like me." Her voice was flat, and I realized I might have hurt her feelings. Guilt bubbled up. I hadn't meant to make her feel bad. I wasn't in the right state of mind for this chat. I was ruining everything.

"No, Mama. Just... that's your life, not mine."

"Your life is airplanes and running around, and what happens when you're really tired, honey? When you're ready to rest? What do you have then?"

"A nice house on the Mediterranean and a cabana boy?"

She sighed, and I could hear the defeat in the sound. "Just let us know where you land this time. And take care of yourself, honey. We love you."

"Love you too." I hung up and stared out the window at the city, wishing I could stop thinking about her words. I tried to hold the idea of a little seaside cottage somewhere, a floppy hat and all the time in the sun I wanted, but the image seemed flat. Empty.

"Airline?" The driver broke through my misery as he turned to look over his shoulder at me.

"Virgin Atlantic," I told him.

Soon we were pulling to the curb and my bags were being unloaded next to me. I paid the driver and thanked him, and then turned to head inside, my heart feeling almost too heavy to carry within my chest.

At the ticket counter, the woman processed my ID and took my bags, directing me to security. I went through the line, doing my best to keep my mind from rolling morosely over the events of the last few weeks, the conversation with my mom. And when I got to the gate, I slumped into a chair, staring out the window at the tarmac. There was something comforting in the sight of airplanes moving here and there. Though this wasn't a Navy base and those weren't jets and cargo planes, it was still a bit like coming home. Especially when I spotted a guy striding confidently across the tarmac below who looked exactly like Brainiac.

I sat up straighter, squinting toward the window, but the man I'd seen had disappeared behind a line of baggage trucks. My mind was playing tricks on me now. It had to have been, because there'd been a second man too, one who looked so much like Mateo that my stomach had actually flipped at the sight of him.

I sank back into the chair again, only to have my name paged from the podium.

"Is there an Annalee Tyson in the boarding area? Miss Tyson, could you please approach the podium?"

I stood, wondering if maybe I'd been upgraded. I picked up my carry-on bag and headed for the counter. "Yes?" I asked, sliding my boarding pass across the counter to the dark-haired woman in the uniform.

She smiled at me and examined my boarding pass. "Miss Tyson, we're going to be boarding certain passengers just a bit early for this flight," she said.

I glanced at the jetway, where passengers from the arriving flight were disembarking. "Okay."

"As soon as we've cleared the aircraft, I'll be escorting you aboard."

This was unusual. "All right," I said. "Is this an upgrade by any chance?" I'd wanted to book first class, but hadn't been able to justify the expense.

"Might be," she said, smiling at me. There was something in her eyes that put me on edge, something I was pretty sure she wasn't telling me.

"Okay. I'm just going to get a soda," I said, pointing to the little gift shop down the corridor. "Be right back."

I headed over to get a Diet Coke, hurrying back to the boarding area just in time to hear my name called again. I presented my boarding pass and the attendant opened the jetway door and waved me ahead. And the weird thing was that as soon as I was through the door and halfway down the jetway, I heard the door close behind me.

This was the strangest pre-boarding process I'd ever experienced. Maybe my airline miles were finally paying off, or they'd gotten wind of the fact I used to fly. I had no idea, but glanced down at the boarding pass the woman had handed me in exchange for mine. It was the same pass, same seat—no upgrade, boo—but there was a note scrawled on it in the attendant's swirly handwriting.

"Head inside the plane and knock on the cockpit door."

What in the world was going on?

I wasn't in a good headspace for practical jokes or pranks. But since half my old squadron mates flew for the airlines at this point, I resigned myself to a reunion. Certainly that's what this would be. I'd smile and laugh at the right parts, pretend my heart wasn't a shriveled black hole inside me, and then get to my seat and put my headphones on, ready to zone out until I arrived in Paris.

I stepped into the silent plane—the attendants hadn't even

boarded yet—and turned toward the cockpit. When I was in in front of the door, I took a deep breath and knocked, preparing to put on the Monroe act again, huge smile plastered over my face.

The knock sounded hollow and loud in the empty jet, and I could hear shuffling on the other side of the door.

When the door opened, my aching heart slipped straight through me, surprise and confusion making all attempts at words utterly pointless.

I managed some kind of strangled sound, and might have shaken my head a little. But mostly, I just stared.

Mateo stood just inside the cockpit, and I stared at the man I'd planned never to see again, the man I knew I'd fallen in love with.

"Annalee," he said.

Chapter 35
Men Weren't Meant to Fly

MATEO

When Annalee first knocked on the door, my heart had leapt into my throat and my skin lit itself on fire as my palms became slick. Now that she stood before me, my breath was coming as fast as if I'd sprinted here from Kasper Ridge, and all the intelligent and compelling things I'd thought of to say to her slid from my mind.

"Annalee," I managed, taken aback as always by her sheer beauty. Here was the woman I'd watched walk away, the one I was sure had taken my heart with her. Her hair was pulled into a low ponytail, and her full ruby lips pressed together with doubt. Her eyes looked tired, full of something wary and unsure—and she'd never been more beautiful.

"I wanted to catch you before you left," I said, feeling like I had a mountain of words I needed to shovel through before I could really make her understand what was in my heart.

"You succeeded," she said, those beautiful eyes wide. "I'm just not sure how. Or why."

"Can I explain?" I gestured her to the first two seats behind her, wide leather chairs in the first-class section of the plane.

She looked at her watch. "I don't have plans until this plane is supposed to take off in about an hour." She slid into the window seat and looked at me expectantly.

"Brainiac flew me here," I started, realizing this was not an important detail, and wishing I could somehow start over.

"Thought you didn't fly," she said quietly.

"I don't. But I had to get here before you left."

She stared at me for a beat, and I felt my heart leap with hope inside my chest. "Go on."

"I didn't mean to get involved with you, Annalee. It was never part of my plan."

She said nothing, but her expression darkened.

"In fact, the first time I saw you, I knew you had the potential to shake my world to pieces. You were so smart, so funny, so confident...and so beautiful. I told myself to stay away."

Annalee tilted her head slightly, blinked.

"But it was probably already too late. And then when we got stranded together. When I talked to you, spent those nights with you—learned who you really are... I was a goner."

The look on her face softened, but the woman I loved still didn't speak. I took a deep breath, steeling myself for the hard part. I sat next to her, facing her, separated by the wide armrest between us and longing to touch her. But I couldn't, not yet.

"I've spent my time—years, actually—trying to make up for

my mistakes. I've had everything all twisted around inside my head. Poppy's death, my daughter's future, my mother-in-law's blame. I let it all stay with me, and it stopped me from moving. It was like being stuck in cement or some kind of invisible net. I knew I was stuck, but it was too hard to figure out how to move through it, get past it.

"But you..." I took a deep breath. "You made me want to figure it out. And I did get through some of it, but god, it was scary. I didn't want to be in love with you, Annalee, because the last time I was in love, the end hurt so much I didn't know if I'd survive."

She nodded, a tendril of her soft blond hair sweeping along her jawline as it escaped the ponytail. "I get it."

"The thing is, it wasn't a choice. I was in love with you before those nights in the cabin. I was in love with you the first time I saw you, I think. Something inside me latched on to something about you, pulled me toward you. And the thing is... I'm just too tired to fight it anymore."

I took a breath, watching for any signs of warning in her beautiful face, not that I would heed them at this point anyway.

"I love you, Annalee. I love you, and I'd really like it if you'd reconsider leaving. Or if you'd at least think about coming back. To me." My voice was thick with emotion, with hope and longing and fear, and I got the last words out in a whisper, feeling desperate for her answer.

Annalee stared at me for a long moment, saying nothing as the air around us seemed to still, atoms halting their movement in wait for her reply.

"You flew here?" she asked.

"Yes." Had she missed the main part of my little speech?

"In a plane."

"Annalee."

"You got in a plane to come tell me all this. You flew for me."

"Yes." I didn't mention the part about nearly throwing up or about Brainiac having to talk me down from panic a few times.

She watched me for a few more seconds, my body coiled as if ready to spring to my own defense should her words not come out the way I hoped they would. It was torture.

"I can't believe you did that," she said, dropping my gaze. The connection between us fractured when she let my eyes go, and I felt the energy begin to seep from me. She wasn't going to discuss the other things I said. It was all one-sided.

Could it be though? Had I imagined everything? Flown all this way for nothing?

She continued staring down at her hands in her lap, and after a second, I realized she was crying, fat tears dropping unheeded from the tip of her nose onto her hands. When she lifted her head to look at me again, those luminous eyes shone and I wanted to pull her into me, to tell her it was okay, that she didn't have to cry. Even if what I was telling her was that it was okay to leave me.

"Mateo," she said in a whisper. "I don't think I want to leave."

"Then don't leave," I said, my heart surging with hope. "Stay here."

"I think I'm running away. Because I'm scared."

"Of me?"

"Of what this might be between us. Of you, in a way. Of your beautiful daughter. Of your life. Of what role there might be for me to play there."

"Whatever role you want." I needed to convince her, to make her want us.

She shook her head and looked so sad I thought I might end up in tears myself. "I don't know how to do any of it. She's just a little girl. She needs a mama."

"She needs adults who believe in her, who can teach her.

She needs examples of the kinds of people she might want to become. She doesn't need you to be her mother, Annalee. She just needs you to care."

Annalee was still crying softly, and I wasn't sure what she was thinking. Had I come all this way just to have my heart torn out again?

I took her hand, twining my fingers through hers. "I'm in love with you," I told her again.

Her lips pressed together into a tentative smile, and she squeezed my hand gently. "I'm in love with you too," she said. "And with Lily, I think."

My body warmed with hope.

"But I'm also completely fucking terrified." She took a deep breath. "What if I do everything wrong?"

"There are no rules. We'll just figure it out as we go."

She took a shuddering breath. "I'm so glad you came," she said. "I don't want to go to Paris."

"You don't?" Happiness was glowing on the horizon like a sunrise and I was doing my best not to hope for too much.

She shook her head, more tendrils escaping the ponytail behind her. "No. I didn't know what else to do."

I tugged on her hand, pulling her into my lap, her legs stretched across the center armrest and her body finally back where it belonged, close to mine.

"We'll figure it out together," I told her again.

Annalee's eyes met mine, and the warm glow I found there put the questions and worries I still felt swirling around inside me to rest.

"I love you," she whispered, tilting her chin up, inviting me closer.

"I love you too," I answered, wrapping her in my arms and pressing my lips to hers. In that moment, the world fell away. The terrifying flight, the pain of her leaving without saying goodbye, the tears streaking my daughter's face, it all disappeared, and all that existed was this moment, this kiss, this love that felt so huge I thought it might be enough to live on forever.

"Ever joined the mile high club?" Annalee asked, pulling away just a breath from the kiss.

"Last time I flew I was eight, and this time Brainiac didn't invite me," I told her. "So, uh, no."

"How long till they come kick us off this plane?"

"No idea," I told her. "But Brainiac said it was ours for a while."

"Then let's be quick."

Annalee kissed me again, fiercely, and swiveled her body so she was straddling me. She wasted no time unbuttoning and unzipping what needed removing and lowering herself onto my straining cock. Her mouth on mine, our bodies connected by heat, friction, and something so much more intense that it felt like my soul was wrapped around her, we confirmed the love we'd just declared for one another. It was quick and hot, and left me panting for breath and wanting so much more.

"When I get you home, I'm taking my time with you," I told her, adjusting her shirt, which was hanging off her beautiful body. "I'm going to strip you naked, lay you out on my bed, and worship every centimeter of you."

"That sounds perfect," she whispered in my ear.

A click echoed through the stillness around us, the sound of the jetway door opening in the distance. Annalee and I reassembled ourselves and stood, and a flight attendant appeared a moment later.

"All good in here?" she asked, giving us a knowing smile.

"All good," Annalee said. "I don't think I'll be traveling with you today after all."

"You sure?" The attendant said. "I could probably get you

that upgrade. Maybe even find an adjacent seat so you don't have to travel alone?" She smiled at me now.

"That's okay," Annalee said. "I don't think I'd find what I was looking for in Paris. Turns out it was actually here, in Colorado."

"Well, that's wonderful," the woman said, beaming at us.

She escorted us back off the plane, and we stood in the waiting area, smiling at each other and holding hands as the flight began to board.

"What now?" She asked me.

"Let's go home."

Chapter 36
TV Can Wait

ANNALEE

Returning to Kasper Ridge (in a private jet, thanks to my pal Brainiac) was a strange experience. After the quick flight, we left the tiny mountain airfield behind us and as the turnaround at the front of the resort came into view, I felt something inside me settle.

Mateo was at my side, holding my hand through the short flight and car ride, which meant that my hand was aching slightly, since describing the man as a 'nervous flyer' was like calling that McDonald's clown guy 'a bit disturbing.'

It was midday by the time we returned, and as we stepped

into the lobby, the familiar sounds of construction and music blasting from the bar greeted us. And for the first time in my life, I felt like I'd come home.

"I need to find Lily," Mateo said softly as we stood near the reception desk. Brainiac had disappeared as soon as we'd stepped inside, leaving us alone.

"Of course." I still wasn't sure where I fit in that equation. Mateo and Lily were a family. And even if I loved this man, and if he loved me, I didn't know what happened next.

"Let's get your bags to your room first, and then you can come with me." Mateo picked up one of my suitcases, and I took the other, trailing it behind me as we stepped into the elevator. I didn't protest, because I wanted to see Lily, actually, and I didn't want to go to my room and be left there with these newly acknowledged thoughts and feelings spinning around my head. I didn't want to be away from Mateo. Not now, not ever.

We deposited my things in the living room and Mateo stepped close to me, eyeing the bedroom door, the big bed lying invitingly just beyond.

I lifted a hand, running it up the front of his soft shirt, over the muscles I'd memorized, the landscape of the body that I visited over and over and in my dreams. But something was missing. I raised my eyes to Mateo's, about to form the question, but I didn't have to.

"I took it off," he said, holding my hand over his chest with his own.

The ring he wore on a chain around his neck was gone. It had never bothered me, not really. How could I resent a love like the one he'd had for Poppy? How could I ever complain about a man loving his wife, the mother of his daughter?

"You didn't have to," I told him.

"It was time," he said. "Time to let her rest, to let that part of my life settle where it belongs. Behind me."

"She'll always be a part of you. Of Lily." I wanted to be sure he knew that I understood—as much as I was capable of understanding this.

"I know. But I don't want anything between us, between you and me and the future." His smile as he uttered these words was soft, careful, as if he wasn't sure how I'd respond.

Love for him rose inside me on a wave of emotion, and I wrapped my arms around him, pressing my forehead to the top of his chest, wanting to breathe him, to feel him, to know him in a way I'd never wanted to understand anyone before. His strong arms pulled me closer, and for what felt like long minutes, we stayed that way, breathing together. Being together.

Finally, my heart so full it felt like something in my chest was literally overflowing, I stepped back, taking his hand. "Let's go find Lily."

He nodded, and we left the suite.

Archie, Lily, and Aubrey were in Archie's suite kneeling around the coffee table, Sasquatch and Antonio seated on the long couch in front of them. The door stood open, so we just walked inside. I moved to drop Mateo's hand, but his fingers tightened around mine, and my heart surged again.

"Daddy!" Lily leapt up and ran to hug Mateo, but her affection for him was cut short when she looked up at me. "You came back!" Her little body wrapped itself around me, and I hugged her back, leaning forward to rub her small back.

Lily squeezed me tightly, then stepped back and took my hand, pulling me to the table. "Look what we're doing."

Unsurprisingly, the map was spread on the table in front of the group, and Archie and Aubrey were staring at the words we'd identified as if they might jump off the table and form a conga line.

"Getting anywhere?" Mateo asked.

"Not really," Aubrey sighed. "I mean, there's something to

do with Rudy Fusterberg, right? There has to be. Between the bear in the bar and the studio he was a part of..."

"This whole thing is very Hollywood," I said, sliding to my knees to look at the words there again.

"This whole thing is very nuts," Sasquatch said, grinning.

"Interesting though," Antonio volunteered.

"So the new blood didn't come up with anything we didn't have?"

"Just one thing," Archie said, reaching for the stack of photographs from the bar, which were in a pile behind him. "Look at this."

The photo in Archie's hand was of a woman who looked vaguely familiar, but I couldn't place her. In the picture, she was glamorous, dark lips and Hollywood curls framing her face as her huge eyes looked adoringly up at Marvin who returned the smile. In the bottom corner of the photograph, the word "Lola" was etched, and the back of the frame, Archie said, had been the symbol we'd matched to the word "Lola" in the poem.

"Who is this?" Mateo asked. "Some starlet?"

"She was in a lot of the old movies," Aubrey said. "That's Annie Lowe."

"Oh right!" I cried. Annie Lowe's name had appeared on a lot of the old movie posters we had found, and she'd had a small role in the movie we'd watched recently, The Map.

"So where does Annie Lowe fit in?" Mateo asked.

"Can I tell them?" Lily chirped, leaping to her feet and bouncing a little with excitement.

"Sure," Archie said, grinning at Lily.

"Annie Lowe was their aunt!" she cried, looking pleased with herself.

I still didn't get it. But Aubrey spelled it out.

"Our aunt Lola," Aubrey said. "Was actually Annie Lowe. But we never knew that, since we never met her. And Uncle

Marvin didn't talk about what she'd done before they got married."

For a brief moment, excitement flared in me, until I realized that this didn't necessarily help.

"So what does that mean?" I asked, looking around the group.

"No fucking clue," Sasquatch said, laughing. "Y'all are Looney Toons."

"It's compelling, though," Antonio said, clearly trying to lessen the sting of Sass's words.

"It means our Aunt Lola was engaged to Rudy Fusterburg before she married Uncle Marvin, for one thing," Ghost said.

"That's right," Aubrey said, snapping her fingers. "Wait, so what does that mean?"

"Not sure, but maybe she's the key." Ghost sat into a big wing chair and leaned back, steepling his fingers in front of his chin.

"Hey Ghost," I said, now that the attention was off the map. "I wondered, would it be okay if I came back?"

"You're already here," he pointed out.

"I mean, to the job? The events director job?" I said.

"Of course," he said. "That's a huge relief actually, because Sasquatch here already pitched me about sixteen ideas that all seem to involve building a soccer stadium."

"I know soccer," the big guy said, shrugging.

"I don't want to put Sass out of a job though," I said, turning to him with an apologetic smile.

"We need all the hands we can get," Ghost said. "He and Antonio have already been helping Brainiac on the lift. Some of the parts came in finally."

"So no television show?" Aubrey asked me.

I shook my head. "No, not for me." All the excitement I'd felt, the pull to some new adventure... it was fading now in the shadow of happiness and warmth inside me, the knowledge that I was home. I'd called Douggie before we'd flown back, and he'd assured me that he would talk with his agent and everything would be fine. "I knew you loved that hunk of man," he laughed. "Get him, girl," he'd laughed.

"I think all I want really, is to stay here," I said.

Lily turned to look at me as I finished speaking, a thoughtful look on her face. "Staying forever?" she asked, stepping close to murmur in my ear. Mateo was watching us, but she stood on the side opposite him, keeping her voice low as I nodded to answer her.

"With Daddy? And me?"

I slid my arm around her little waist and pulled her closer to my side, letting myself feel her warmth, allowing myself to breathe her little girl scent. "That's the plan," I said. "Is that okay?"

For a second, she was still, leaning into my side, breathing but not speaking. And then she was in front of me, throwing her arms around my neck and pressing her little face into my neck.

"I think she's glad you're not going anywhere," Mateo said, leaning in. The rest of the group was pretending to be studying the map on the table, but I knew they were all paying attention.

"I'm glad too," I said, speaking loudly enough that all the nosey eavesdroppers didn't have to strain to hear.

For once in my life, I was glad to be staying in one spot. Glad to be putting down something that felt like roots, and more surprisingly—to me, at least—glad to be part of a family.

Mateo and I had a lot of things to figure out, and there was nothing official to designate me as part of his little family, but at least I wasn't terrified of the thought anymore.

I held Lily in my arms, felt the solidity and strength of Mateo by my side, and let the joy inside me suffuse every cell of my body, and I looked around at the other family I hadn't known I needed. These people at Kasper Ridge, my old friends and those I'd just met, they'd become everything a family should be, and I realized I'd been running all this time from something I wanted with all my heart.

Late that night, Mateo was tucking Lily into bed in the suite upstairs, and I waited in the living room, talking quietly on the phone.

"I want you to come visit, Mama. You'll love it here."

My mother had been surprised to get my call, and it made me realize I hadn't been the best of daughters. "You've never been too excited to have us invade your life before, darling. Are you sure?"

"I don't know if this will make sense," I tried. "But I think I always thought you'd come and try to pull me back into the life you thought I should have."

"What, you thought I'd storm onto a Navy base and demand that you go back to doing pageants?" Mama laughed lightly, and I realized how silly my fears really had been.

"It wasn't that, exactly. I mean, yes, partly that." I took a breath. "I think I just always imagined something different for myself, but I didn't know what it was. And until I found it, maybe I worried that I'd give up, that coming home might be easier than continuing to search."

"And coming home would be so bad?" Mama sounded sad now.

"No," I said, exploring the feelings I'd long been too afraid to look at carefully. "It wasn't that. But home has a lot of memories, and when I'm there, I feel a little bit like I'm becoming a previous version of myself again. Someone weaker. Less capable."

"Okay, Annalee, I'll say it one more time. Maybe you're ready to hear it now. What happened with that boy was not your fault. It was a terrible tragedy, and I'm so sorry that it happened right in front of you. But it was not your fault. Let it go now, sweetheart."

I knew she was right, and for the first time in my life, I thought maybe I could let it go. I let out a long breath. "Will you come, Mama? You and Daddy? There's a grand opening party in November."

"Maybe we'll wait until it's a little quieter. Are you coming home for the holidays?"

"What if you came here?"

There was a pause, and then Mama said, "I think we might like that. Let me talk to Daddy and your sister. She's so busy with those kids I don't think she'll even notice if we aren't there."

She would. And she'd hold it against me. "Maybe she could come too."

"You want four little kids running around your fancy hotel?" Mama laughed, and I thought of Lily, how much she'd enjoy having some friends her own age up here.

"I think that would be great," I said honestly. I wasn't ready to tell Mama about Mateo and Lily—I didn't know exactly what I'd say was happening anyway—but by Christmas I hoped I would be.

Mateo stepped out of the bedroom just as I was saying good-bye. I slid the phone onto the coffee table, surprised to find how much I really missed my mother.

"Lily's asking for you," he said, striding across the room. "You okay?"

"Just talking to my mom." I stood to face him. "Is Lily okay?"

"She just wants you to tuck her in," he said. Fear threatened to rise in me at the thought of this, but then I thought of little Lily, her trusting face and swinging pigtails, and my fear turned to something else entirely.

"I'd love to." I kissed Mateo quickly, loving the warm manly scent of him and the way his rough face rubbed mine, and then I headed for the bedroom.

Lily's eyes were drifting shut, but a sleepy smile spread across her face as I entered. Her stuffed tiger was pulled close against her chest. "Annalee," she said in a whisper.

"Good night, Lily," I said, sinking down to sit beside her and brushing a lock of hair from her cheek. "Sweet dreams."

She smiled at me then, a warm expression so full of trust and affection that I thought my heart might have shuddered a little inside me.

"I'm so glad you stayed," she told me.

"Me too," I said honestly, feeling amazed and honored that this was my life, that I was here, with these people I loved.

"I love you," she said quietly, her little eyes drifting shut.

"I love you too," I whispered, turning just as Mateo's dark shadow filled the doorway. "I love you both."

I rose and walked toward the man in the doorway, the man who'd made me realize that loving people was risky, as I'd always believed, but that the payoff was more than worth the fear. He wrapped me in his arms, and we stood there in the near-darkness, breathing, loving. Being together.

Also by Delancey Stewart

Want more? Get early releases, sneak peeks and freebies! Join my mailing list here or scan the QR code and get a free story!

The Kasper Ridge Series:

Only a Summer

Only a Fling

Only a Crush

Only a Secret

The Singletree Series:

Happily Ever His

Happily Ever Hers

Shaking the Sleigh

Second Chance Spring

Falling Into Forever

Singletree Box Set 1

Singletree Box Set 2

The Digital Dating Series (with Marika Ray):

Texting with the Enemy

While You Were Texting

Save the Last Text

How to Lose a Girl in 10 Texts

The Text Before Christmas

The Digital Dating Box Set

The MR. MATCH Series:

Prequel: Scoring a Soulmate

Book One: Scoring the Keeper's Sister

Book Two: Scoring a Fake Fiancée

Book Three: Scoring a Prince

Book Four: Scoring with the Boss

Book Five: Scoring a Holiday Match

Mr. Match: The Boxed Set

The KINGS GROVE Series:

When We Let Go

Open Your Eyes

When We Fall

Open Your Heart

Christmas in Kings Grove

www.ingramcontent.com/pod-product-compliance
Lightning Source LLC
Chambersburg PA
CBHW071742190726
48292CB00003B/844